THE GOOD, THE BAD, AND THE UNCANNY

SIMON R. GREEN

ACE BOOKS, NEW YORK

THE BERKLEY PUBLISHING GROUP
Published by the Penguin Group
Penguin Group (USA) Inc.
375 Hudson Street, New York, New York 10014, USA
Penguin Group (Canada), 90 Eglinton Avenue East, Suite 700, Toronto, Ontario M4P 2Y3, Canada
(a division of Pearson Penguin Canada Inc.)
Penguin Books Ltd., 80 Strand, London WC2R 0RL, England
Penguin Group Ireland, 25 St. Stephen's Green, Dublin 2, Ireland (a division of Penguin Books Ltd.)
Penguin Group (Australia), 250 Camberwell Road, Camberwell, Victoria 3124, Australia
(a division of Pearson Australia Group Pty. Ltd.)
Penguin Books India Pvt. Ltd., 11 Community Centre, Panchsheel Park, New Delhi—110 017, India
Penguin Group (NZ), 67 Apollo Drive, Rosedale, North Shore 0632, New Zealand
(a division of Pearson New Zealand Ltd.)
Penguin Books (South Africa) (Pty.) Ltd., 24 Sturdee Avenue, Rosebank, Johannesburg 2196,
South Africa

Penguin Books Ltd., Registered Offices: 80 Strand, London WC2R 0RL, England

This is a work of fiction. Names, characters, places, and incidents either are the product of the author's imagination or are used fictitiously, and any resemblance to actual persons, living or dead, business establishments, events, or locales is entirely coincidental. The publisher does not have any control over and does not assume any responsibility for author or third-party websites or their content.

THE GOOD, THE BAD, AND THE UNCANNY

An Ace Book / published by arrangement with the author

PRINTING HISTORY
Ace hardcover edition / January 2010
Ace mass-market edition / January 2011

Copyright © 2010 by Simon R. Green.
Cover art by Jonathan Barkat.
Cover design by Judith Lagerman.

ISBN: 978-0-441-01977-9

ACE
Ace Books are published by The Berkley Publishing Group,
a division of Penguin Group (USA) Inc.,
375 Hudson Street, New York, New York 10014.
ACE and the "A" design are trademarks of Penguin Group (USA) Inc.

PRINTED IN THE UNITED STATES OF AMERICA

10 9 8 7 6 5 4 3 2 1

continued . . .

Just Another Judgement Day

"Another unrestrained ride through the Nightside . . . The pace is fast, and the climax . . . satisfies. Fans of urban noir will want to discover this series if they have not already done so."
—*Monsters and Critics*

"Perhaps my favorite of all of these invented magical neighborhoods that have spawned in one series or another . . . Taylor is fast becoming one of my favorite private eyes." —*Critical Mass*

"Simon R. Green delivers up yet another roller-coaster ride through the dark fantasy nightscape of the Nightside, throwing an opponent at John Taylor who is truly out of his weight class . . . [It] is certain to please Green's legions of fans, offering a strong new tale . . . recommended." —*SFRevu*

"There's plenty of the usual action and sarcastic humor that make this series a real standout. This time around, there's also a good deal of serious discussion about the nature of Good and Evil, and the consequences of each . . . A trip to the Nightside is always a good time, especially with John [Taylor] and Suzie Shooter as guides." —*CA Reviews*

The Unnatural Inquirer

"Sam Spade meets Sirius Black . . . inventively gruesome."
—*Entertainment Weekly*

"Fast paced and amusing, as well as packed with inventive details." —*The Denver Post*

Hell to Pay

"If you're looking for fast-paced, no-holds-barred dark urban fantasy, you need look no further: the Nightside is the place for you." —*SFRevu*

"A real treat . . . Highly entertaining and with an ass kicker of a plot, this may be my favorite of the series yet."
—*Crimespree Magazine*

Sharper Than a Serpent's Tooth

"This is Green's tour de force culmination of the Nightside books. Anyone who's enjoyed the series to date absolutely must read this installment. Highly recommended." —*SFRevu*

Paths Not Taken

"A fantastic fantasy . . . action packed." —*Midwest Book Review*

Hex and the City

"Urban fantasy with a splatterpunk attitude, a noir sensibility, a pulp sense of style, and a horror undercoating."
—*The Green Man Review*

"The Nightside saga takes a huge leap forward . . . It's a big, turbulent stew, but Green is a master chef . . . a terrific read."
—*SFRevu*

Nightingale's Lament

"Filled with supernatural creatures of various sorts, the action leavened by occasional bits of dry humor." —*Chronicle*

"Strong horror fantasy." —*The Best Reviews*

Agents of Light and Darkness

"I really enjoyed Green's first John Taylor novel, and the second one is even better. The usual private eye stuff—with a bizarre kick." —*Chronicle*

"The Nightside novels are a great blending of Lovecraft and Holmes." —*Midwest Book Review*

Something from the Nightside

"The book is a fast, fun little roller coaster of a story!"
—Jim Butcher

"No one delivers sharp, crackling dialogue better than Green."
—*Black Gate*

The good, the bad, and the uncanny.
We're all in there somewhere.

This is the Nightside.

Hidden away deep in the hollow heart of London is another city, another world, another reality. Where it's always night, always dark, always three o'clock in the morning; the hour that tries men's souls. Rain-slick streets, gaudy neon signs the exact colours of childhood candy we always knew was bad for us. Bars and clubs and private establishments, where you can find everything you're not supposed to want. Love for sale on every street-corner, love, or something like it. And the constant roar of traffic that never, ever stops.

Angels and demons lurk in shadowed alleyways, arranging deals and making decisions never to be shared with Humankind. Nightmares go walking in borrowed flesh, and not everything that looks back at you with human eyes is really human. Who watches the watchmen? Who preys on the predators? Who gives a damn, in the night that never ends?

I'm John Taylor, private investigator. Tall, dark of eye, and handsome enough at a distance. I take the cases no-one else will touch, because I have a special gift for finding things. Most of my clients say they want me to find the truth; but they don't always mean it. I wear a long white trench coat, like a knight in cold armour; and I have fought monsters, in my time.

You can find monsters in the Nightside, and gods, too, if they don't find you first. Forbidden knowledge, appalling pleasures, sex and death and everything in between; all yours for the asking. As long as you remember: buyer beware. If you can't spot the patsy in the deal, it's almost certainly you.

This is the Nightside. Don't say you weren't warned.

ONE

Into the Dragon's Mouth

I was out and about that night, taking my trench coat for a walk, when a sudden fog came rolling down the street towards me like a grim grey tidal wave. I stopped, and studied its progress cautiously. We don't get many fogs, in the Nightside. We get lots of rain, and thunder-storms, and the occasional hail of frogs, but we don't really do weather, as such. Weather and seasons are part of the natural order of the world, and we don't really do natural either. So a sudden fog always means trouble for someone.

People on the street were already running ahead of the fog, or disappearing into sheltering doorways, as the thick pearl grey wall rolled relentlessly on, enveloping clubs and shops and soaking up the neon light, till only the merest Technicolor glints showed through, like so many half-blinded eyes. A growing silence moved with the fog as it ate up all the

3

life and laughter in the street. I could see dim shapes moving, caught in the thick mists, struggling slowly like insects caught in hardening amber. The fog smeared itself across shop-windows, filling the night and hanging heavily on the air, surging forward in sudden, billowing clouds. Up close, the pearly grey mists were full of shimmering sparks and uncertain shapes that came and went in a moment. I seriously considered running.

This had all the makings of a flux fog.

Such things are dangerous. A flux fog means the corners of the world aren't properly nailed down any more, and reality is up for grabs. Inside a flux fog, all certainties are thrown into question, and all the possibilities that ever were are suddenly made equal. Take the wrong turning, in a grey world where every turn looks just like every other, and you could end up walking out of the fog into a whole new place. With no guarantee you'll ever find a way home again. Everything looks blurred and out of focus in a flux fog because you're seeing a dozen different dimensions, a hundred possibilities, for every object or person or direction. People and places can change subtly even as you approach them; familiar faces can become strangers, and in the blink of an eye you're trapped in a world that never knew you. The only real defence against a flux fog is not to be there when one manifests.

I should have known better than to be out and about on such a night. The weather forecast had been *Changeable*, with a side order of *On your own head be it*. But I felt the need to go out, to walk up and down the Nightside, to see what there was to be seen and think a few very private thoughts. Some thoughts can only be properly considered when you've removed yourself from your comfort zone. A melancholy had come upon me over a period of weeks, and I wasn't sure why. Things were actually going well, for a change. I was wealthy enough that I could pick and choose my cases, pursuing only those that interested me; and I was respected enough that no-one had tried to kill me in weeks. And Suzie and I were . . . closer than ever.

I had everything I'd ever dreamed of. So why was I so restless? Why was I waiting . . . for the hammer to fall?

Suzie was out pursuing a case of her own, hunting down some poor bastard for the bounty on his head, and the house had seemed very still and quiet without her in it. I'd felt strangely agitated, disturbed, uneasy . . . as though someone, somewhere, had me in his gun-sight. So I left the house and went out for a walk, to think and brood, and hopefully tempt any possible enemy out into the open, where I could get at him.

And what I got, for my trouble, was a flux fog.

The mists really were getting quite close now. People stepped out of the grey wall before me, vague and indistinct, their details only firming up as they left the fog behind them. A giant teddy bear in a World War I British Army uniform looked confusedly about him, clutching his rifle with his furry paws. A scientific person in a pristine white lab coat stalked right past me, gabbling to himself in low Coptic. And a gaggle of Russian tourists in *Chernobyl Health Spa* T-shirts started to take photographs of me, before they realised who I was and decided to take a sudden interest in something else instead.

Nothing out of the ordinary, for the Nightside, where some days you can't trust anyone or anything to stay the same for ten minutes in a row. All the people here have some nasty little secrets, something cold and unpleasant clutched greedily to their bosoms, some special need or fascination that could only be revealed and satisfied in the neon-lit streets of the Nightside. A private face behind every public mask, a hidden meaning peeking through whatever words they choose to share with you. Even I had turned out to be . . . not who I thought I was.

Lilith's son . . .

The flux fog surged forward, filling the street, and I opened my arms to it, embracing the bitter, tingling mists as they rolled over me. A reckless, stupid thing to do; but the restlessness was so great in me, I felt a desperate need to do something, anything, out of character, just to prove to myself that I was still in charge of my life. That I was still making the decisions. The mists felt hot and clammy, like the steam in a sick-room, where the fever burns like madness and inspiration all at once. Shadowy shapes skittered all around me, like sharks circling a body in the water; and somewhere far away a great bell made of ice tolled the hours before dawn.

And then, just like that, the fog was gone. The street was back, in all its wild and gaudy details, the clubs and bars and private establishments as loud and raucous as ever. The bright primary colours of the neon signs blazed as sleazily as ever, and the huge oversized Moon shone coldly in the clear night sky. People spilled back out onto the pavements, once again intent only on tracking down their own particular heavens and hells, their very own private rewards and damnations. Nothing had changed, least of all me. I lowered my arms, feeling faintly foolish and obscurely disappointed. The flux fog hadn't touched me. Perhaps because of my not-altogether-human nature; perhaps because it was afraid of me. Or perhaps because it wouldn't deign to touch anyone who wanted it . . .

Why was I so restless, that night of all nights? Why did I want so badly for my life to change? Was it because I'd finally got everything I ever wanted, and all I could think was . . . *Is this it?*

Perhaps fortunately, my mobile phone rang, playing Mike Oldfield's "Tubular Bells." I finally got rid of the *Twilight Zone* theme; you can run some jokes into the ground. I took out my phone, hit the exorcism function to keep out the really determined ad mail, and did my best to speak cheerfully and normally.

"Hi, there! You have reached John Taylor, private investigator, hero for hire, and female impersonator for private functions. This may or may not be a recording. Speak now."

"Oh God, you're in one of your moods again, aren't you?" said my secretary, Cathy. "I don't know why you ever try to sound cheerful; you know you're no good at it. I, on the other hand, am always bright and cheerful and charming because I am young and fresh and still relatively unsullied."

She had a point. Cathy was so unrelentingly cheerful I used to think she dosed herself morning, noon, and night with every drug known to man, but no, it was just her. There ought to be a law.

"What do you want, Cathy?" I said patiently. "You're interrupting my quality time."

"Oh, you're not going to believe this one, boss."

"What have you done this time?"

"Nothing! Or at least nothing you need to worry about. But you won't believe who just phoned the office, looking to hire you . . . An elf! Really! You could have knocked me down with a French tickler. Not only has an elf lord come to the Nightside, which is weird and scary and disturbing enough in itself, but he wants you to solve a case for him! How cool is that?"

"Which particular elf lord are we talking about here?" I said, since one of us had to be practical and professional in this conversation, and it clearly wasn't going to be Cathy.

"Says he's the Lord Screech; but you can bet good money that's not his real name. Elves lie like they breathe. They only come into our world to mess us over."

"Of course," I said. "It's all they've got left. What exactly does this putative Lord Screech want me to find for him?"

"Wouldn't say," sniffed Cathy. "Too far up himself to discuss details with a mere underling. Says he'll be at the Dragon's Mouth for the next two hours if you'd care to drop by for a little chat. No mention of money. But . . . he's an elf! When did you last hear of one of them lowering himself to ask a mere human for help?"

"Never," I said. "Which would suggest that not only is this case going to be impossible, unethical, and quite mind-bogglingly dangerous, but I'll probably end up stabbed in the back by my own client."

"Well, of course," said Cathy. "I thought that was all understood when I said, *Your client is an elf.* But come on, boss, we are talking major bragging rights here! You could dine out on this for months! John Taylor, the private investigator so special that even the high-and-mighty elves come to him to solve their problems! We could have new cards made!"

"Still," I said, "why the Dragon's Mouth? That's a seriously unpleasant place, even for the Nightside. What would an elf be doing there? Or does he know . . . that I know the Dragon's Mouth? That once upon a time, I knew it very well."

"You used to frequent the Dragon's Mouth, boss?" said Cathy, somehow managing to sound scandalized and delighted at the same time. "But it's . . ."

"The Nightside's premiere drug den," I said. "You never knew me in my dog days, Cathy; when I was down-and-out and on the run from everyone, including myself. I swore I'd never go back . . . but if that's where the elf is, then that's where I'm going. If only because I can't have our crafty and underhanded elf lord thinking he has an advantage over me. No-one tells me there's somewhere I can't go, not even me."

"You're weird, boss."

I shut down the phone and put it away. I'd gone out into the night looking for changes, and it seemed I'd found some. I'd been thinking about my future, but it seemed my past wasn't finished with me yet. I thrust both hands deep into the pockets of my trench coat, took a deep breath, and headed for the Dragon's Mouth, and the deepest, darkest part of the night.

Never trust elves. They always have their own agenda.

There are places you just don't go in the Nightside. Either because they're so dangerous you know you're going to have to fight your way in, and probably out, or because they're so extreme, so shameful, and so damned sickening that no-one with any sense would have anything to do with them. There are bad places, dangerous places, and unhealthy places; and then there's the Dragon's Mouth.

Tucked away casually in a shadowy side street not far from the old main drag, the club's exterior really is a huge dragon's head, some thirty feet tall and twenty wide, its huge gaping jaws forming the entrance. Rumour had it the dragon had been petrified centuries ago by the gorgon Medusa herself. In which case, I hated to think what they were using for the back door. The wide stone head was a smooth dull grey, untouched by time or weather. The eyes were deep, dark hollows. Great jagged teeth pointed up and down, like stalagmites and stalactites. There were no exterior guards; just walk in, whenever you please. All are welcome, for as long as their money or credit holds out. Anything goes, any need satisfied, enter at your own risk, and abandon hope all ye . . . Well, I'm sure you know the rest.

I strolled unhurriedly between the two long rows of teeth and descended the winding stone stairs into the belly of the beast, the huge stone chamber spread out beneath the street. It was years since I'd last been here, a lifetime. It was yesterday. Sometimes you do things to yourself so bad that the memories have barbs and never let you go. I'd known what the place was, all those years ago, and what it could do to me, but I'd descended into hell anyway. I had come here because what it offered . . . was what I wanted. The slow, sweet suicide of addiction.

I was so much younger then, and beset on all sides by threats and questions and destinies I couldn't face any more. So I ran away, from friends and enemies alike, buried myself in the delightful depths of the Dragon's Mouth, and gave myself to a very harsh and demanding mistress. I'd still be there, if Razor Eddie hadn't come and got me out. No-one says no to the Punk God of the Straight Razor. I stayed with him a while, with all the other homeless who washed up in Rats' Alley. I'd thought I couldn't fall any further. Until Suzie Shooter came looking for me, for the price on my head; and I ran headlong from the Nightside and everything in it, with Suzie's bullet burning in my back.

I thought I was done with the Nightside forever, but destiny called me home, where I belonged, with all the other monsters.

I descended the smooth stone steps into the great cavern below, and it all looked just as I remembered. As though I'd merely stepped out for a moment, and all the last years of my life had been only another smoke dream. I stopped at the bottom of the steps and looked about me, fighting to keep my face calm and unconcerned. The stone chamber was packed with people, standing and sitting and lying down, but the whole buzz of conversation was little more than a susurrus of whispers. You didn't come to the Dragon's Mouth to talk.

The air was thick with a hundred kinds of narcotic smoke, and already my lips and nostrils were going numb. You could experience a dozen different highs just strolling round the room, and long-buried parts of me stirred slowly, awakening, remembering. I took a deep breath. The smoky air smelled of sour milk and brimstone. I smiled slowly, and I knew it wasn't a pleasant smile.

Some of the people there recognised me. They smiled and nodded, or scowled and made the sign against the evil eye; and some crept further back into the concealing shadows. But nobody said anything, and nobody did anything. Held tightly in the jealous arms of their own particular mistresses, they trusted the club's staff to see that they remained undisturbed. There was never any trouble in the Dragon's Mouth because on the few occasions anyone was stupid enough to start anything, old Mother Connell would take measures. Very extreme and unpleasant measures.

She sat where she always sat, behind an ornately carved Restoration desk, right at the bottom of the entrance steps.

11

You couldn't see the top of the desk for all the piled-up currency, gold, jewels, and credit cards. Mother Connell sat at her ease in a frighteningly huge padded chair; four hundred pounds of overwhelming femininity wrapped in a purple toga topped off with a long, pink feather boa, draped loosely around her huge, wattled neck. Sometimes the boa stirred, as though it were alive, or dreaming. Mother Connell dominated anywhere she was, just by being there, through the sheer force of her appalling personality. And her complete willingness to make use of her mallet-sized fists at the first hint of any unpleasantness.

Harsh and sweaty under an obviously fake curly blonde wig, her wide red face was marked by heavily mascaraed eyes and a scarlet gash of a mouth, along with heavy jowls that disappeared into the pink feather boa. I always thought she looked like she'd just eaten half a dozen drag queens for breakfast. She had a smile for everyone because a smile cost nothing; but it wasn't a pretty sight. Her huge hands moved restlessly over the piled-up wealth before her, endlessly counting and sorting and rearranging it. In a rare moment of companionship, she'd once told me that when the cash really came rolling in, there was so much that she didn't have time to count it; so she weighed it.

She looked up and caught my eye. Mother Connell never forgot a face and never took any good-bye as final. Her scarlet lips pulled back to reveal yellow teeth, and she beckoned me over with one meaty hand. Her voice was deep and harsh, like a dog growling.

"Hello again, Mr. T. Been a while. Still looking for your Shanghai Lil?"

"That was long ago, in another land, and besides, the

wench is dead," I said. "I understand you're letting in elves these days?"

Her smile disappeared in a moment. "Hard times, Mr. T. Decadence and debauchery isn't what it was. I blame television."

"Tell me at least you didn't let him pay you with faerie gold."

She cackled briefly. "Not likely, Mr. T. He had a Master-Card."

"How very appropriate," I murmured. "Where can I find this elf, Mother Connell?"

She stabbed a meaty finger at the back of the room, her heavy underarm swinging ponderously. "In the smoking section, Mr. T. Do us all a favour; get him the hell out of here. He's lowering the bleeding tone something awful."

"Well, naturally," I said.

I waggled my fingers in a good-bye, and she grinned back at me like a shark scenting blood in the water. I turned away, with a certain sense of relief, and moved off into the cavern, drifting deeper into the depths of the Dragon's Mouth. No-one paid me any attention, as they all were sunk deep in their own personal heavens and hells. But one man saw me, and knew me, and came striding daintily out of the smoky mists with his professional smile of greeting fixed firmly in place. No-one knew precisely how old the Host was, or even if he was, technically speaking, human; he'd been with the Dragon's Mouth since it opened, over a century and a half ago. The Host was there to make you feel welcome, to see to your every need, and to see that you got everything that was coming to you. He'd find you somewhere comfortable, help you with the pipe or the pills, or the needle and the tourniquet, whisper suggestions in your ear when you looked to be hesitating, and encourage you to try things you'd never even contemplated before. He'd cuddle you when the shakes were bad, hold your hair back as you vomited, and take you for every penny you had. And when you died in the Dragon's Mouth, his would be the last face you ever saw. Still smiling.

Do I really need to tell you why?

He was currently wearing the very best suit Savile Row had to offer, complete with an old-school tie I was pretty sure he wasn't entitled to wear. He'd painted his face stark white with arsenic; his smiling mouth was crimson with heavy lipstick, and his dark shining eyes never blinked once. His jet-black hair had been slicked down so fiercely it looked painted on, and a small silver ankh hung from his left ear-lobe. His every movement and gesture were elegance personified, and he moved through the world as though everyone in it was merely a supporting player to his star turn.

The Host could get you anything, anything at all. And the worse it was for you, the wider he smiled. The Host was always delighted to be of service. He'd been only too happy to supply me with what I thought I needed, all those years ago. He drifted to a halt before me, bowed ever so politely, and clasped his pale, long-fingered hands together across his sunken chest.

"Well, well," he said, in a happy, breathy voice positively brimming with artificial bonhomie and fake sincerity. "Back again, Mr. Taylor? How nice. We're always happy to welcome back one of our straying sons. What can I get you, Mr. Taylor? Your usual?"

"No," I said. "I'm not here for that. I'm here to meet someone."

His dark red smile widened, just a little. "That's what they all say. Don't be shy, Mr. Taylor; you're amongst friends here. There's nothing to be ashamed of in the Dragon's Mouth. Indulge yourself. It's what we're here for."

"It's not what I'm here for," I said steadily. "I'm here on business. So stand aside."

He didn't move, his unblinking eyes fixed on mine, his gaze full of a malign intensity. "No-one ever leaves the Dragon's Mouth, Mr. Taylor. Not really. They only pop out for a while, then they come back. Who else knows you as well as us; who else can provide you with what you really need? You belong here, Mr. Taylor; you know you do. Come with me. Let me lead you to your old cubicle. It's still here. Nothing's changed. Let me prepare the needle for you and pop up a vein. You never really left; the world outside was just a cruel dream. You've always been here, where you belong."

I laughed right in his face, and he actually fell back a step. "Dream on," I said. "I'm a lot more than I used to be."

The Host rallied almost immediately. "Are you sure I can't offer you a little taste, Mr. Taylor? On the house, of course."

"Don't tempt me," I said.

The Host stepped gracefully to one side, bowing his head, admitting defeat. For the moment.

"Be seeing you, Mr. Taylor."

"Not if I see you first," I said to his elegantly retreating back.

I looked around the chamber, and various significant details loomed up out of the slowly swirling smoke. The old place hadn't changed since I was here last. Hiding from a world that had broken and defeated me, in pretty much every way there was. I hadn't so much lost hope, as thrown it away;

because hope hurt too much. The sheer weight of my life had become too much to carry, and I couldn't stand to see my reflection in the eyes of my friends. I'd failed; at everything that mattered and a few things that didn't. So I came here, to the Dragon's Mouth, asking only for pain's ease and forgetfulness. For the one thing drugs could give you that was better than pleasure—the cold, quiet comfort of feeling nothing at all.

There were hanging silk curtains and embroidered standing screens, to provide privacy for those who still cared about such things. Tables and chairs and camp beds, scattered in little clusters. Shadowy grottos and cells cut deep into the dark stone walls. Blood and piss and vomit on the floor. And all around me, men and women and other things, lost in dreams and might-have-beens. Dying, by inches . . . but I couldn't find it in myself to feel much for any of them. No-one comes to the Dragon's Mouth by chance. Everyone knows what happens here. You have to want it, and choose it, in the same way you'd choose a gun or a noose or the razor's blade.

And I had wanted it so very badly once upon a time.

I shook my head hard. I'm not normally one for dwelling in the past or regretting old mistakes. The tainted smoke curling on the still air was getting to me. I moved forward, making my way carefully between the packed tables and chairs, and stepping over the occasional dim shape on the floor; looking about me for the elf. A few people turned their backs as I passed them. Either they knew me, or they didn't want to know me. I didn't recognise any faces.

Two Hydes were fighting in a pit gouged raggedly from the stone floor. Overmuscled forms, with taut skin and bulging veins, they slammed together again and again, tearing at each other with clawed hands and bared teeth. Blood and sweat coursed down their distorted forms, and they grunted and snarled like beasts, while a few languid spectators roused themselves to lay bets on which Hyde would survive. The dead Hyde would be recycled, so as not to waste any of the drug. Junkies know everything there is to know about making a drug go further.

A cyborg from some future time-line was main-lining a fierce and nasty future drug called Blood. Tech implants protruded from his grey flesh, discharging sudden bursts of static. His eyes glowed golden as they rolled up into his head, and his slack mouth was full of metal teeth. You can fill the future with all the high tech you want, but people will still be people.

A long row of camp beds had been pushed up against one wall, and a dozen or so pretty young things stared sightlessly up into the smoky air, enjoying the complete out-of-the-body experience, courtesy of the banned African drug taduku. Blasted loose from the chains of their bodies, their minds were free to drift into the past or the future or any number of alternate dimensions or realities. Sometimes they came back, and sometimes they didn't. You can probably imagine what happens to the bodies of those who don't come back.

Brother Frank was experimenting with Angel Breath again, the old deep fix, trying to separate out the various levels of his consciousness so he could have conversations with himself. You had to be careful around Brother Frank. He did so love to spike a drink, so to speak.

A huge cage with reinforced iron bars held those who had chosen to indulge in the ancient alien drug known as Revert. A sly and deceitful drug that could throw your evolution into

17

reverse, transforming you into the Neanderthal state, or even further, if you could stand it. In the cage, amongst the heavy, low-browed figures, there were other, even more disturbing shapes.

And, finally, a small and rather furtive group were smoking Martian red weed from hookah pipes. Devotees claim it helps you think in whole new ways. Smoke enough of the stuff, and you can think like a Martian. Smoke too much, and your body will actually turn into a Martian. And then everyone around you will rise up and club you to death because even the Nightside has its standards.

A couple of soft ghosts wandered through the thick air, hand in hand, looking for anything familiar. They were vague, indistinct, half-transparent, their very existence worn down and eroded by too much travelling in other dimensions. Human once, they had gone too far and seen too much, and now they could no longer remember how to find their way home, or even what home had been like. The details of their faces had grown smooth and doubtful, like the statues of cemetery angels worn down by time and the elements. The smoke ghosts drifted here and there, desperate for a familiar face or an accent, asking in their soft, distant voices of cities and peoples and worlds that no-one had ever heard of.

The patrons of the Dragon's Mouth flapped them away with heavy hands, or ignored them completely. The soft ghosts should have known better than to look for help here, but they were attracted to the altered states of consciousness like moths to a flame. One of them tugged gently at my sleeve, trying to attract my attention, but I shrugged it off. I'd spotted my elf.

I was heading straight for him when someone moved

abruptly forward to block my way. I stopped short, because it was either that or walk right over him, then paused to consider the man before me. I knew who he was almost at once, though the years had not been kind. Carnaby Jones, the Wide-Eyed Boy, infamous dandy and free spirit of the old King's Road, had fallen far from what he once was. His T-shirt and jeans were clean enough, but he looked as if someone else had dressed him. His old muscular frame was gone, the flesh sunk right back to the bone, and his skin was a dull, unhealthy yellow. The skull showed clearly behind the taut skin of his face, his deep-set eyes were lost and murky, and his thin-lipped smile held all the malice in the world. He smelled bad.

I could still remember when the Wide-Eyed Boy had been the best and bravest.

"What do you want, Carnaby?" I asked politely.

He sniggered loudly. "No time for old friends, John? Nothing to say to the old friend you abandoned and left behind? The one who brought you here, and taught you the ropes, and introduced you to pleasures you never knew existed?"

"I forgave you for that long ago," I said. "We're both different people now. Is that a tinge of purple I see in your eyeballs, Carnaby? Been injecting through the tear ducts because you've run out of veins? How could you have fallen so far?"

"Practice," he said, his grin widening to show rotten teeth. "You're looking good, John. Really. Very . . . healthy. What made you think you could just walk back in here and stroll amongst us with your nose in the air? You owe me, John. You know you do."

"You want me to take you out of here, I'll do it," I said. "You want help, I'll get you the best there is."

"I don't want anything from you! Except to see you pay for what you did."

"What did I do, Carnaby?" I said patiently.

"You broke the rules, John! You got out! No-one's supposed to get out of here. That's the point."

"I had help," I said. "Take my hand, Carnaby. Really. I mean it. The only one keeping you here is you."

He looked at me sideways, still smiling his unpleasant smile. "You got out, and now you're a big man in the Nightside. Oh yes, the news trickles down, even to places like this. Word is you're a rich man, too. So how about a little something, for an old friend? How about a hand-out, how about the shirt off your back, how about everything you've got!"

He was spitting the words out now, his whole wrecked body shaking with years of pent-up, carefully rehearsed spite and hatred. I sensed old Mother Connell stirring behind her table, and raised one hand to stop her. Because once upon a time the Wide-Eyed Boy really had been a friend of mine, had really had it in him to be the very best of us. Drugs don't just destroy who you are; they destroy all the people you might have been.

So I stepped forward, grabbed his bony head firmly with both hands, and held his gaze with my own. He tried to break away, but there was no strength left in him. He tried to look away, but I had him. I concentrated, and he cried out miserably as all the old scabs on his forearms broke open, and dark liquids oozed out and trickled down his arms. Everything he'd ever taken, every last nasty drop of it, ran out of him, and he cried like a baby at the loss of it. When I was finished I let him go, and he fell in a heap before me.

"There," I said. "You're clean. Free as a bird. So you can

leave, or you can stay; it's all up to you. And don't say I never did anything for you."

I left him there and headed for the elf.

He was sitting alone at a small table, smoking opium through a hollowed-out human thigh-bone. Just because he could. There was a circle of open space around him, despite the crowded conditions of the Dragon's Mouth, because even the kind of people who habituated a place like this didn't want anything to do with an elf.

Long and long ago, humans and elves lived together on the Earth, sharing its wonders and resources. But we never got on. There were battles and wars and horrible slaughters, and in the end we won by cheating; we outbred the pointy-eared bastards. They gave up and left our world, walking sideways from the sun, moving their whole race to another world, another reality. The Sundered Lands. The few elves you see walking the world today are rogues, outlaws, remittance men. They live to screw us over because that's all they've got.

This particular elf watched me approach and lazily blew a perfect smoke ring at me. Followed by half a dozen increasingly complex smoke shapes, culminating in a great ship perched on a rising wave, complete with billowing sails and shaking rigging. But he was only showing off, so I ignored it. I pulled up a chair and sat down opposite him, careful to keep the whole of the table between us.

"So," said the elf, in a voice like a cat drowning in cream and loving every minute of it, "here you are. Lilith's son."

"Actually," I said, "I take more after my father. I'm John Taylor."

21

"Of course. And you can address me as Lord Screech, Pale Prince of Owls."

"But that's not your real name."

"Of course not. To know the true name of a thing is to have power over it. But for the purpose of this transaction, Lord Screech will do."

"Because the owls are not what they seem?"

"Quite."

I looked him over. Screech was inhumanly tall and almost impossibly slender, with the usual slit-pupilled cat's eyes and sharp, pointed ears. His skin glowed like fine porcelain, so pale as to be almost colourless, and his quick smile showed pointed teeth behind the rose pink lips. He wore long oriental robes of a shimmering metallic green, complete with a stiff high collar that rose behind his head, and his long white hair had been swept up in tufts on either side of his elongated skull, like an owl's. I was tempted to make a Flock of Seagulls joke, but he wouldn't have got it.

And besides, it would have dated me.

"Why ask for me?" I said, directly.

"You have a reputation for arrogance, style, and occasional viciousness," said Screech. "You might almost have been an elf."

"Now you're just being nasty," I said. "And why meet here, of all places?"

"Because I do so love to watch humans degrade themselves," Screech said easily. "Throwing their lives away for such pitiful rewards. No elf would ever lower himself to anything as small as this; even our sins have to be magnificent."

"Tell me what you want," I said. "Or I'm out of here."

"Always so impatient," said Screech, laying aside his bone

pipe. "Always in such a hurry. Comes of being mortal, I suppose. Very well, Mr. Taylor, I shall talk, and you will listen, which is of course the proper state of affairs between elf and human. I am presently passing through the Nightside on a matter of importance. It is imperative I complete my journey without being stopped or in any way detained along the way. I am an emissary between the two warring factions of Faerie."

"Hold everything," I said, leaning forward despite myself. "Go back, go previous; run that by me again. The Fae are at war with each other? When did that happen? And why haven't we heard about it?"

"Because it's none of your business."

"It is now," I said. "Or you wouldn't need my help."

"Life is imperfect," said Screech.

"All right; why pass through the Nightside at all?"

"Because this appalling locality is the nearest thing we have to neutral territory. I can see I'm going to have to fill you in on a few of the background details. How very tedious. In the beginning, long before human history began and we were all myths and legends . . . Queen Mab ruled over the Fae, and she was mighty and magnificent and terrible to behold in her glory. Under her rule we spread and prospered; but it didn't last. How could someone of such a magnitude as Mab have foreseen the rise of the vermin called Man? She underestimated you, and lost the war, and was deposed, by Oberon and Titania.

"They dragged her off her Throne and threw her down into Hell; and there she stayed for many centuries, while Oberon and Titania ruled the Fae in her place, in the Sundered Lands. But Mab got out; and after so long in the Houses of Pain, her vengeance was terrible to behold. She cast Oberon and Titania down, to take her place in Hell, and re-established herself as the one true rightful ruler of the Fae. Or as many of us as were left after she'd finished purging the unfaithful.

"But then Oberon and Titania fought their way out of Hell and took up residence in Shadows Fall, in the land under the hill, and have since amassed a mighty power of rebellious elves, determined to take back the Sundered Lands by force of arms. Aren't families embarrassing when you have to explain them to strangers?

"Anyway, civil wars are always costly, in all too many ways, and both sides have been persuaded to step back from the brink. For the moment. I have been acting as emissary between the two rival Courts, and after much . . . discussion, we have a Peace Treaty. It won't last—such things never do—but hopefully it will buy us time for more reasonable voices to make themselves heard. Or perhaps some public-spirited person will assassinate one or other of the Courts. I need you, John Taylor, to find me a safe way across the Nightside, from this distressing location to the furthest boundary, and the Osterman Gate. Where I might finally take my leave of this . . . human world, in favour of some more civilised reality.

"You must understand, Mr. Taylor, there are many here who would like nothing better than to see me dead, and the Treaty destroyed, for a whole variety of reasons. These unprincipled villains include certain elves on both sides who want war for personal and political reasons, who can't or won't forgive past slights . . . and then there are all those people who hate elves and would delight in the spectacle of our slaughtering each other. This very definitely includes the Nightside's current Overseer, Walker; who has set his people to harrying and threatening my progress. Apparently he has decided it is in Humanity's best interests that the elves remain divided and, preferably, destroy each other. A very . . . practical man, your Walker."

The elf stopped talking and looked at me. I considered the matter, taking my time. My first impulse was to get up and leave. Well, actually, get up and sprint for the exit. Getting involved with elves is never a good idea, and getting caught between two warring factions struck me as only marginally less dangerous than playing Russian roulette with a fully loaded gun. There's just no way you can win. And on top of all that . . .

Never trust an elf.

I'd heard rumours about Queen Mab's return, and everything Screech had said had a dreadful plausibility to it, but he had to be lying about something, even if only by omission. Because that's what elves do.

"Why should I help you?" I said bluntly. "You and your kind have always been the enemies of Humanity. Maybe Walker's right. Maybe elf killing elf is in our best interests."

"What makes you think our war would take place in the Sundered Lands?" said Screech, smiling pleasantly. "No; we'd fight our battles in your world, where the extensive collateral damage wouldn't bother us in the least."

"Good point," I conceded. "All right; suppose I do take this on. How do you propose to pay me?"

"Not with any of the usual means of payment," said Screech. "You wouldn't trust any of them, and quite rightly.

"I propose to pay you . . . with information. I know something you don't know. Something that you definitely need to know. Because it involves a real and present danger to the whole of the Nightside and because it involves you personally. Something very old and very powerful and quite appallingly terrible has come to the Nightside. You'll know the name when I say it; though it isn't what you think it is. Get me safely across the Nightside to the Osterman Gate, and I'll give you its name. Believe me, John Taylor; you need to find this thing before anyone else does."

I looked at him thoughtfully, saying nothing. *Never trust an elf . . .*

"If you wanted to pass unnoticed through the Nightside," I said, finally, "why come as an elf and draw attention to yourself? Why not hide your true nature behind a glamour and pass yourself off as just another tourist?"

"Appear as a human?" said Lord Screech, looking down his nose at me. "I wouldn't lower myself. I have standards. Do we have a deal, Mr. Taylor?"

"You're almost certainly not who you say you are," I said. "You're probably not even what you claim to be. And you're proposing to pay for my services with a secret that may or may not turn out to be of any practical use. Have I left out anything important?"

"Only that any number of truly unpleasant individuals will quite definitely try to kill the both of us all the way to the Osterman Gate," the elf said cheerfully. "But then, that situation's normal for you, isn't it?"

"What the hell," I said. "I've got nothing else interesting on at the moment. But if your precious secret turns out to be a crock of shit, I will quite definitely rip both your pointy ears off and use them as can openers."

"Oh, it's a wonderful secret," said the elf, smiling. "Vitally important and damnably significant. You're really going to hate it."

I got up from the table, and Screech rose to his feet in one long, graceful movement. He was still smiling, which is always a disturbing thing in an elf.

One of the Hydes from the pit came storming towards us, sweeping tables and chairs and their occupants out of his way with great blows from his muscular, blood-soaked arms. He'd taken a hell of a beating from the other Hyde, but already the old drug was closing his wounds for him. His fierce gaze was fixed on the elf. Carnaby Jones was right behind him, urging him on. And a dozen or so inhabitants of the Revert cage brought up the rear, carrying improvised weapons. Carnaby sneered at me.

"Did you think I'd be *grateful*?" he said flatly.

I glanced quickly about me. Mother Connell was already out from behind her table, her massive hands closing into impressive fists, but by the time she'd forced her way through the packed crowds, it would probably all be over, one way or the other. The Hyde loomed up before us, a great wedge of bone and muscle with blood on his breath and gleeful murder in his eyes. Screech took a graceful step forward, and punched the Hyde in the throat. The sheer impact of the blow sent the Hyde staggering backwards, and the crunching sound of shattering trachea was horribly loud in the sudden quiet. Screech watched interestedly as the Hyde sank to his knees, clawing desperately at his destroyed throat, dying by inches. Carnaby let out a wordless cry of rage and waved the Reverted men forward. I stepped up and stared the head Revert right in the eyes, stopping him in his tracks. Huge and brutal, only half-way human, he couldn't meet my gaze.

He backed away, swinging his low-browed head from side to side, then he turned and lumbered back to the safety of the cage. The others followed him. And Carnaby Jones was left standing all alone.

"Shall I kill him for you?" said Screech.

"No," I said. "I'm not feeling merciful. Let's get out of this shit hole. And this information of yours had better be worth it."

"Get me to where I need to be, and I promise I'll tell you something to your disadvantage," said Lord Screech.

Some nights you just shouldn't get out of bed.

TWO

Hot Pursuit in a Cold Town

Outside the Dragon's Mouth, the air was fresh and sharp and full of familiar scents. All kinds of cooking, from all kinds of cultures; blood and sweat and musk blasting out of the dance halls; the lingering reminders of a thousand different kinds of sin. I took a deep breath to clear my head. Getting Lord Screech all the way across the Nightside to the infamous Osterman Gate would have been tricky and dangerous enough at the best of times, but with Walker and all his various people out and about, keeping under the radar was going to be more than usually difficult.

The Osterman Gate is an ancient crystal amulet the size of an elephant, and the only dimensional gateway in the Nightside that leads directly to Shadows Fall; that remarkable little town in the back of beyond where legends go to die, when the world stops believing in them. And now, it seemed, home to the elven Court in exile. Normally, you got to Shadows Fall by the Underground rail system, but Walker's people would have all the stations staked out by now. Along with the Street of the Gods, the World Beneath, and all the other subterranean routes and hidden paths. Walker was nothing if not thorough. So, unfortunately, all that remained was the most dangerous route of all. The roads.

There are many roads leading in and out of the Nightside, and wise people have nothing at all to do with them. The traffic that roars up and down our streets hardly ever stops, and it's better that way for everyone. There are cars and trucks, ambulance chasers and motorcycle messengers, horse-drawn equipages and futuristic vehicles that often don't have wheels or windows or any regard for the rules of the road. Every single one of them in a hell of a hurry to get where it's going, usually to somewhere even stranger and more dangerous than the Nightside.

Ambulances that run on distilled suffering, ice wagons that carry blocks of frozen holy water, and ghost trams that stop for no man. Articulated vehicles as long as city blocks carrying hazardous and forbidden materials, silent hearses carrying the kind of cargo that has to be fought back into its coffin at regular intervals; and not everything that looks like a car is a car. There are things in the traffic that feed on slower things. Sometimes I look at the main roads, and I don't see traffic; I see a jungle on wheels.

Which is why no-one with any sense uses the roads unless he absolutely has to.

I don't own a car. I have my own ways of getting places. But when I do need one, I throw myself on the kindness of strange friends. I got out my phone and called Dead Boy. An old friend and occasional partner in crime, Dead Boy owned a truly magnificent car that had strayed into the Nightside from some future time-line. It could beat up anything on four wheels, and had never even heard of road safety. But after I waited patiently through the dialling chant, all I got was Dead Boy's usual recorded message.

"Hi. I'm dead. Call back later."

So I frowned, tapped my foot thoughtfully, and considered who else might be available and up for a little motorised mayhem. It wasn't a terribly long list, and it didn't take me long to get to the bottom. I sighed and entered the number for Ms. Fate; the Nightside's very own transvestite crime-fighter. A man who dressed up as a super-heroine to kick the crap out of bad guys. She's actually very good at it; and she has a really remarkable car. It's just that I find her continual bright-eyed girl-guide enthusiasm somewhat trying . . .

"Hi, John!" she said, her voice rich and warm as always. "In trouble again, are we?"

"How did you know?" I said, a bit suspiciously.

"John, my phone is preprogrammed to recognise your voice. It sets off all sorts of warning bells and a siren, because let's face it, sweetie, you're always in some kind of trouble."

"How would you like to drive me and my elven client from one side of the Nightside to the other, all the way to the Osterman Gate, almost certainly fighting off attacks by assorted bad guys from beginning to end, and help prevent a major war into the bargain?"

She laughed. "You always did know how to show a girl a good time. Did you say . . . elven?"

"Yes. Don't ask me to explain, or I'll start to whimper. It's complicated."

"My fee just doubled. Shall we say . . . twenty per cent of what you're getting?"

I grinned. "I don't have any problem with that."

"Fabulous, darling! I'll slip a few extra nasty tricks into my utility belt, fire up the Fatemobile, and be with you in two shakes of the best false boobies money can buy."

There wasn't anything I felt like saying in response to that, so I shut down my phone. I was about to put it away when it rang. I looked at it for a moment. Sometimes you just have a feeling . . . I answered the phone, holding it a cautious distance away from my ear.

"This had better not be who I think it is."

"John, dear boy, this is Walker. You need to stop what you're doing and go home, right now. This is none of your business."

"He's my client," I said. I didn't know how Walker knew I was involved with the putative Lord Screech; but then, Walker knows everything. I think that's actually part of his job description. Along with keeping the peace and enforcing the status quo in the Nightside by any and all means necessary. Either way, he should have known better than to give me orders.

"You can get other clients," Walker said reasonably. "Walk away, John. I've already signed the elf's death warrant. I'd hate to have to sign another."

That was Walker for you. He might or might not hate to do it; but he'd do it. Walker was all about getting the job done.

"You know I never let a client down," I said.

"Of course, dear boy. I'm only keeping you talking so my people can pinpoint your current location . . . John? What are you doing back at the Dragon's Mouth?"

There was something in his voice. It might have been concern; but you can never be sure with Walker.

"I'm fine," I said. "The client chose the meeting place."

"Typical elf. He knew what it meant to you. Yet another reason why you shouldn't trust him. I know you pride yourself on being loyal to your clients, John, but he won't be loyal to you. He can't. He's an elf."

"The principle still stands," I said. "I don't have many, so I have to stick with what I've got. We're off on a little road trip, Walker, off to see the worlds. Try and keep up."

"This is no joke, John. I've been forced to take on some really serious people, to see this through."

"Send the best you've got," I said. "And I'll send them home crying for their mothers."

Walker sighed into my ear, like a parent disappointed by a stubborn child. "You've been listening to the elf, haven't you, John? You know you can't trust anything an elf says. I am the only one who knows what's really going on here."

"Doesn't matter," I said. "If he's on the opposite side to you, I must be doing the right thing."

"All these years of butting heads," said Walker. "And you haven't learned a damned thing."

The phone went dead. I looked at it for a moment, to see if anyone else felt like calling and sticking their oar in, then I put the phone away. Of course I knew Lord Screech couldn't be trusted. He was an elf. But I'd given him my word, and my word was good. I looked up and down the street. Ms. Fate had better get a move on. Walker hadn't been joking about pinpointing my position through my phone.

There wasn't anywhere handy I could use as a shelter. The clubs and bars in this part of town were so down-market, the bouncers were outside chucking them in, and they forced you to order your drinks at gunpoint. And there was no way I was going back into the Dragon's Mouth.

"Is there any particular reason why you're ignoring me?" said Lord Screech.

"Because I'll get lied to less that way," I said, not looking at the elf. "I know all I need to know."

"Walker was quite right. Never trust anything an elf tells you. We always lie—except when a truth can hurt you more. Or when the truth can be made to serve our best interests over yours. I don't care about you, or Walker, or any other human, except where you can help or hinder my mission."

I didn't ask how he knew it was Walker on the phone.

"If you're trying to be disarming, it isn't working," I said. "And don't even try to be charming. I've got protections against that."

"Why are you helping me, John Taylor? When you know you should know better?"

I looked at him for the first time. "Because I'm intrigued. And not by the terrible secret you've offered as payment, whatever it may or may not turn out to be. I've spent my whole life dealing with terrible secrets. No, what intrigues me is why a high-and-mighty elf lord should endanger himself by coming to the Nightside, then beg help from a human. Even one as special as me. So I'll go along with you, do my best to get you to where you need to be . . . and no doubt your true purpose will become clear along the way."

"I wouldn't put money on it," the elf said cheerfully.

Perhaps fortunately, we were interrupted at that point by the approaching roar of a powerful engine. We both looked round and stepped back a little as the Fatemobile surged out of the traffic and slammed to a halt right in front of us. On every side, hardened sinners on their way to infamous dens of iniquity stopped, to get a better look at the Fatemobile. A good twelve feet long and almost as wide, Ms. Fate's crime-fighting motor car was a magnificent machine, with low, powerful lines in a retro sixties style, complete with tall rear fins, a prominent afterburner, and acres and acres of gleaming chrome. It was a shocking fluorescent pink from bonnet to bumper, and had big fluffy wheels. In fact, it wasn't so much pink as *PINK!* And instead of the usual silver winged victory figure on the front radiator, the Fatemobile boasted a silver wee-winged faerie in a basque and suspenders.

Ms. Fate might have heard of taste, but only as something other people had. Boring people.

"I like it!" said Lord Screech.

"You would," I said.

The heavy driver's door swung open with a puff of compressed air, and Ms. Fate emerged from her car via a single elegant movement I couldn't have copied without throwing my whole back out. Tall and leanly muscular, Ms. Fate wore a black leather super-heroine outfit, cut tightly to show off her long legs and false bosoms. Heavy boots and gauntlets, and a proud horned cowl. Her green eyes shone brightly through polarised eye-slits, and her mouth was a brilliant red. Her utility belt was a bright yellow, presumably so she could find it in the dark. She crashed to a halt before me and struck a pose that was only slightly self-mocking.

"And here I am, to save the day! Ms. Fate, at your service, rogues, villains, and creatures of the night a speciality. Ask me about my special rates for criminal conspiracies. How are you, John?"

"All the better for seeing you," I said. "Where's your cape? I always think you look so more authentic with your cape."

"In the back seat. I have to take it off when I'm driving; I find it restricts my movements too much."

Ms. Fate is the real deal. A genuine old-school super-heroine who just happens to be played by a man.

"We really do need to get a move on," I said. "Walker's people are already on their way here. So fire up the Pink Panther mobile, stomp on the pedal, and it's everything forward and trust in the Lord all the way to the Osterman Gate. Stop for nothing and no-one, and I hope all your car's armaments are loaded for bear because we're going to need them."

"You know how to sweet-talk a girl," said Ms. Fate. "Aren't you going to introduce me to your elven friend?"

"This is Lord Screech," I said. "Only he probably isn't. Think of him less as my client and more as cargo to be transported. I'd lock him in the boot if I could trust him out of my sight that long."

"Well," said Ms. Fate, smiling challengingly at Screech. "An elf. How . . . exotic."

The elf lord gave her a formal bow, with all the trimmings. "Delighted to meet you. You're a man."

"Not when I'm on duty," said Ms. Fate. "Is my secret identity going to be a problem?"

"Not at all," said Screech, smiling easily. "Like all my kind, I delight in all forms of deceit and disguise, and glory in the joys of transformation. We've never understood this human preoccupation with normality. Where's the fun in that?"

"Definitely time to be going," I said. "When an elf starts making sense . . ."

Ms. Fate laughed and snapped her fingers at the Fate-mobile. All the doors swung open. Ms. Fate headed for the driving seat. I looked at Screech.

"You want to do rock, scissors, paper to see who rides shotgun?"

"Only people I trust get to sit beside me in the Fate-mobile," said Ms. Fate.

"I'll get in the back seat," said Screech.

"Mind my cloak," said Ms. Fate.

I settled into the passenger seat while Screech folded his long body almost in two to fit through the backdoor. Sitting down, he had to lean forward to keep from banging his head on the roof, and his knees came up to his chin. He still looked insufferably dignified and aristocratic, but that's elves for you. The Fatemobile's interior was pretty much as I remembered. Lipstick red leather on all the seats, a high-tech dashboard complete with computer displays and weapons systems, and a steering wheel covered in ermine. A bonsai pine tree perched on the dashboard served as an air freshener. Ms. Fate touched the ignition pad with a leather-clad fingertip, and the whole car trembled eagerly.

"Are there many super-heroes in the Nightside?" said Screech, from between his raised knees.

"We prefer the term *costumed adventurers*," said Ms. Fate, running quickly through her car's warm-up checks. "Pretty much everyone and everything turns up here eventually, and there have always been a few of us, making a stand for justice and revenge and the right to kick six different colours of crap out of the bad guys. I think we do it for the challenge. No-one does villains like the Nightside. Right, John?"

"Archetypes and icons have always felt at home in the Nightside," I said. "But super-heroes and super-villains are a bit too innocent to do well here. I think we disappoint them, with our endless shades of grey rather than their preferred black-and-white morality. There have always been a few costumed heroes; the Mystery Avenger, the Lady Phantasm, the Cutting Edge . . ."

"And the villains?" said the elf, hopefully.

"Again, we tend more towards colourful characters," I said. "The Painted Ghoul, Jackie Schadenfreude, Penny Dreadful . . ."

"And remember that awful little poseur, Dr. Delirium?" said Ms. Fate. "Today the Nightside, tomorrow the world?"

"Of course I remember," I said. "Walker had Suzie and me toss his nasty little arse out of the Nightside. Last I heard, he was sulking somewhere in the Amazon rain forest, swearing vengeance on the world and trying to build his own private army through ads in the back of *Soldier of Fortune* magazine. This is what comes of uncles leaving you far too much money."

"You work for Walker?" said Screech.

"Sometimes," I said. "When he's not trying to have me killed. It's complicated. It's the Nightside."

"Heads up, people," said Ms. Fate. "Company's coming."

They came marching down the street towards us, and everyone else hurried to get out of their way. Striding arrogantly in perfect formation and perfect lock-step, carrying heavy truncheons and pistols holstered on both their hips, in black-and-gold uniforms with reinforced helmets; Walker's very own shock-and-awe troopers. I felt obscurely flattered that Walker had sent his own personal heavies to stop me. It showed a certain respect for my capabilities.

Walker's job was to keep the lid on things, and to do that he could call on support from the Army, the Church, and pretty much anyone else he felt like, along with any number of specialists. But he wasn't usually one for displays of brute force; he tended more towards dividing and conquering and *Let's you and him fight*. He only sent in the shock-and-awe troopers when he absolutely positively felt the need to stamp on everyone in sight, as an object lesson to others. He must see Lord Screech's Peace Treaty as a threat to the Nightside's status quo . . . but still, he shouldn't have done it. He must have known I'd take it personally.

I did a quick headcount, and came up with thirty heavily armed specimens, heading right for us. Under normal circumstances, sending thirty armed men to take down one elf, one super-heroine, and me might have seemed somewhat excessive; but as I've said before, we don't do normal in the Nightside. These might well be hard-faced, hard-hearted, hardened soldier types; but in the end they were only military men, and we . . . were so much more. They broke into a trot as they spotted the Fatemobile, hefting their truncheons eagerly.

I just knew we weren't going to get along.

The three of us stepped out of the car and stood together, studying the advancing bully-boys. They all had that look . . . of men who'd been thrown out of the SAS for excessive brutality; of men who didn't know the meaning of the word *fear*, or *self-restraint*; of men who would get the job done whatever it took. Idiots with muscle, basically. Training's all very fab and groovy, but it only works in the sane, everyday world. In the Nightside, we depend more on violent improvisation and downright nasty weirdness.

Someone in the front rank spotted me, and I saw a ripple

pass through the ranks as my name worked its way back. They all swapped their truncheons to their left hands, and drew their guns with their right. Heavy, long-barrelled pistols, loaded with dum-dums if they had any sense. I smiled, a little. Walker must have told them about me, but they clearly hadn't listened. So, time for my party trick. I raised my hands, called on an old well-rehearsed magic, and took all the bullets out of their guns. The bullets fell in streams from my upraised hands, to jump and clatter on the ground at my feet. As tricks go, I couldn't help feeling it was getting just a bit predictable, but I think people have come to expect it and would be disappointed if I didn't use it at some point. Sometimes I'm a victim of my own reputation.

The shock-and-awe troopers could tell the guns in their hands were empty by the sudden change in weight, and they holstered them quickly. Without slowing their advance, they transferred their truncheons back to their right hands. A good move. You can't take bullets out of a stick. I looked behind me, casually, in case there was an obvious exit route, but the street was blocked off by a crowd of fascinated onlookers, taking photos and placing bets. One guy had even taken advantage of the crowd to set up a fast-food stall, selling wriggling things on sticks.

Ms. Fate finished fastening her midnight blue cloak about her shoulders. It suited her. The cape made her look more like an experienced crime-fighter and less like a pervert in a fetish suit. The heavy leather cape swirled about her as she drew a handful of razor-sharp silver shuriken out of her belt. In that moment, she looked every inch the real thing; because she was.

"We could drive off," I said. "Thus avoiding unnecessary blood and suffering. Just putting it forward as a possibility . . ."

"Don't be silly," said Ms. Fate, making fists inside her gauntlets so that the leather creaked loudly. The knuckles were reinforced with steel caps. "I have my reputation to consider."

"Sorry," I said. "Don't know what came over me. Don't suppose you've got any battle armour built into that costume?"

"Of course not. It slows me down when I'm fighting. You really mustn't worry about me, John. It's sweet, but just a touch patronising. Worry about those poor bastards."

Her right hand whipped forward, with a practised snap of the wrist, and a silver shuriken flashed through the air to bury itself in the nearest trooper's left tit. It punched right through his body armour and buried itself deep in the pectoral muscle. Blood spurted on the air as the force of the blow slammed him back onto his arse. Well trained, though, he didn't make a sound as his fellow troopers trampled right over him in their eagerness to get to us.

"Some people would take a hint," said Ms. Fate. "But I can see we're going to have to do this the hard way. Up close and personal."

"Best way," said Lord Screech.

I looked at him, and couldn't keep from raising an eyebrow. "Are you seriously proposing to involve yourself in a common brawl? I didn't think your kind lowered themselves to simple fisticuffs and putting the boot in."

"We don't, usually," said the elf. "But we never miss an opportunity to put mere humans in their place."

And he and Ms. Fate marched purposefully forward to strike terror into the hearts of the ungodly. I stayed right where I was, considering my options. I've never been much of a one for brute force, mainly because I've never been very good at it. I had no doubt I'd have to get personally involved at some point, but I thought I'd wait and see what Ms. Fate and Lord Screech had to offer first.

The shock-and-awe troopers clearly didn't take a costumed super-heroine seriously, right up to the moment she hit their advancing front line like a grenade. She punched out one man, back-elbowed another in the throat, swung around and took out two more with a sweeping karate kick. Shocked cries of pain and horror filled the night as she waded right into the troopers, breaking heads and noses, beating them up and knocking them down, and making it all look easy. The troopers quickly rallied, striking out viciously with their truncheons, but somehow Ms. Fate was never where they thought she should be, and they did more damage to each other than they did to her.

Ms. Fate had trained long and hard to be a costumed crime-fighter, and it showed.

Lord Screech, on the other hand, was every inch the magnificent amateur; a man who never practised because he didn't need to. He seemed simply to stroll into the mayhem, and men started dropping to the blood-stained ground. He moved languidly, gracefully, through the confused pack of armed men, and every time his hand shot out, there was the sound of breaking bone and cartilage, and blood flew everywhere. He moved so quickly none of the shock-and-awe troopers could even touch him.

I sat on the bonnet of the Fatemobile, cheering my colleagues on but not so loudly as to draw unwelcome attention to myself. Screech and Ms. Fate didn't seem to need my help. Until a new pack of troopers, twice the size of the original, came racing round the corner, and charged forward to join the fight. I sighed. Given that Walker was every inch a product of the old public school system, he seemed to have great difficulty in grasping the concept of playing fair.

Screech and Ms. Fate moved quickly to stand back-to-back, surrounded by broken and bloodied figures crawling painfully about on the street. They could have run back to the safety of the Fatemobile, but that wasn't their style. Ms. Fate was breathing hard, the leather over her fake breasts rising and falling, but her gloved hands were full of shuriken, and her cowled head was proudly erect. Screech wasn't even breathing hard. He flicked drops of blood from the tips of his elegant fingers and glared arrogantly at the approaching troopers. But there had to be a good sixty armed men heading right for them, and the odds weren't good.

So I got up off the bonnet, walked casually forward to join Screech and Ms. Fate, waited till the charging troopers were almost upon us, then used a variation on my bullet-removing trick to rip all the fillings, crowns and bridgework right out of their mouths. The troopers skidded to a halt, clutching at ruined, bloody mouths, making quite distressing and pitiful sounds of pain and horror. Screech and Ms. Fate looked at me inquiringly. I explained what I'd just done, and Ms. Fate got the giggles. Screech nodded approvingly, as though I was a rather backwards pupil who'd finally done something right. I stepped forward, and cleared my throat loudly to get the troopers' attention.

"Yes," I said cheerfully. "That was me. Now, be good little shock-and-awe troopers and trot off back to Walker, or I'll show you another disappearing trick, involving your testicles and a series of buckets."

They looked at each other, put away their various weapons, and trudged off to tell Walker I'd been mean to them.

And probably to ask if he knew a good dentist. They looked rather sullen and sulky, as though we hadn't played the game by refusing to be helpless victims.

"Spoil-sport," said Ms. Fate, her breathing almost back to normal. "I was just getting warmed up."

"That was a really nasty trick, Mr. Taylor," said Screech. "Almost worthy of an elf."

"Let's get back to the car," I said. "We need to remove ourselves from the vicinity, at speed, before Walker decides to send someone or something really dangerous after us. Those poor fools were just a shot across the bows, to get our attention."

"And," said Ms. Fate, "now he knows what car you're using. So much for the element of surprise."

We all piled back into the Fatemobile, Ms. Fate detaching her cloak and tossing it onto the back seat, where it enveloped Lord Screech. Ms. Fate slapped at various controls, the automatic seat belts did themselves up, and she gripped the ermine-covered steering wheel with her gloved hands.

"Atomic batteries to power, turbines to speed!" she yelled joyously, and slammed her foot down.

The Fatemobile peeled out so fast it took a minute for its shadow to catch up, and bullied its way into the streaming traffic through sheer bravado and force of character. The acceleration pressed me back into my seat, and the sudden turns clanged my eye-balls together. Screech finally freed himself from the folds of Ms. Fate's cape and leaned forward.

"Atomic batteries? Is she joking?"

"Who can tell?" I said. "This is the Nightside. We do things differently here."

"You humans and your toys," said Screech. "I think I'll take a little nap. Wake me up when we get to the Gate."

• • •

We shot through the Nightside at breath-taking speed, over-taking most things, intimidating others, and shouldering aside anything that didn't get out of the way fast enough. The Fatemobile might look like a contender for *Top Gear*'s Most Effeminate Car of the Year Award, but it moved like a guided missile, and had enough built-in weapons systems to more than punch its weight. Ms. Fate wasn't above using the front-mounted machine-guns to clear the way ahead if she recognised anyone she disapproved of, and she tossed a con-cussion grenade through the open window of a taxi-cab when the driver was rude to her. He must have been new. Any-one else would have had more sense. Or at least sense enough to maintain a safe distance. The various bars and clubs all merged into one long blur as we streaked past them, the neon signs a long multi-coloured smear. The Fatemobile's motor roared like a beast unleashed, and there wasn't a thing on the road that could match us.

It wasn't until we were directed off the main road and onto the side routes that our real troubles began.

Walker had set up roadblocks at all the major intersec-tions leading to the Osterman Gate, heavy fortifications topped with barbed wire, leaving only narrow gaps for the traffic to file through. Every barricade was manned with heavily armed and armoured shock-and-awe troopers. Only Walker would have dared interfere with the flow of traffic through the Nightside, and even he couldn't hope to keep it up for long without risking open mayhem and madness; but it did what it was supposed to do. It forced us off the main roads and onto the lesser-known and lesser-travelled routes.

Roads that took you through the darker territories, where the really wild things lived.

Ms. Fate was quickly lost and disorientated. You can't rely on a sat-nav in a place where directions can be a matter of choice, and reality rewrites itself when you're not looking. I concentrated on the Osterman Gate, keeping its location fixed in my mind, even as the roads twisted and turned before us. We were in the dog latitudes now, in the raw and savage parts of the Nightside that most tourists never see. Where you can find all manner of terrible things, if they don't find you first. The traffic was just as heavy, though maybe a little faster and better armed, and Ms. Fate swore constantly under her breath as she fought to keep up with everything else. I guided her through back routes and hidden paths, forced this way and that by blocked-off exits, but always edging closer to our goal. Walker might have his traps and his barricades, and his spies on every street-corner; but I was born in the Nightside, and no-one knows its streets better than I.

We were heading through Chow Down, where we put the seriously extreme ethnic restaurants (cuisine red in tooth and claw), when Ms. Fate glanced in her rear-view mirror and made a clucking noise of disappointment.

"Take a look behind, John; we seem to have acquired unwanted suitors. Really uncouth types."

I turned around in my seat and looked behind me. Screech gave every indication of being fast asleep, his mouth hanging slightly open. I looked past him, through the rear window, and winced. Walker had put Hell's Neanderthals on our tail. Now, that was just mean. There were twenty of the massive, hairy creatures, riding souped-up, stripped-down, chopper motorcycles. Great muscular specimens of another kind of human, brought to the Nightside from the ancient past via some travelling Timeslip, and put to work by anyone who needed brawn untroubled by much brain. Hell's Neanderthals were always ready to do security, body-guarding, or menace for hire, for anyone with hard cash to offer.

They wore long, flapping coats made from the tanned skins of enemies they'd defeated. And eaten. They wore Nazi helmets, lots of trashy jewellery, and a curious mixture of all the major religious symbols. They also wore lengths of steel chain wrapped around their bulky torsos, to use as flails in close combat. Their leaders had swords sheathed on their backs, and I knew from experience that they would be brutal jagged butcher's blades. Hell's Neanderthals don't do subtlety.

They moved up fast behind us, their outriders lashing out with steel-tipped boots at anyone who got too close. I could hear the pack-leaders hooting and howling at each other in their prehuman language, and something in those brutal, primitive sounds made all the hairs on the back of my neck stand up. I must have made some kind of noise myself, because Screech's eyes snapped open. He turned languorously to look out the rear window and pulled a face.

"And I thought humans were ugly . . . Nature can be very cruel to some people. Any chance we can outrun these evolutionary disasters?"

"Not in this traffic," said Ms. Fate. "It's so tightly packed I can't build up any speed, while those motor-bikes are weaving through the vehicles behind us. It's times like this I wish I'd invested in that air-to-surface missile system I saw in *Motors of Mass Destruction* magazine. Find me an open road, John, and those creepy bastards can eat my radioactive dust, but as it is . . . Prepare for boarding, chaps. And do try to keep them from chipping the paint-work . . ."

"Give me a rundown on the car's defences," I said. "What have you got that's new and nasty?"

"Not a lot, I'm afraid. The machine-guns, of course, but only at the front . . . The grenade launchers and the nerve-gas dispensers really need refilling; you know how expensive they are to maintain . . . And a few other bits and bobs, but that's basically it. I'm a street fighter, John; I don't really do that whole *death from afar* thing. I've always prided myself on being an old-fashioned hands-on sort of girl, dispensing personal beatings to bad guys."

"Isn't there anything you can do?" I said.

"Oh sure! I'll put on some Evanescence; that should put us in the right mood."

As the music blasted from the in-car speakers, I remembered why I only ever called on Ms. Fate for transport when there was no-one else available.

A motorcycle's roar contended fiercely with the music as a Hell's Neanderthal pulled up alongside. He matched his bike's speed to the car's and grinned nastily at me through my side window, showing off brutal yellow fangs. He came in really close, reaching for the length of steel chain wrapped around his barrel chest, and I slammed open the side-door with all my strength behind it. The door rammed into the Neanderthal, and he suddenly disappeared sideways as his bike overturned, leaving him hooting loudly in surprise and pain as the road came up terribly fast to meet him. I looked back as he shot back down the road under his bike, in a shower of sparks and spurting blood, then his cries were cut off as his own people rode right over him. They came howling after us, waving their steel chains in circles above their heads.

One of them pressed in close, right on the Fatemobile's bumper, and Ms. Fate slammed on the brakes. The other bikers sped past us, caught by surprise, but the rider behind couldn't react quickly enough, and his front wheel connected with the rear bumper. The bike kicked and dug in, and threw the Neanderthal violently forward over the handle-bars and onto the car's boot. He clung fiercely to one of the pink tail fins, his bandy legs dangling behind in the slip-stream, then he pulled himself forward and up onto the roof, hooting and howling wildly. A jagged steel blade punched down through the roof, the long blade narrowly missing Screech. The elf grabbed the blade with one bare hand and snapped it off, leaving the Neanderthal nothing but the hilt. He jumped forward onto the bonnet, whirled around, and showed us his blocky teeth in a nasty grin. And while he was busy feeling proud of himself, Ms. Fate hit the brakes hard again, and the rather-surprised-looking Neanderthal was thrown tit over arse off the bonnet and onto the road, where we ran over him.

Up ahead, the other Hell's Neanderthals had turned themselves around and were now roaring back, weaving in and out of the approaching traffic while waving their various weapons in the air. Ms. Fate opened up with the forward-mounted machine-guns and mowed them down. The night was full of the sounds of gunfire, and the road was full of blazing motor-bikes and dead Neanderthals. Eventually, Ms. Fate ran out of targets, so she shut the guns down and cruised on in quiet satisfaction.

"What depressingly stupid creatures," she said, after a while.

"Evolution is wasted on some people," Screech said solemnly.

"Oh . . . shit," said Ms. Fate.

"What? What?" I said.

I looked back again; even more Hell's Neanderthals were coming. Walker must have press-ganged every rogue Neanderthal in the Nightside. I counted forty before I gave up, and more were joining the chase all the time. I was beginning to grow somewhat annoyed with Walker. Time to show him what I could do when I really got annoyed and put my mind to it. I concentrated, firing up my special gift. My inner eye slowly opened, my third eye, my private eye; and my gift made clear to me all the things that could go wrong with a motorcycle. And then it was the easiest thing in the world to reach out, find what was nearly wrong with each motorcycle, and push them all over the edge.

Some bikes crashed, some exploded, and quite a few went up in balls of flame, burning fiercely bright against the night. Neanderthal bikers were thrown through the air, roasted with their machines, or blown apart into scattered pieces quickly churned up by the passing traffic. In a few moments the whole pack was gone, nothing left behind but bits and pieces of wrecked machines and ruined riders. I sank back into my seat, closing my eyes. Using my gift so widely really took it out of me.

"Hardcore, John," said Ms. Fate. I couldn't tell from her voice whether she approved or not, and I didn't feel like looking at her.

"Turn the music down," I said. "I've got a headache."

• • •

I don't like to use my ability too often. It takes a mental and a physical toll, and sometimes a spiritual one, too. I don't like to think of myself as a killer, just a man who does what's necessary, and I only ever act in self-defence . . . But sometimes the Nightside doesn't care what you want. And so you do what you have to, and live with it afterwards as best you can.

I don't like to use my gift too often because the candle that burns twice as bright burns half as long; and I do blaze so very brightly when I send my mind out, into the night. I can't use it too often without killing myself by inches. And I have relied on my gift so very often these past few years. There are days when it feels like I'm only held together with duct tape and will-power.

But some days you don't have a choice. Ms. Fate needed directions, and I was way past the point where I could do it from memory. So I fired up my gift again and sent my mind soaring up out of my body, to look down upon the Nightside from above, and See the whole dirty mess stretched out below me. Walker's roadblocks and barricades showed clearly in the night, and I sent Ms. Fate running this way and that to avoid them. We were making progress, but the Osterman Gate was still a long way off.

My head ached abominably, and my chest felt like it was full of razor blades. There was blood in my mouth, filling faster than I could spit it into a handkerchief. More blood dripped from my nose and seeped out from under my eyelids. It was getting hard to think clearly. I shut down my Sight,

closed my inner eye, and slumped in my seat. I knew better
than to push myself so hard, but the job decides what's necessary, not me.

Whatever Lord Screech had to tell me, it had better be
worth it. Or I would drag his nasty arse right back to Walker
and dump him at his feet.

Ms. Fate was darting glances at me, clearly concerned, but
she knew better than to say anything. She understood the
price we have to pay to be the kind of people we have chosen
to be. (I saw him naked once, in a sauna. He had scar tissue
like you wouldn't believe.) If Lord Screech was aware of what
his precious mission was doing to me, he kept it to himself.
He just looked out the windows, admiring the scenery and
smiling happily to himself, occasionally singing along to the
music in the car. Figures he'd like Amy Winehouse.

I was half dozing when I suddenly realised we were slowing, and my head snapped up as we eased to a halt. Ms. Fate
was leaning forward, peering over the steering wheel at the
road ahead. I sat up straight and looked, too, but I couldn't
see anything immediately threatening.

"What is it?" said Screech. "Why have we stopped?"

"It's the traffic," said Ms. Fate. "Where's it all gone?"

She had a point. We were on a minor road, in a distinctly
shabby area, but even so, there should have been more than
the mere trickle of cars slipping past us. The pavements were
empty, too, hardly a tourist or a punter to be seen anywhere.
When this happens in the Nightside, it can mean only one
thing. Something really bad is about to occur, and people
with any sense have removed themselves from the vicinity
until it's all safely over.

"It's Walker," I said. "He must have shut down the side streets to block us in."

"What do we do?" said Screech.

"Get ready," I said. "Something's coming."

The werewolves came out of nowhere, dozens of them, streaming out of the side streets, racing down the main road, bursting out of the clubs and bars on either side of us. Huge, bestial shapes, with long, hairy bodies that were still vaguely, disturbingly, human. Muzzles full of teeth, and hands and feet tipped with vicious claws. Inhuman muscles bulged along their lupine frames. They were ahead and behind and all around us even as I realised what was happening. The first ones to reach us swarmed all over the Fatemobile, and it shook and juddered under their weight.

"Move move move!" I yelled, and Ms. Fate put the hammer down. The Fatemobile squealed off down the road, accelerating wildly. Some of the wolves fell off, but others clung to the roof, sinking their claws deep into the metal to hold them in place. The rest of the pack came running after us, inhuman strength driving their speed well past natural limits. The Fatemobile went faster, and so did they. Claw tips punched through the roof above me, as the werewolves fought to gain enough purchase to rip the roof open like a tin can and get at the meat inside. Ms. Fate yelled something entirely unladylike at them, and sent the Fatemobile swerving dangerously back and forth, trying to shake them off. They clung on, pounding their great fists on the metal, howling the joy of the hunt to the oversized Moon above.

More werewolves were running along beside us, easily matching our speed, occasionally reaching out mockingly to trail their claws down the side of the car. That made a sound like screeching, like screaming. The whole pack caught up with us in a few moments, surrounding the car and forcing us to drive in a straight line.

The werewolves stuck close to the car, sometimes leaping right over it in the sheer joy of the chase. Dark red tongues lolled from elongated muzzles, and great toothy grins showed on every side. They could have stopped us anytime, but wolves live for the chase. They were playing with us now, and we all knew it. One jumped up onto the front bonnet, sat down on the pink metal, and laughed soundlessly at us. Ms. Fate slammed on the brakes, and he rolled suddenly backwards, somersaulting twice before falling off the front of the car and being crushed under the weight of the on-coming Fatemobile. I looked out the back mirror, just in time to see him rise, and pull his broken body back together, and come running after us again.

"Do you have any silver bullets for your guns?" I asked Ms. Fate.

She shook her head quickly. "Maybe a dozen silver shuriken left in my belt. Don't suppose you've got a silver dagger?"

"Not on me," I said.

"Don't even ask," said Screech.

A whole bunch of werewolves threw themselves in front of the Fatemobile, and we screeched to a halt as they grabbed the front wheels and the undercarriage, forcing the car to a stop. The pack was running in circles around us by then, jumping and leaping and howling beneath the huge Moon. Long, jagged rents appeared in the car's roof as the wolves above us went to work. One wolf reared up beside Lord Screech, and punched the side window. The reinforced glass shattered, leaving a jagged hole through which a huge hairy hand came clawing, reaching for the elf, who calmly grabbed the hairy arm with both his slender hands, and broke the arm in three places with quick, efficient moves. The werewolf yelped piteously, and snatched its arm back. Screech kicked the side-door open and left the car so quickly he was little more than a blur. He grabbed the nearest werewolf, lifted it off the ground and turned it over, and broke its back across his knee. He threw the broken body aside, tore out another wolf's throat with his bare hand, then grabbed another and used it as a club to beat other wolves.

He was hurting them, but he wasn't killing them. They healed almost immediately and came at him again. And the moment he slowed down, they would be all over him.

A werewolf hauled open the driver's seat so quickly he ripped it right off its hinges. Ms. Fate's hand snapped forward, and a silver shuriken sprouted suddenly from the wolf's left eye. He howled horribly and fell backwards, turning half-human again as the pain maddened his mind and he lost control. Ms. Fate stepped quickly out of the car, a shuriken in each hand, and dared the werewolves to come to her. They prowled back and forth before her, showing her their teeth, wary of the silver; waiting for her to drop her guard for just one moment.

A wolf pulled open the door next to me, hauled me right out of my seat, and threw me into the road. I curled up instinctively and hit the ground rolling, but the impact was still enough to knock the breath right out of me. The werewolf loomed over me, snapping its long jaws mockingly. Up close, it smelled really bad, a harsh, rank mixture of musk and blood and wet dog. And then it must have got something of my scent, because it hesitated, and lowered its wedge-shaped head for another sniff. Because of circumstances not easily explained, I have some diluted werewolf blood in me. Not enough to make me were, but enough to accelerate the healing process. The werewolf could smell it on me; and while he was trying to figure that out, I punched him in the throat, hard enough to feel cartilage crack and break under my knuckles. The werewolf fell back, fighting frantically for breath as it scrabbled helplessly on the ground. I rose painfully to my feet and kicked him hard in the balls and in the head, to give him something else to think about.

I looked about me. Werewolves were swarming all over the Fatemobile, tearing bits off it and pissing on the roof, but the reinforced armoured frame was still keeping them out. One of the tail fins had been bent right over, and long runnels of pink paint had been torn away all down one side. One wolf grabbed at the silver figure on the radiator, then howled miserably as his hand caught fire.

Ms. Fate was still spinning and kicking and lashing out with the silver shuriken in her hands, but she was getting tired, and the werewolves surrounding her weren't. Screech danced and pirouetted gracefully through the heart of the mayhem, but for every wolf his elven strength put down, more rose up to take its place. He was strong and he was magical; but he wasn't silver. Ms. Fate and Lord Screech were fighting well and fiercely, but the odds were stacked against them.

Which meant, as usual, that it was all down to me.

People say that werewolves only fear silver, but that's not strictly true. There's one thing they fear even more, because it rules their lives. I concentrated again, raised my gift, and reached out to the oversized Moon that hangs over the Nightside. It took me only a moment to find the right ultraviolet frequency in the moonlight and change it subtly; and just like that, the whole damned pack howled and shrieked as the change raged through them, stripping them of tooth and claw and fur . . . and suddenly the street was full of naked men and women, running for their lives. Except for those who didn't react fast enough and got the crap kicked out of them by Ms. Fate and Lord Screech.

They soon ran out of victims and returned to the car. Ms. Fate wept bitter tears of rage and frustration as she saw what had been done to her beloved Fatemobile.

"Look what they've done to my precious! One door gone, windows smashed, the paint-work ruined . . . Bastards! I'll have their hides for this!"

"Bad doggies," I said tiredly, and slid slowly back into my shotgun seat. Ms. Fate and Screech looked at me, then at each other, and got back into the car without saying anything. For all the damage it had taken, the Fatemobile started up the first time, and we roared off down the empty street.

We caught up with a few fleeing naked figures, and Ms. Fate made a point of swerving to run them down.

I dozed some more, half dreaming, as the car made its way steadily through half-deserted streets. Apparently our reputation preceded us. I woke up only when we eased to a halt again. I looked around quickly, but the quiet side street was entirely free of Neanderthals, werewolves, or anything else obviously dangerous. Ms. Fate tapped her fingertips thoughtfully on the steering wheel, looking straight ahead. She seemed to be considering something. She turned to look at me, then stopped, and clucked in a motherly way. She produced a tissue from her utility belt and mopped some of the blood from my face.

"You look like shit, John," she said. "This isn't doing you any good. Tell me it's not as bad as it looks."

"It's not as bad as it looks," I said.

"Very good! Now try saying it like you mean it. I never knew using your gift screwed you up this badly."

"It's not something I advertise," I said.

"Should I call Suzie Shooter?"

"Don't you dare! She'd turn this whole area into a blood-bath." I looked around me. "Where are we, exactly?"

"I was wondering that," said Screech, from the back seat. "I am in a bit of a hurry, you know."

"If he says, *Are we there yet?* feel free to hit him with something large and spiky," I said. "Why have we stopped again?"

"Because we've come to the edge of a different territory," said Ms. Fate. "This whole area is currently under the rule of a new Mr. Big, name of Dr. Fell. If we try to cross without advance permission, we'll have to fight our way through his army as well as Walker's."

I scowled, struggling to concentrate. My head was pounding. "I didn't think there were any Mr. Bigs left, after the Walking Man paid his grand visit to the Boys Club. I thought he wiped them all out."

"Not everyone was there that night," said Ms. Fate. "The few that survived the Walking Man massacre wasted no time in taking over the old territories and expanding their influence. Dr. Fell is still very much alive and running this whole area like his own private kingdom. I'm surprised Walker hasn't sent someone around to slap him down."

"Walker has always believed in dealing with the devil you

know," I said tiredly. "Sometimes literally . . . As long as this Dr. Fell sticks to his own territory and doesn't make waves, Walker will do business with him." I frowned. "Dr. Fell . . . The name rings a bell, but I can't place him. Was a time I knew all the major scumbags in town . . . Talk to me, Ms. Fate. Tell me things."

"He wasn't really anyone, until the Walking Man wiped out most of the competition," said Ms. Fate. "Just one more freak with a nasty gift and an itch for power. No-one seems to know who or what he was before he came to the Nightside, but since he came to power here, he's made a name for himself for ruthless efficiency, money laundering on a grand scale, and general weirdness. They say he can See through the eyes of all those who work for him, so he always knows what's going on throughout his territory. All the lesser scumbags pay tribute to him, to be allowed to operate here. And anyone who passes through has to pay a toll to him personally. Now, I could just put my foot down, drive like the devil, and hope he's got nothing fast enough to catch us . . . but there are stories. And I don't think me or my lovely car are in any condition to fight a running battle if it all goes wrong. It might be . . . expedient just to stroll into his presence, give him the money, and avoid a lot of unpleasantness."

"This Dr. Fell worries you," I said. "What makes him so different?"

"Dr. Fell is seriously weird," said Ms. Fate. "Even for the Nightside. I would have taken him down myself, just on general principles . . . but there is that whole private-army thing he's got going. A girl should know her limitations."

"I don't pay tolls," I said. "Normally. But I think you've got the right of it. None of us are in any shape to fight off armies. So, we go in politely, act diplomatically, and see if we can sweet-talk the scumbag. Screech, you'd better stay in the car."

"I am deeply hurt by your insinuation," said the elf. "I can be diplomatic if I have to be. I am an emissary, after all."

"All right, you can come in with us," I said. "But *don't kill anybody*. Unless I start something first."

"Well, really," said Screech. "What do you think I am, a barbarian?"

"No," I said. "You're an elf. Which is worse." I looked at Ms. Fate. "Same to you, only less so. I've no doubt we're going to see some distressing things in Dr. Fell's court, but patience and dignity at all times. We can always go back and give him a good arse kicking some other time."

"I have had . . . disagreements with some of Dr. Fell's people, in the past," Ms. Fate said carefully. "Really quite vicious and bloody disagreements, on occasion."

"Oh, this is going to go really well," I said.

We drove a short distance until we came to what was obviously Dr. Fell's place of power. We all got out of the Fatemobile, and I took a long thoughtful look at it while Ms. Fate activated what was left of the car's security systems. From the outside, Dr. Fell's court looked like just another shabby night-club, with boarded-up windows and a really quite understated neon sign—*The Penitent*. The whole place could have used a lick of paint and quite possibly a tetanus injection. The only signs of life were the bouncers outside the firmly closed front doors, two huge golems in oversized tuxedos. They looked very professional and quite staggeringly dangerous. The only sure way to take down a stone golem is with a road drill.

The fresh air had revived me, or the werewolf blood in me was kicking in, and I actually felt half-way human as I headed for the club entrance. I was in the mood to spoil someone's day, and the bouncers would do as well as anyone. Their heads turned slowly in unison, accompanied by low, grinding sounds. I nodded to them briskly, and they stared silently back with their empty stone faces.

"John Taylor and friends, here to speak with Dr. Fell," I said. "And don't give me any crap about appointments or I'll make you targets for every pigeon in the Nightside."

"There aren't any pigeons in the Nightside, John," said Ms. Fate. "Something eats them."

"Yes," I said patiently, "I knew that, but very probably they didn't, until you told them. Now I have to come up with a whole new threat."

"Ah," said Ms. Fate. "Shutting up now."

"You're not on the list," the stone golems said in unison, in low, grating voices.

"I rarely am," I said. "But I think you'll find Dr. Fell will want to see me anyway."

The two blocky heads turned slowly to look at each other; there was a silent conference, then two empty faces ground back to look at me.

"Go right in," they said together. "Dr. Fell will have words with you, and your friends."

"Wonderful," Ms. Fate said brightly. "Doesn't sound at all intimidating."

Lord Screech sniffed loudly, stepped forward, and thrust a single long finger deep into the blank stone face of the nearest golem. With a few quick gestures, he etched long, sweeping furrows into the stone, giving the golem a nice happy face. He gave the other golem a sad face, then stepped back to regard his handiwork. He nodded, satisfied.

"Never take sass from the hired help."

"Can't take you anywhere," I said.

"Dr. Fell really isn't going to like that," said Ms. Fate.

"Good," I said. "Now, when we get in there, stick close to me, don't pee in the potted plants, and act civilised. If anyone's going to start anything, it's going to be me, and I really don't like to be upstaged."

I led the way forward, and the dull grey entrance doors slowly swung open before us. Above the doors, the neon sign had changed to read *Suffer for Your Sins*. Nice touch, I thought. Beyond the entrance doors lay a sparse and spartan lobby with cracked plaster walls and a grubby wooden floor. On the far side of the lobby was another set of double doors, apparently made of solid brass. I walked right up to them, but they didn't open on their own. I gave them an experimental push, and they swung slowly backwards, a few inches at a time, their hidden counterweights utterly silent. A bright light flared in the widening gap between, too painful to look at directly. I couldn't see a thing through it, so I waited for the gap to widen enough, then marched forward with all the confidence in the world. And a complete willingness to look down my nose at anyone who wasn't actually a member of a major pantheon.

Ms. Fate strode proudly beside me, like the renowned crime-fighter she was, and Lord Screech . . . was Lord Screech.

The moment we passed through the doors, the light sank back to a bearable level, and Dr. Fell's curious court was revealed before us. It looked like a circus, seen from the other side. A dark carousel of strange delights and twisted grotesques, candy-coloured clowns with painted-on leers, and malformed supermodels with a strange, wounded glamour. Cold-faced men in smart leisure suits sat stiffly in oversized chairs, surrounded by pretty boys and hard-faced girls in all the more extreme fashions of decades past. All of this was set against a selection of colour schemes that were shockingly bright and almost painfully clashing.

There was no music, no background entertainment; only a constant buzz of whispered conversation.

Every face turned to look at us, but though the whispers continued, no-one had anything to say to us. They looked us over with blank, expressionless faces, staring like so many dead people, as though all the life and passion and independence had been beaten or intimidated out of everyone present. Many of them held champagne glasses in their hands, but no-one seemed to be drinking. They all looked like they'd been standing in Dr. Fell's court forever and might stand there forever more. They weren't his courtiers, or his acolytes, or even his army; they were his, to do with as he would.

Here and there, light flared up suddenly in this pair of eyes or that, and I remembered that Dr. Fell was supposed to be able to See through them. So I smiled cheerfully about me, determined to give him a good show. I heard the heavy brass doors close behind me, but I didn't look back.

Ms. Fate struck a super-heroine pose at my side, her leather fists resting on her black-clad hips, just above the utility belt. Her dark cloak swirled slowly, dramatically, about her. It was a tribute to her reputation and her sheer presence that she didn't look in any way camp or amusing. The dried werewolf blood spattered across her leathers probably helped. Lord Screech struck a carelessly elegant pose on my other side, his bored expression suggesting he was slumming just by being there, and everyone present should feel honoured that he had deigned to stop off on his way to somewhere far more interesting. Typical elf, in other words.

And I . . . stood straight and tall in my white trench coat, and let everyone get a good look at me. I was John Taylor, and that should be enough for anyone.

Dr. Fell's foot-soldiers bothered me. I'd spotted them right away. Every crime boss and Mr. Big had them; young men with a lean and hungry look, eager to advance in the organisation by demonstrating just how much more vicious and extreme they were than their colleagues. Attack dogs, with good suits that couldn't quite hide the bulges of holstered guns and other weapons. There were quite a few of them, lined up casually in the crowd between me and their boss. Nothing I hadn't seen before, and even wiped the floor with on occasion . . . but these were different. It was in their eyes . . . He was in their eyes.

Supermodel types moved listlessly through the packed crowd, sporting garish little numbers and strangely styled gowns, offering trays of drinks and nibbles and the very latest chemical delights. They were all pretty as a picture, criss-crossing the room in simple patterns, moving in perfect unison, like flocking birds. They smiled widely, all the time, the only smiles in that place of whispers and staring eyes; but smiles too perfect and unwavering to be real. Sometimes guests would reach out to caress or slap their perfect bodies, and sometimes a girl would be pulled down to sit on someone's lap, and the smiles looked even more unreal.

This was Dr. Fell's carnival court, just so many living dolls for him to play with.

The man himself sat above them all, on the traditional raised dais, posed stiffly on a chair fashioned from human bones bound together with strips of mummified human muscle and tendon. Supplied, no doubt, by his many deceased victims. In a faded mourning suit, Dr. Fell was a tall, thin presence, with dull grey skin and a hideously mutilated face. Half a dozen naked women stood in a semicircle behind his hideous chair, all of them malformed or abnormal in various unpleasant ways. Missing parts, twisted limbs, gouged-out eyes. You only had to look at them to know they'd been made, not born, that way. They were the way they were because it amused Dr. Fell that they should be. Some of them held knives, some held guns, and some held nasty-looking magical weapons. All of them possessed a strange dark glamour and a dangerous attraction. Dr. Fell's personal body-guards and assassins.

I was beginning to remember where I'd heard his name before; and I didn't think we were going to get on.

Dr. Fell had burned out his own eyes with a white-hot crucifix. Now his scorched and shrivelled eyelids were sealed together under two great cross-shaped scars. He came to the Nightside as a rogue vicar and gave up his eyes in search of a greater Vision. Whatever he Saw, it changed his allegiance completely. Rumour had it he'd looked into a mirror . . . And the man who'd come here to rage against the darkness ended up embracing it. He wore a crown of thorns, pressed down hard onto his forehead, and rivulets of dried blood ran down his sunken cheeks.

All the time I was considering Dr. Fell, he studied me through the eyes of his people.

I started forward and an aisle opened up, a narrow passage

through the crowd to lead me right to Dr. Fell. Ms. Fate and Lord Screech strode along beside me, but Dr. Fell only had eyes for me. A hand reached out from the crowd to tug at Ms. Fate's cape. She punched the man out without even looking round. He made no sound as he fell, and no-one else showed any reaction. A hunchbacked girl lurched forward into the aisle, blocking our way, and we had to stop or run over her. She was bent almost in two by the gnarled mass that ran the length of her spine, clearly visible thanks to her backless dress. She raised her head as high as she could, to smile at Screech.

"You're so beautiful," she said, in a voice like a little girl's.

Screech smiled upon her. "Yes," he said. "I am. You, however, are not a natural hunchback. This was done to you. Why?"

"Because it amused Dr. Fell," she said. "There is no greater purpose, no greater reward. He looks upon us with his divine Sight, and we become what he Sees, what we truly are. He says it is only fitting that our exteriors match our interiors. He lets us be . . . what we really are."

"Typical human bullshit," Screech said briskly. "You're like this because he can't bear to be the only monster here. And that is not acceptable to me."

He took the young woman by the shoulders and shook her hard. She convulsed in his grip and cried out as the bones in her back snapped and cracked loudly, rearranging and restoring themselves. The hunch sank down into her flesh and was gone, all in a moment. Screech let go of the woman and she straightened up, slowly and disbelievingly, until she stood straight and tall before us all. She looked at Screech with awe and wonder and naked gratitude in her eyes, but he just waved her away. The chorus of whispers around us rose briefly, then fell back to its usual disturbing background noise. I looked at Screech, and he shrugged.

"I can't abide small cruelties," he said, to no-one in particular. "Only the greatest sins are worthy of indulgence."

He sounded as arrogant as ever, but I liked him rather better in that moment. Not that I'd ever tell him.

A hulking figure appeared suddenly before us, blocking the narrow aisle. He wore a ruffled silk shirt over knee-length shorts, and his face was painted like a debauched clown. Rattles and dollies and clutches of blood-stained children's finger bones hung from his belt. Two ugly horns thrust up out of his forehead. He opened his mouth to speak, but Screech cut him off.

"You, on the other hand, aren't nearly ugly enough for what you really are. In fact, your entire existence offends my aesthetic sensibilities."

He snapped his fingers crisply, and the man exploded. Bits of flesh and bone flew over a distressingly large area, spatter-ing the clothes of pretty much everyone in the crowd. Inter-estingly, although many of them pulled disgusted faces and made appalled sounds, not one of them fell back by so much as a single step; and though the general whispering rose up loudly on every side, no-one protested. I wondered if they could. Ms. Fate looked at Lord Screech.

"Nice trick. You couldn't have used it on the werewolves?"

"Only works on people," said Screech. "The wolves are too far from baseline Humanity to be affected."

"Leaving aside why you'd want a spell that only worked on people . . . do you think you could teach me that trick?"

"Not if you want to remain human. Though I can't think

why anyone would want to. You are such small and limited things."

"Still kicked your arse in the last war," said Ms. Fate.

"Children, children," I murmured. "You're not at home now . . ."

"John Taylor," said Dr. Fell, and everything stopped. The whispering cut off sharply, and his dry, dusty voice seemed to echo unpleasantly in the new silence. He leaned forward slightly, and I couldn't tell if the soft, creaking sounds came from him or his awful chair. "Approach me, John Taylor. We have so much to talk about."

"We do?" I said, not moving.

"We are both men of vision. Men of power, and of destiny. Fate brought you to me, John Taylor."

"No," I said. "A Fatemobile."

I strode forward to stand at the base of the raised dais. Ms. Fate and Lord Screech had to hurry to keep up with me. I'd had enough of Dr. Fell and his corrupt court, and I wanted this over and done with. Up close, he looked like a museum exhibit. A preserved specimen of something really nasty, only kept around to remind us of past mistakes. He smelled faintly of burned meat, as though some part of his scarred face was still burning. He smiled slowly at me, ignoring my companions. I didn't smile back.

"Dr. Fell," I said flatly. "Not at all pleased to meet you. Sorry if it's taken me a while to get around to you, but you know how it is . . . Things to see, people to do, and complete and utter scumbags to put in their place. Busy, busy, busy."

"Calm, polite, and diplomatic, remember?" Ms. Fate murmured in my ear. "We're here to beg a favour unless you want to start a war."

"Haven't decided yet," I said. I looked Dr. Fell over, unhurriedly. "So, from rogue vicar to crime lord. I don't know why you people keep coming here; you must know it isn't good for you."

"I came here to test my faith," said Dr. Fell, apparently undisturbed by any of the things I'd said to him. "And I fell from my high station. Sometimes it feels like I'm still falling and always will be."

"I never know what to say when people say things like that to me," I said. "So, moving right along . . . I will be passing through your territory. I thought it only right and proper to pop in and tell you."

"You wish to beg my permission and pay tribute?"

"No," I said. "I don't do the begging thing, and I don't have any loose change on me. I'm just here to be polite."

"You come into my court, into my domain, you speak roughly to me, and you bring with you a deviant and an elf," said Dr. Fell, his dry, scratchy voice entirely without emotion. "You mock me, Lilith's son."

"Why does everyone keep going on about Mommie Dearest?" I said. "All right, my mother's a Biblical myth, and she nearly killed everyone in the Nightside, but can we please all get over that and move on? I have achieved a great deal in my own right, you know."

"We are aware of your sins," said Dr. Fell. His pursed, dried-up mouth moved in something that might have been a smile. "Did you really think we would allow one such as you . . . to travel unmolested in our territory? *Sinner . . .*"

"If there's a sinner here, I'm looking at him," I said. "The more I see of you and your people and your operation, the more I think you need shutting down with extreme prejudice.

I will get around to you, but it doesn't have to be now. Look the other way while I pass through your territory, and you can live to intimidate the impressionable another day."

"Which part of *Let's not piss off the complete and utter loony because he's got his own private army* did you have trouble grasping?" Ms. Fate hissed in my ear. "If this is your idea of diplomacy, you should write the Diplomatic Mail Order School and demand your money back."

"I had hoped for more from you," said Dr. Fell. "We are both men of vision, Mr. Taylor, men who have learned to See the world for what it is rather than what most people would have it be. I had hoped, after all this time, to find a kindred soul . . . but no matter." He turned his head slightly, so that his blind eyes fixed on Ms. Fate. "You can be reconstructed, deviant, returned to what you were meant to be. You shall earn redemption here, through long and painful penance. But the elf . . . is an abomination. It has no soul. Destroy it."

Without warning or outcry, the whole crowd fell on us, arms outstretched, hands like claws. And every one of them had someone else looking out of their eyes. Ms. Fate threw down some pellets she'd unobtrusively palmed from her belt, and great clouds of choking black smoke billowed up, confusing our attackers. Lord Screech flexed his long fingers like a piano player about to attempt a difficult piece, then stabbed his left forefinger at one attacker after another. Men and women exploded, or melted and ran like candle wax, or burst into flames. People died as fast as the elf could point, but still they fought their way through the smoke to get to us.

Because they belonged to Dr. Fell, who cared for nothing but that his will be enforced. When rogue vicars go bad, they go all the way.

I was tired, my head hurt, and I could still taste blood in my mouth, but I needed my gift again. If only so I could stop Screech killing people who might yet be salvaged. So I concentrated, forced open my reluctant inner eye, and fixed my Sight on Dr Fell. Everyone has a secret fault, a hidden weakness, a spiritual Achilles' heel, and it didn't take long to find Dr. Fell's. I reached out in a direction I sensed as much as Saw, and found the mirror that Dr. Fell had stored there; the original mirror he'd looked into, with his new Sight. I brought the mirror to his court, and placed it right beside him, a tall, standing mirror in a simple wooden frame. Dr. Fell's head turned slowly, almost reluctantly, to face the mirror; then he screamed shrilly as he Saw again the thing that had made him burn out his own eyes and banish the mirror rather than See it again. He stood up sharply, the bone chair falling backwards as he faced his reflection. Everyone in the court stood very still, watching him with their own eyes.

I could see Dr. Fell's reflection looking back at him, and it took me a moment to realise what was different about it. The Dr. Fell in the mirror still had his eyes. And as we all watched, the reflected image reached out of the mirror and grabbed Dr. Fell. He shrieked horribly as the long arms wrapped around him, and he kicked and struggled with all his strength as the reflection dragged him slowly, lovingly, into the mirror. In a moment he was gone, his screams suddenly shut off, and all that remained on the raised marble dais was an overturned chair and a mirror—with no-one reflected in it.

All around, men and women shook their heads tentatively, as though to assure themselves there was no longer anybody else in there with them. Some looked scared, some delighted; most looked lost, as though they no longer knew what to do without someone else to tell them. The six naked body-guards sat together on the dais, hugging each other and crying. Some of the foot-soldiers looked at me angrily through Ms. Fate's slowly dispersing smoke. A few even started forward, but I waggled a finger at them, and they stopped. Lord Screech sniggered beside me.

"It's over," I said loudly. "Go home. Get your lives back. But . . . if I hear any nonsense about reinstating the tolls and the tribute, I will come back and find a mirror big enough to hold every damned one of you."

No-one tried to stop us as we left.

We were all the way through what used to be Dr. Fell's territory and out the other side before the flying carpets came after us. Walker had picked up our trail. A whole fleet of the things came swooping down, brightly coloured, rippling fluidly as their riders steered them expertly in and out of the traffic that once more filled the road. The carpets could have flown right over them, but where was the fun in that? Riders fly carpets because they're dangerous, and even in the midst of an important mission, they couldn't resist a chance to show off their skills. This bunch were so cocky they weren't even wearing helmets.

They crouched proudly on their flapping carpets, riding the updrafts, holding all kinds of weapons. It appeared Walker wasn't interested in simply stopping us any more.

Ms. Fate put the pedal to the metal, and the Fatemobile leapt forward as though it had been goosed, but the carpets shot after us at impossible speed. And since they were entirely magical, their riders weren't even bothered by the slip-stream.

They shot in and out of the traffic lanes, weaving in and out of the paths of the slower-moving vehicles, closing in on us with loud hunting cries.

The first few pressed in close behind us, and bullets ricocheted from the Fatemobile's reinforced pink exterior. Two riders swept down low to cut at our tyres with long, curved scimitars, only to recoil, baffled by the fluffy wheels. They fell back as they lost concentration, and slipped in behind us. Ms. Fate snapped a toggle on the dashboard, and the Fatemobile's afterburner roared into life. A jet of flame incinerated both carpets in a moment, and the burning riders fell screaming to the road, swiftly put out of their misery by the following traffic. I looked at Ms. Fate.

"Hardcore."

"No-one messes with my ride," she sniffed. "And can I just point out that you will be paying for all repairs out of what the elf's paying you?"

I thought of what the elf was paying me. "You'll get your fair share," I said. "Though you may have to take it in kind."

Ms. Fate looked at me suspiciously, then concentrated on her driving. The afterburner had given us an extra burst of speed, but the carpets were already catching up, and more gunfire raked the rear of the car, which shuddered under the impact. Somebody back there had a really big gun.

A carpet rider spotted a gap in the traffic and shot forward to fly alongside. He grinned at me through my window and produced a gun. Ms. Fate tapped the brake, and he shot on ahead for a moment. While he was busy controlling his speed, I lowered my window, reached out, and grabbed a trailing thread I'd spotted hanging from the rear of the carpet. I pulled on the thread until I had a decent length, then lassoed it around a handy lamp-post. The thread spun around the steel post often enough to hold it firm, and I gave the signal to Ms. Fate. She accelerated, and the carpet poured on the speed to keep up with us; the rider didn't notice that his carpet was unravelling until there wasn't enough left under his feet to support him, and he crashed to the road with a very satisfying look of surprise on his face. And was immediately run over by a horse and cart.

Two carpets descended from above, and landed on the Fatemobile's roof. Lord Screech kicked open the rear door and swung lithely out. He steadied himself on the door rim with one hand, reached up, seized an ankle with his other hand, and threw the guy off into the traffic. Screech then pulled himself up onto the roof. Ms. Fate hit another toggle on her high-tech dashboard, and the whole roof became transparent. I didn't know it could do that. Lord Screech had acquired a long, blazing sword from somewhere. The remaining carpet rider looked like he'd rather be anywhere else, but he met the elf with a long blade of his own. The two of them duelled back and forth across the roof while Ms. Fate sent the car sweeping rapidly back and forth from one lane to the next. More carpets closed in, heading for the car's roof. Screech ran his opponent through with a casually elegant thrust, kicked the dying man off the roof, and loudly challenged all comers to come and do something about their murdered colleague.

One of the carpet riders took the sensible approach and opened up on the elf with a machine-gun. But somehow none of the bullets could find Lord Screech. He laughed in the rider's face, extended a single finger, and the rider's carpet caught fire. He was still alive when his length of burning cloth hit the road; but the on-coming traffic took care of that.

There were still dozens of carpets coming up behind us and closing in fast.

I had no choice but to raise my gift again. It was like trying to lift a murderously heavy weight that got heavier with every attempt, but I did it. I reached out with my gift, searching for the spell that kept the carpets flying; only to find there was no individual magic involved, but rather a complex web of spells that would take me ages to understand and undo. So instead, I did what I should have done at the beginning, and used my gift to find the nearest Timeslip that could transport us directly to the far side of the Nightside and the Osterman Gate. I'd put off doing it because there were so many dangers involved. Timeslips don't always go where you think they do; the time differentials are so complex you could come out the other end days or even weeks in the future. Worse still, there are all kinds of things that live inside Timeslips and prey on those who pass through. Only damned fools, certain extreme sportsmen, and truly desperate people ever enter a Timeslip by choice; but I needed this road trip to end, and end soon, before my gift burned me up completely.

I yelled a warning to Ms. Fate at the wheel, and Lord Screech on the roof, concentrated all my remaining strength; and a Timeslip opened up before us. Nothing subtle or complex about this one, only a great rip in space and time, and a huge glowing tunnel for Ms. Fate to steer into. The Fatemobile roared forward into the savage rotating energies, and, just like that, the Nightside and the pursuing carpets were gone, and we were hurtling down a shimmering corridor with no beginning and no end. Screech swung down from the roof and dropped into the back seat. Even elves have enough sense to be cautious when it comes to Timeslips.

Great bells were ringing all around us, voices screeched and howled, and from somewhere came the sound of huge engines straining, fighting to hold back some incomprehensible threat.

And then the Fatemobile shot out the other end of the Timeslip, and Ms. Fate swore harshly and slammed on all the brakes. The car screeched to a halt, stopping only a few yards short of the massive barricade blocking the street before us. It rocked to a complete halt, amidst the unpleasant smell of scorched fluffy tyres, while I glared through the cracked windscreen at the man standing so elegantly before us. He raised his bowler hat to us, politely and entirely without irony, and smiled complacently.

"Nice try, John," said Walker. "Everyone out, please. End of the line."

Ms. Fate looked at me, but I shook my head tiredly. No point in fighting any more. We'd done all we could. The three of us stepped out of the Fatemobile. The car looked like it had been through hell, but it had held together and got us here safely. I patted the scarred pink bonnet fondly, as if it were a horse that had run a good race. Ms. Fate, Lord Screech, and I formed a stubborn silent line before the Fate-mobile, and waited for Walker to come to us. As always, he gave every appearance of being the perfect city gent, in a neat suit, complete with bowler hat and umbrella. Only those of us who found it necessary to deal with him on a regular basis knew exactly how devious and deadly he could be. A hundred or more of his shock-and-awe troopers were lined up by the barricade, covering us with their guns.

"Any ideas?" said Ms. Fate. "I'm feeling rather out of my depth, and distinctly outgunned."

"Relax," said Lord Screech. "They're only human. Except possibly Walker; we've never been too sure about him."

"He's human," I said. "The best and the worst of us, wrapped up in one underhanded package."

"Ah, John," Walker murmured. "You know me so well."

"You could have taken us at any time," I said, too tired even to be properly outraged. "You let us exhaust ourselves fighting your proxies, waiting for me to be dumb enough to use a Timeslip, all of which you'd interfered with to deliver us here. Of course. It's what I would have done." I looked at Screech. "If you've got any explodos left in your finger, feel free . . ."

"If I did, I wouldn't be foolish enough to use it on Walker," said the elf. "He's protected."

"Can we at least try talking reasonably?" I said to Walker. "I know the odds are against it, but we have been able to find common ground in the past."

"That's right, John," said Ms. Fate. "You talk reasonably to Walker, and I'll be right behind you. So I can use you as a human shield when the shooting starts."

Lord Screech stepped forward, suddenly seeming more arrogant, noble, and inhuman than ever. All the troopers' guns moved to follow him. Walker leaned on his umbrella and gave Screech his full attention.

"Hold hard and stand amazed," said the elf, in a carrying, sonorous voice. "I hold all answers here, and it is I who must bar confusion. Let it be known by all that I am not Lord Screech, Pale Prince of Owls, but yet still an elf of great renown and vital importance."

"You're not who you claimed to be?" said Walker. "Really, you do amaze me. An elf who lies—who would have thought it? I don't give a damn who you really are; just give me the damned Peace Treaty. Or we can take it from your cold dead fingers, if you prefer. Guess which I'd enjoy most?"

I looked at Screech. "Who are you? And why do I know I'm not going to like the answer?"

"Maybe you're psychic," said the elf, with a smile and a wink.

His glamour disappeared like a cut-off song, and the whole world seemed to shake and reassemble itself, as Lord Screech gave way to the real elf, and his true form. I think we all gaped, just a little. In place of the typically tall and slender Lord Screech, we were now faced with an elf almost twice as tall as any of us, but bent over by a hunched back that pulled one shoulder down and forward, ending in a withered arm and a clawed hand. The rest of his form was smooth and supple as a dancer, but his hair was grey, his flesh was the colour of old bone, and two elegant horns thrust up from his heavy brow. He wore a pelt of some animal fur that blended into his own hairy torso, and his legs ended in cloven hooves. He was noble and elegant and almost unbearably inhuman. He grinned widely, his deep-set eyes full of mischief.

"Of course," I said. "I should have known. The only elf that is not perfect. Puck."

"Indeed," he said, in a cold, lilting voice. "Who else but I, that wild rover of the speckled night, could pass freely between two elven Courts and yet pay allegiance to none? Loved by both, trusted by neither, able to speak and hear the things no other elf could be suffered to know? I am Puck, that merry wanderer of the Nightside, and I have led you all in a sweet and merry dance, to suit mine own purposes. I do not have the Peace Treaty, Lord Walker. I never did. Another elf has it, one of lesser renown but great craft, and he has

passed quietly and unobserved through the Nightside, hidden and protected behind a most powerful glamour, while I
have been so very visible, alongside the infamous John Taylor,
holding your attention all this while. That other elf has now
gone through the Osterman Gate with the Peace Treaty, and
my part in this game is done. Be a good loser, good Walker."

Walker considered this for a long moment, while I
reminded myself, yet again, *Never trust an elf.*

"I could still have you shot," said Walker. "If only on general principles."

"You could try," said Puck. "But even if you did somehow
succeed, you would but provide the one common cause that
could unite all elves to go to war with the Nightside. I may
not be perfect, but I am still royal; and an insult done to me
is an insult to all the Fae."

"Oh, get out of here," said Walker, smiling just a little.
"Before I run you all in for loitering with intent."

He turned his back and strode away, waving at his troopers to accompany him. I felt like shouting after them as to
who was going to dismantle their bloody big barricade; but
I thought I'd pushed my luck enough for one day. I turned
to Puck.

"I really don't like elves," I said.

"You're not supposed to," said Puck. "Merely marvel at our
cunning and be dazzled by our brilliance."

"You want a slap?" I said.

"Never trust an elf," said Ms. Fate. "They always have their
own agenda."

"Well, quite," said Puck.

"That's it," said Ms. Fate. "I am out of here. I let my lovely
car be ruined because of you! I risked my life for you!"

"Of course," said Puck. "That's what humans are for."

I really thought I was going to have to stand between them, for a moment. Ms. Fate glared at me.

"I'll be waiting for my cut of your fee. And the next time you need a ride, call somebody else."

She stomped back to the Fatemobile, threw herself through the space where the door used to be to slip behind the steering wheel, fired up the engines, and roared away. I considered Puck thoughtfully.

"So," I said. "Here we are. Mission accomplished, more or less. Now tell me what you promised I need to know."

"Something bad is coming to the Nightside," said Puck, and there was something in his eyes, in his voice. If he hadn't been an elf, I would have said he was afraid. "Something very old, and very powerful. You'll know the name when I say it, but in this at least, trust me when I tell you that it is not what you think it is, and never was. You must find it and make it yours, John Taylor. Or everything you have done will have been for nothing."

"Why?" I said. "What's coming? What is it, damn you?"

He leaned forward, to whisper the name.

"Excalibur."

THREE

Familiar Faces, Come Round Again

I headed for home, via the Underground. I must have been looking more than usually grumpy, because everyone gave me lots of room. A few of Walker's security people were still hanging around the station entrance, but they made a point of looking the other way. I ended up sitting in a carriage on my own, indulging myself in a quiet brood. At least the trains are always on time in the Nightside. Supposedly because if a train does arrive late, the System Controller takes it out the back and shoots it, to put all the other trains in a properly motivated frame of mind.

I still didn't feel like going home, so I went to Strange-fellows, the oldest bar in the world; where everybody knows your game. Not actually the sleaziest bar in creation, but pretty damned close. It was just another night in Strange-fellows. The Witches of Woking were out on a hen night, getting tipsy on Mother Superior's Ruin and reanimating the bar snacks so that they scampered back and forth on the table before them. Someone had got the Water Witch of Harpenden drunk by sneaking up behind her liquid form and injecting it with a horse hypodermic full of neat gin. You could actually see the ripples running up and down her as she giggled, lurching splashily between the tables, watering everyone's drinks in passing. At another table, two vaguely humanoid robots from some future time-line were sucking on batteries and farting static.

A young woman wearing far too much make-up was wailing for her demon lover, because he'd just dumped her and gone off with her best friend. A stone cherub from a nearby graveyard was checking its investments in the *Financial Times*, and frowning a lot. A newly reborn vampire was sitting sadly at a side-table, staring at the glass of wine before him, wine that he'd ordered but couldn't drink. He was telling anyone who'd listen that he hadn't wanted to come back as a vampire, that he'd tried so hard not to come back . . . but he got so bored just lying in his coffin. So here he was now, with gravedirt still clinging to the good suit they'd buried him in, trying to come to terms with all the normal, everyday things he'd never be able to do again.

He didn't need to worry. If he kept up the self-pity routine long enough, someone would ram a stake through him if only to shut him up.

I leaned on the bar, and waited for the barman to get around to serving me. Alex Morrisey owned and ran Strangefellows, and didn't believe in being hurried. He was currently busy with a minor Norse deity at the other end of the long bar and was putting a lot of effort into ignoring me, but I was used to that. It was his little way of reminding me that I still hadn't paid off my bar tab.

Beside me on the bar an upturned top hat juddered briefly, then a pale, elegant hand emerged, waggling an empty glass plaintively in request for a refill. The magician had been in there for some time now, and we still hadn't figured out a way to get him out. Damn, that rabbit had been angry. Never do a magic trick with a pookah. Further down the bar, two white-robed Sisters from the Order of Saint Strontium were getting stroppy over glowing Half-Life cocktails, and everyone else was giving them plenty of room. Any other bar would have banned them, but Alex liked having them around to irradiate some of the more elderly bar food.

I leaned patiently on the bar, glad of a chance to do a little quiet thinking. As cases go, the elven client's had been particularly annoying. Chased half-way across the Nightside, attacked from all sides at once, and not a penny richer at the end of it. Just a word of warning, a name out of legend. Excalibur . . . I supposed I shouldn't be so surprised. Everything turns up in the Nightside eventually. Except . . . Excalibur never had before. Why now, and where had it been all this time? I was pretty sure the Collector never had it, if only because he'd never have stopped boasting about it. Could the sword's reappearance into history be connected to Merlin Satanspawn's recent final death? Or could it be heading here through a Timeslip, direct from King Arthur's time? The trouble with the Nightside is that it offers so many more possible answers to a question than anywhere else.

Excalibur.

It isn't what you think it is, and it never was.

Sewer Man Jack arrived at the bar beside me, smelling

strongly of several different colognes and spotlessly clean. It wasn't his fault that a kind of awful psychic aroma seemed to hang around him anyway; but that's what you get from working in the Nightside's sewers. You wouldn't get me down there on a bet. With all the weird sciences and strange magics fizzing and shaking and detonating all over the place, it's hardly surprising so many failed experiments end up flushed down the sewers. Where they have been known to combine with the wildlife and kick them way, way up the evolutionary ladder. Which sometimes leads to the need for the Sanitary Brigade, with their really big guns and flame-throwers. Operatives like Sewer Man Jack get to earn their combat pay.

Sewer Man Jack's party trick is to blow smoke rings. Only he does it by lighting his farts. And he wonders why he isn't invited to more parties . . .

"Busy night, John?" he said politely.

"You could say that," I said. "Yourself?"

"Just finished dealing with another would-be Phantom of the Sewers. I blame that Lloyd Webber musical myself. Then there was the giant ants last month. Still, every time you think you've got it bad, someone's always ready to tell you something worse. I was just chatting with the Sonic Assassin, outside the Time Tower. Word is, the Collector has thieved a whole new kind of time-travel device, from some far-future museum; a device that can project his consciousness into any person in the Past, Present, and Future. So now he can track down his precious rarities in complete anonymity. Must be very dispiriting, having everyone shoot at you the moment you show your face . . ."

"So basically, anyone could be the Collector now," I said. "That is seriously spooky. I just went through something similar with Dr. Fell. You can't trust anyone to be who they claim any more. As if the Nightside wasn't paranoid enough already . . ."

Sewer Man Jack looked at me interestedly. "You finally had a run-in with Dr. Fell? What happened?"

"I happened—to him," I said.

"You worry me sometimes, John," Sewer Man Jack said sadly, and he moved away.

Alex Morrisey finally drifted my way and poured me a glass of wormwood brandy without waiting to be asked. I looked at it.

"What's wrong now?" said Alex. "It's a clean glass. Because I know you're fussy about things like that."

"Nothing wrong with the drink," I said. "I was just wondering if I'm becoming predictable. Never a good idea, in the Nightside. Start falling into familiar routines, going to the same place, always ordering the same drink, and you can bet good money someone will figure out a way to take advantage."

"Oh, shut up and drink your drink," said Alex. "This bar already has a resident gloomy bugger, and it's me."

Alex was dressed all in black, as usual, in mourning for the way his life had turned out. He also wore a black beret, to hide his spreading bald patch, and designer shades, in the mistaken belief that they made him look cool. Alex was born miserable and hadn't improved with age. He gave short measures, always got your change wrong, and mixed the most distressing cocktails in the world. Wise men avoided the bar snacks. On the other hand, he put up with people and behaviour that wouldn't be tolerated for a moment anywhere else, and viciously enforced a general truce that made

Strangefellows one of the few real neutral grounds in the Nightside.

Alex and I go way back. We're friends, sort of. It's complicated.

I pushed the wormwood brandy determinedly to one side. "What else have you got, Alex?"

"A fast-receding hair-line, lower-back pains, and you really don't want to hear about my bowel movements."

"I shall slap you in a moment, and it will hurt. I meant, do you have anything more interesting in the booze department that you might feel like recommending? I'm in the mood for something . . . different."

"Well, you could try the Valhalla Venom," said Alex. "I got a job lot, cheap, because no-one in the Adventurers Club felt brave enough to try it. So far, everyone here has wimped out, too. I have a feeling it's something to do with the way the bottles sweat blood."

"Pour me a glass," I said. "A big glass, with a lead-lined straw."

Alex raised an eyebrow. "You're in one of your moods again, aren't you? Just sign this release form naming your next of kin while I open the bottle with my special long-handled tongs."

The drink, when it arrived, turned out to be a pale amber liqueur. It didn't seethe or try to eat its way through the glass, so I took a good sip. The liqueur rolled languidly across my tongue, and then hit me between the eyes with a half brick and mugged my taste-buds. It was like drinking a whole summer orchard at once. But after my trip to the Dragon's Mouth this was strictly amateur hour. I took another good sip, and Alex smiled triumphantly out across the crowded bar.

"Look! He's actually drinking it! Pay your bets!"

"It's good," I said. "Vicious, but good. Why not try a glass with me?"

"Because I've got more sense." Alex leaned forward companionably across the polished bar. "It's coming to something when the most exciting thing in this bar is betting whether or not a new drink will make your head explode. It's been really quiet here lately, and you know how dangerous that can be. There's always something, of course . . . minor things, like snakes getting into the Real Ale barrels and improving the flavour . . . And there's no rats in the traps, which mean something's eating them again . . ."

"How are you and Cathy getting on?" I said casually. "You know, my teenage secretary who is barely half your age, of whom I am inordinately protective?"

"Surprisingly well," said Alex. "I keep waiting for the other thunderbolt to drop. I have a horrid suspicion I might actually be happy when she's around, and I'm not used to happy."

"She *is* a lot younger than you."

"I know! Half the bands I like had split up before she was even born! And she's never even heard of half the old television shows I watch on DVD. And she will insist on trying to cheer me up."

I had to smile. "I could have told her that was a lost cause."

"I don't know," said Alex. "There's this thing she does in bed . . ."

"Change the subject right now," I said.

"All right. Have you seen the state of Agatha?" Alex gestured bitterly at his pet vulture, currently perched on top of the old-fashioned cash register, giving everyone the evil eye.

"Look at the little slut. Twenty months pregnant, which is going it some for a vulture. God alone knows what she had sex with, or what she'll eventually produce. There's a pool going, if you want to lay some money down . . ."

And then he broke off and stared out across the bar, his jaw actually dropping. I turned to look, and winced. There are some people who, when they walk into a room, you know there's going to be trouble. Alex's ex-wife came striding through the packed bar with her usual intimidating attitude of complete self-confidence, not in the least bothered that she'd just entered the kind of place where most angels have more sense than to tread. She was tall, lean, and wore her power business outfit like a suit of armour. She had a hard-boned face that expert, understated make-up entirely failed to soften, under close-cropped platinum blonde hair. People got out of her way without even realising why they were doing it because she so clearly expected it of them. She slammed to a halt at the bar beside me, gave me a quick look over, and sniffed loudly.

"Hello, John. Been a while. You're looking very yourself. But then, you never did have much ambition."

"Hello, Agatha," I said. "Not often you choose to grace us with your presence. What brings you to this low dive, all the way from the great counting-houses of the business sector? Did they give you time off for good behaviour?"

"That'll be the day," she said. "So, still playing at being a private detective?"

"And very successfully," I said. "How about you? Still playing at being a human being?"

She gave me a cold, unblinking glare. "You always did take his side."

"Hey," I said, "I have to drink here. How's your boy toy accountant?"

"Rodney is fine. Doing very well. Up for junior partner, actually. And he's only three years younger than me. How's your psycho gun-nut girl-friend?"

"Fine," I said. "I'll tell Suzie you asked after her."

Agatha's cold, superior smile disappeared, and she turned abruptly away to give her full attention to Alex.

"Hello, Alex. Still determinedly down-market, I see. And still wearing black."

"Only until someone comes up with a darker colour," he said. "What are you doing here, Agatha? I didn't think you liked people from your new life knowing where you came from."

"Into every life a little slumming must fall," said Agatha. "I've brought you your monthly blood money."

She took an envelope from an inner pocket and slapped it on the bar between them. Alex snatched it up.

"Do I need to count it?"

"It's a cheque, Alex. No-one uses cash any more."

"I do. Credit has no place in a bar. Why deliver the alimony in person, Agatha? You've always sent a messenger before."

"Because I heard about you and your latest," said Agatha, smiling sweetly. "A teenager, Alex? You always did like them young and impressionable."

"At least I like them alive!" snapped Alex.

My head came up sharply at that, but neither of them had time for me now. They were glaring at each other so fiercely they were all but incinerating the air between them.

Agatha gave Alex her best superior smile. "Do I really

need to remind you of the terms of our agreement? If you choose to marry again, you're on your own, Alex. No more money."

"Typical of you, to think of that first," said Alex. "And you've got a hell of a nerve, criticising me on my choice of lover. You cheated on me with Merlin!"

"Hold everything," I said. I knew better than to get involved, but this was too good to miss. "You had sex with *Merlin*, Agatha? Our very own dead but not departed enough sorcerer, Merlin Satanspawn? The one who used to be buried under this bar? That is so tacky . . ."

"You didn't know him like I did," said Agatha. "He was so much more mature than Alex."

"Only in the sense that cheese gets mature if you leave it lying around long enough," said Alex. "The back-stabbing bastard! He possessed my body so he could have sex with you! It took me ages to figure out why I kept waking up in odd places. You cheated on me using my own body!"

"And he was so much better in bed than you," said Agatha.

Women always fight dirty.

Alex started to reach for one of the many unpleasant weapons he kept behind the bar, then stopped himself. "Get out of my bar, Agatha. My life is none of your business any more."

"I'll go where I please! I still have a lot to say to you . . ."

"No, you don't. Leave. Or I'll show you one of the nastier magic tricks I inherited from Merlin Satanspawn."

Agatha hesitated, then sniffed loudly, turned on her heel, and stalked out of the bar. I looked thoughtfully at Alex. He might have been bluffing, or he might not. Alex looked at me.

"I might have known she'd turn up, after you mentioned meeting her sister Augusta Moon at the Adventurers Club."

"Big woman, Augusta," I said. "Very . . . hearty."

"She fancies you," said Alex.

"I'd rather stab myself in the eyes with forks."

I retired to a private booth at the back of the bar, with the bottle of Valhalla Venom and a glass, so I could drink and brood in peace. Never get involved in domestic disputes. Whatever you say, you're going to be wrong. One of the many reasons why I don't do divorce work. I could still remember Alex and Agatha when they first got together. We were all a lot younger then. They were so happy, so full of life, so sure of all the great things they were going to do. Their love burned in them like a fire, and I was so jealous, so sure I'd never know anything like it. Agatha and I never really got on, but we pretended for Alex's sake.

When the end came it came quickly, and apparently out of nowhere. Agatha walked out on Alex because he wouldn't, couldn't, leave the bar; and she was determined to get on in the world and make something of herself. She'd never hidden her streak of naked ambition, but it was still a shock when she just disappeared one evening, in pursuit of her dreams. She never looked back. Never contacted any of her old friends. She was going places, and we weren't. I didn't know about the Merlin business; I don't think anyone did. But it wouldn't surprise me if she engineered the whole thing, just to make sure Alex wouldn't try to stop her leaving. Agatha always was the practical one in their relationship.

I really hoped the thing with Alex and Cathy would work

out. Even in the Nightside, miracles can happen. Look at me and Suzie Shooter. I sure as hell didn't see that one coming. We were closer than ever now. It still surprised me, sometimes, to wake up and turn over in bed and see Suzie lying there beside me, sleeping happily. I took a long drink of the Valhalla Venom and wondered if that was why I'd been feeling so unsettled. Was I feeling the need to have a proper grown-up life, to go along with my grown-up relationship? Agatha might be right about one thing. Maybe it was time to stop playing at being a private eye and do something that mattered with my life.

Or, it might be time to have another drink and stop thinking so much. Yes; that felt right. I filled my glass to the rim. Larry Oblivion appeared out of nowhere and sat down opposite me without even waiting to be asked. I glared at him, and he stared calmly, coldly, back. You'd think, after all my time in the Nightside, that I'd be used to seeing dead people; but sitting and talking with the risen dead is never easy. Doesn't matter whether it's an old friend like Dead Boy, or a business rival like Larry Oblivion . . . There's just something about a walking, talking corpse that puts my spiritual teeth on edge.

Larry Oblivion, an average-looking man in an expensive suit, with a pale, washed-out face under flat straw blond hair. He was dead and didn't care who knew it, so he didn't bother to disguise some of the more distressing aspects, like not blinking often enough and breathing only when he needed to talk. He'd been murdered by his own partner and brought back as some kind of zombie; and he was still bitter about it. Larry was probably the best-known private eye in the Nightside, next to me. The Dead Detective. The Post-Mortem

Private Eye. He ran his own Investigations Bureau, did a lot of corporate work, and advertised in all the right places. It must kill him that I made more money than he did. I smiled, politely, and offered him my glass of Valhalla Venom. He shook his head curtly.

"I don't drink. I'm dead."

"No need to be obsessive about it," I said. "Dead Boy eats and drinks and . . ."

"I know what that degenerate does!" said Larry. "Some of us have more dignity."

"Some of us have more fun," I said. "What do you want, Larry? I have important drinking and brooding against the injustices of the universe to be getting on with."

"I want you to find my missing brother, Tommy. You do remember Tommy, don't you, Taylor? Went missing during the Lilith War, when he was supposed to be under your protection? Still missing after all this time, presumed dead. I don't believe that. I won't believe it. I'd know if he was dead. He's still out there, somewhere, maybe lost, maybe hurt . . . and you're going to find him for me, with your amazing gift."

"I did what I could to protect him," I said. "There was a lot going on, and in any war . . . bad things are going to happen. There were crowds; there was fighting. A wall collapsed over Tommy; then . . . the press of fighting moved us all away." I didn't tell Larry about the half-mad mob that fell on Tommy's half-buried body. I didn't tell him about the screaming. "I went back later, when it was all over, but there was no trace of him anywhere. Why come to me now, Larry, after all this time?"

"Because Hadleigh has decided to get involved."

The name seemed to drop into a sudden silence, and heads rose sharply all around us. Some people got up and left; others just disappeared into thin air. And all through the bar, there was a general feeling of *Oh shit* . . .

Everyone in the Nightside knows the history of the three Oblivion brothers. If only because knowledge is so often self-defence. Their father was Dash Oblivion, the famed Confidential Op, private investigator back in the thirties. Their mother was one Shirley den Adel, the Lady Phantasm, a costumed adventurer from the same period. They had their first son, Hadleigh, soon after they were married. Then they went time-travelling in 1946 in pursuit of an escaped war criminal, the Demon Claw. They followed him into a Timeslip, and when they came out again, it was 1973.

They had two more boys, Larry and Tommy. During their long absence, Hadleigh had gone his own way and made a name for himself, outdoing even his parents' reputation. He represented the Authorities in the Nightside, much like Walker, all through the sixties and into the seventies. Hadleigh . . . was the Man. Taught Walker everything he knew. But then . . . something happened. No-one knows what, or if they do, they're not talking, which is almost unheard of in the Nightside. Hadleigh was never the same afterwards. He went a bit strange . . . and left the Authorities to walk forbidden paths.

There *are* forbidden paths, even in a place like the Nightside. Certain doors and ways that are sealed off, locked, and guarded—closed to all but the most powerful and the most stubborn. Not because they're so dangerous or because so many who go in don't go back . . . The Nightside has always believed that everyone has a right to go to hell in their own way. The problem is that some of those who come back return strangely changed and horribly altered.

People talk in whispers of the House of Blue Lights, where many are tempted in but only a few come out; and when they do, they aren't even remotely human any more. They're Blue Boys. People who've been hollowed out to make room for something else. They study our world through human eyes, and they play with us as though we're just toys. They have appetites, too . . . Nasty appetites. Walker has them killed the moment they're identified, but the bodies take a lot of killing, and they're always empty. When things get really bad, and Walker decides there are too many Blue Boys loose in the Nightside, he orders a cull. He bangs the drum and waves handfuls of money around, and we all come running. The bounty hunters, the assassins, and concerned citizens like me, who just want the bloody things off our streets. The pay is good, the risks are appalling, and no matter how many we kill, there are always more Blue Boys . . .

Suzie looks forward to the culls. I think they're her idea of an *all-you-can-kill* buffet.

Blue Boys. Dr. Fell. And now, the Collector. All of them looking out at the world through someone else's eyes. It's moments like this I wonder if Someone is trying to tell me something . . .

Hadleigh Oblivion went underground after he left the Authorities—all the way underground. He descended into the world beneath the world, into the sombre realms; and there he studied at the Deep School, the Dark Academy. The one place you can go to learn the true nature of reality. Most people fail the course. They die, or go mad, or both. Like the infamous Sigismund, the Mad Mathemagician. I worked with him on one case, when he was simply known as Madman. Last I heard he was still sleeping peacefully in his cocoon. No-one's sure exactly what will come out of it, but Walker's arranged an armed guard, just in case.

However, a few extraordinary souls do make it all the way through the course and return to the world above disturbingly powerful and strangely transformed. Like Hadleigh Oblivion. He walks in the shadows now, between Life and Death, Light and Dark. Or perhaps above them. Hadleigh Oblivion, the Detective Inspectre, who only ever investigates crimes and cases where reality itself is threatened. So if he'd decided to get involved . . .

"Oh shit," I said.

"Exactly," said Larry Oblivion.

"Why didn't he show up during the Lilith War?" I said, to avoid saying a whole lot of other things. "We could have used his help."

"Who says he didn't?" said Larry. "There was a lot going on. And Hadleigh has always operated on a far bigger stage than us. Did you never wonder why Heaven and Hell didn't get directly involved in the Lilith War? Do you really think your mother could have kept them out if they'd wanted in? We were knee-deep in angels when they came here looking for the Unholy Grail."

"I didn't start the Angel War!" I said, perhaps a bit loudly.

"Never said you did," said Larry.

"Sorry," I said. "I'm a bit touchy about that. Carry on."

"The point is, there are rumours that Hadleigh intervened, to keep the angels out and let us take our own shot at winning the War."

I looked at him for a long moment. "Could he really do that?"

"Who knows? Who knows what they made him into, down in the Deep School? He's the Detective Inspectre now."

"Good point."

"Enough about Hadleigh; I'm here to talk about Tommy."

"All right," I said. "Let's talk about Tommy. The existential private eye, who specialised in cases that might or might not have happened. A good soul, but not terribly bright."

"No," said Larry. "Or he wouldn't have trusted you to look after him. But this isn't only about him. The more I looked into Tommy's disappearance, the more I learned of other people who'd just . . . vanished in the aftermath of the Lilith War. I've compiled a list, of Major Players and minor players who've dropped off the radar. No reason, no motive, no trace of them anywhere. And these were people who could look after themselves. Names you'd know, or recognise. I have to wonder; did someone take advantage of the chaos that followed the War, to . . . remove certain people? It's taken me some time to put this list together, but I'm convinced it means something. There's a definite connection between all the people on this list. Take a look."

He passed me a sheet of expensive monogrammed paper. As his hand briefly touched mine, the skin was so cold it almost burned me. As though his dead flesh sucked the warmth right out of mine. I didn't snatch my hand back, but I took the sheet from him as quickly as possible. The thick paper crackled loudly as I unfolded it. Thirty-seven names, all more or less familiar. Some of them jumped out at me: Strange Harald the Junkman, Bishop Beastly, Lady Damnation, Sister Igor, Salvation Kane, and Mistress Murmur.

People good, bad, and in between. Some I'd worked with, some I'd known, and some I'd cross the street to avoid. But all the people on the list were, I knew, powerful personages in their own right.

"Okay," I said, "I'll bite. What do all these names have in common?"

"They all knew Tommy," said Larry. "Every single one of them."

"Tommy did get around." I thought about it. "Who is there powerful enough to make all these people disappear?"

"Maybe someone interested in removing potential competition," said Larry. "But . . . why Tommy? He wasn't interested in becoming famous, or important, or powerful. All I can see is that he moved in the same circles as these people. I need to know what happened to my brother, John, and I need to know why. Will you work with me on this case?"

"No money, right?"

"You owe me, John. You promised me you'd look after him."

"So I did. All right; let's do it. I have wondered whatever happened to Tommy Oblivion."

"Is Suzie Shooter available to work with us?"

I raised an eyebrow. "Expecting trouble?"

"Always."

"Unfortunately, no. Walker has her out on the fringes, hunting down a bounty. Old Mother Shipton's set up another baby-cloning clinic, and Suzie's been sent to shut her down with extreme prejudice. Mother Shipton has her own private army, so that should keep Suzie happy for a while. You really expecting serious opposition?"

"Yes," said Larry. "And she's the one person I could think of who wouldn't be intimidated by Hadleigh."

"How do you feel about him?" I said carefully. "I mean, he's your brother."

"I don't know what Hadleigh is any more. Some of the stories I've heard . . ."

I nodded. We've all heard stories about the Detective Inspectre. Few of them had happy endings.

"I've lost one brother," Larry said abruptly. "I won't lose another. Tommy . . . should never have become a private eye. He only did it to please our father. And because he'd acquired his special existential gift. He won it in a poker game, you know, bluffing with a pair of threes. No-one could believe it. I was right there when it happened, and I still can't believe it. I asked him to come and work with me, in the Bureau. So I could teach him the ropes, look after him till he was ready to stand on his own two feet. But Tommy . . . always had to go his own way. Maybe he was right. In the end, I couldn't even protect myself from my own partner."

"Why come to me?" I said, after a moment. "When you do, after all, have a whole Bureau of your own people to call on?"

"Because none of them are up to this," he said flatly. "Hell, maybe even the infamous John Taylor isn't up to going head to head with Hadleigh Oblivion. But I can't do this on my own. I need heavy-duty backup, in case it all goes . . . Besides, you owe me. You promised me Tommy would be safe with you."

"Yes," I said. "I did. You'd think I'd know better than to make promises like that." I looked at him for a while. "You've never . . . approved of me, Larry. Why is that?"

"Because you're not a real investigator. Not like me, or my father. We do the job the way it's supposed to be done: taking statements, gathering evidence, putting the clues together to get a result. You have a gift that does half the work for you, and for the rest you rely on guesses, intuition, and intimidating the truth out of people. You're not a professional, only a gifted amateur. I'm only prepared to work with you on this because, if we do cross paths with Hadleigh, I need to be able to fight fire with fire." He suddenly leaned forward to fix me with his cold blue eyes. "I need your gift to find Tommy."

"I've already tried," I said. "Right after the War, and many times since. Did you think I didn't care? Tommy was my friend. But I can't locate him anywhere. He's not dead, or my gift would have showed me his body. But I can't See him anywhere in the Nightside."

"How can anyone hide from you?" said Larry.

"Good question. He hasn't left the Nightside; I did some asking around. But he's not here." I considered Larry carefully. "Of course, I'm not the only one at this table with a special gift, am I? You have a magic wand, Larry. An elven wand. What did you do for the Fae, Larry, that Queen Mab gave you an elven weapon?"

He looked straight back at me, not blinking, unnaturally still in his seat. "How in God's name did you find out about that?"

"You'd be surprised at some of the things I know." I actually found out by eavesdropping at a party, but I wasn't about to admit that. "And, I just worked with Puck."

"You do get around, don't you?" said Larry. And that was all he would say.

I decided to change the subject, for the moment. "You're part of the new Authorities. Why not go to them for help?"

"Because Hadleigh's involved. That makes it family business."

"A thought has just struck me," I said. "And not a very pleasant one. Could Hadleigh be responsible for all these disappearances?"

"I can't believe he'd harm his own brother," said Larry. "I can't afford to believe that."

"He's your brother," I said. "Are you scared of him, Larry?"

"Of Hadleigh? Oh yes . . . We got on quite well, when I was young. He was more like a really cool uncle than an elder brother. But then he went away, to the Deep School, and when he came back . . . I couldn't even stand to be in the same room as him. None of us could. Just to look at him . . . was like staring into the sun. People aren't supposed to blaze that brightly. I don't know what the Detective Inspectre is; but he's not the Hadleigh I knew. I'm not even sure he's human any more."

Time to change the subject again.

"So," I said. "You don't drink, you don't eat, and you don't . . ."

"No," said Larry. "I don't. I'm dead. I don't need the distractions and illusions of life."

"So what do you do?"

"I keep busy. To avoid brooding on the realities of my condition."

"You don't like being dead? I'm told there are advantages . . ."

"I don't sleep. I'm cold all the time. When I touch something, it feels like I'm wearing gloves. I never get tired, never get out of breath, never feel anything . . . that matters. I can't feel any of the things that make us human. No *advantages* are worth that."

"If you hate being a zombie so much," I said carefully,

"why do you keep going? There are any number of people in the Nightside who could . . . put you to rest."

"I know," said Larry. "I've talked to some of them. But I have to go on because I'm afraid of what might come next. I did a bad thing once, when I was young and stupid. I did a terrible thing . . . so I have to go on until I can put things right again." He shook his head slowly. "It's the wand. It always comes back to the wand."

"What did you do, Larry?" I said. "What did you do to earn your wand?"

"I brought Queen Mab up out of Hell."

"What?" I said. "How? And more importantly, why? Mab is one of the great old monsters! Everyone knows that!"

"I didn't know what I was getting into! I thought it was just another job. I wasn't a private eye back then. Just a treasure-hunter, trying to make a name for myself. And I always was a fool for a pretty face."

FOUR

Larry Oblivion, Treasure-Seeker

I never told anyone this story, said Larry Oblivion. *Whom could I tell? Who would believe me, and believe that it wasn't my fault?*

Only those who have been damned to Hell while still alive can be brought back up out of Hell, and restored to the lands of the living. To do this, you need a hellgate, a go-between, and one poor damned fool to play the patsy.

I was a lot younger then. Thought I knew everything. Determined not to follow in the footsteps of my famous father. I wanted a bigger adventure, something more glamorous. I wanted to be the Nightside's Indiana Jones, digging up forgotten treasures from their ancient hiding places and selling them for more money than I could spend in one lifetime. I spent a lot of time in the Nightside's Libraries, digging patiently through discarded stacks and private collections, sifting through diaries and almanacs and very private histories. Looking for clues to point me in the right direction and set me on the trail of significant valuable items that had slipped through history's fingers. There have always been treasure-hunters in the Nightside, but I flattered myself that no-one had ever taken such a methodical approach before. Sometimes all you have to do is look carefully.

I'd just turned twenty, and I'd already had a few triumphs. Tracked down some important items. One of the original seven veils, from when Salome danced before her father for the head of John the Baptist. A set of dentures made up of teeth taken from the skull of the Marquis de Sade. And one of Mr. Stab's knives. Nothing big, but enough to start a reputation, put some decent money in my pockets.

I needed to find something special, something important, something to make people sit up and take notice. The Holy Grail, or Excalibur, or Merlin Satanspawn's missing heart. Think big, and you'll make it big. I had a lot of sayings like that, in those days.

I was drinking a nice chilled merlot in the Bar Humbug that night. A small and very exclusive place, for ambitious young people on the way up. A civilised watering hole for every bright young thing prepared to do absolutely anything to get to the top. Kind of place where you swap business cards instead of names, smile like a shark, and preen like a peacock; and slip the knife in so subtly that your mark won't even notice till you're gone. The Bar Humbug was comfortable rather than trendy, with richly polished oak-panelled walls, padded booths to drink in, and only the most pleasant music in the background. Refreshingly normal and refined, for the Nightside. An oasis of calm and serenity, and never very full, because people don't come to the Nightside for calm and serenity.

Place was run by a sweet-natured old lady in tweeds, pearls, and pince-nez. Grey-haired, motherly, mind like a steel trap when it came to money. Miss Eliza Fritton; always pleasant, always obliging, and not one penny on credit, ever. Only used the shotgun behind the bar when she absolutely had to. She used to run a private girls' school, back in the day. Until the pupils burned it down and sacrificed half the staff in a giant wicker man. *Such high-spirited gels,* Miss Fritton would say, wistfully, after her second port and lemon.

I was talking with the Beachcomber that night, a dry old stick with a military manner who turned up surprising amounts of treasure by spending all his time in the little curiosity shops and junk emporiums that are always springing up like mushrooms in the Nightside. They handle all the lesser flotsam and jetsam that washes up here through Timeslips, or in the pockets of tourists and remittance men from other dimensions and realities. Most of it worthless, of course, but the Beachcomber could find a king penguin in the desert. And teach it to talk before he sold it. He'd had a good week, so I let him buy me drinks and listened patiently while he boasted of his triumphs in a dry, understated way.

"A Shakespeare first folio, of *Love's Labour Redeemed.* A betamax video of Orson Welles's *Heart of Darkness.* An old 45 by the Quarrymen, though played half to death, I regret to say. I do so love alternative histories. Though I believe I could have lived quite happily without seeing the nude spread featuring a young Hugh Hefner, from a 1950s copy of *Playgirl.* Oh, and a rather interesting ash-tray, made out of a werewolf's paw. Nice little piece, with the disconcerting habit of turning back into a human hand every full Moon. Rather upsetting, I suppose, if you happened to be stubbing out a cigarette in it at the time."

I was waiting for him to run out of breath, so I could slip in a few exaggerated claims of my own, when I happened to glance over his shoulder as a very pretty girl walked in. Young and fresh and bubbling over with high spirits, she marched into the bar as though at the head of her very own parade. She wore a tight T-shirt and tighter jeans, with cowboy boots and all kinds of bangles and beads. Skin so clear it almost glowed, huge dark eyes, a scarlet mouth, and close-cropped platinum blonde hair. Without even trying, she took my breath away. Now, pretty girls have always been ten a penny in the Nightside, but she . . . was different.

Conversations died away on all sides as she stopped in the middle of the bar and looked around. All the young dudes perked up, ready to catch her eye, only to be utterly dismissed as her gaze settled on me. She trotted happily forward to join me, and the Beachcomber allowed himself a small, disappointed sigh. He moved away gracefully, to find someone else he could button-hole. I was clearly spoken for. The girl swayed to a halt before me, smiling brightly. Up close, I could see that her T-shirt bore the legend *If You Have to Ask, You Can't Afford It.* And that she wasn't wearing a bra under it. I smiled easily back at her, as though this sort of thing happened to me every day, and gestured for her to park her cute little bottom on the abandoned bar-stool beside me. She dropped onto it with a happy squeak and fixed me with her huge eyes.

"Don't get comfortable here, dear; you're not staying," said

Miss Fritton, in a cold tone I couldn't remember her using before. "We don't serve your kind. Oh yes, I can see right through you; don't think I can't."

The girl pouted prettily and batted her heavy eye-lashes at me. "I can stay, can't I, sweetie?"

"Of course," I said.

Miss Fritton sniffed loudly. "None so blind," she said. "It'll all end in tears, but no-one ever listens to me." She gave the girl a stern look. "No trouble on the premises, young lady, or I'll set the dogs on you."

She moved off to the other end of the bar. I was a little put-out. I'd never known Miss Fritton to turn anyone away while they still had some of her money in their pockets.

"Does she actually have dogs?" said the girl.

"Only metaphorically," I said.

"Hi!" the girl said brightly to me, dismissing Miss Fritton with a careless shrug. "You're Larry Oblivion, I'm Polly Perkins, and you're very pleased to see me! Because I am about to make you rich beyond your wildest dreams."

"Ah," I said. "It's a business deal, is it?"

My disappointment must have showed in my face because she giggled delightfully and squeezed my left thigh with a surprisingly powerful grip.

"Business first, pleasure later. That's how the world works, sweetie."

"Exactly how are you going to make me rich?" I said, trying hard to sound tough and experienced.

"You're a treasure-hunter," Polly said briskly. "Everyone knows that. And I know the location of a treasure so splendid that just breathing its name in your ear will bring tears of joy to your eyes and a definite bulge in the trouser department."

"What do you think you've found?" I said politely. "Has someone sold you an ancient map, perhaps, or a book with a sealed section? You can't believe everything you buy in the Nightside. Some of these cons go way back. Oh, all right, go on, astound me. What have you found, Polly?"

"Word is, you have a special interest in Arthurian arte-facts," said Polly.

I brightened up, despite myself. "What is it, the sword in the stone?"

"Even better," she said. "The sword's original owner. Ah, I thought that would make you sit up and take notice. I know where we can find the Lady of the Lake, frozen for centuries in a block of ice. Preserved against the ravages of Time, since the days of King Arthur. Frozen in her own lake, after Excalibur was returned to her, after the fall of Camelot. Imagine the possibilities if she could be released from her icy tomb! The things she could tell us, of the Age of Arthur. Think of our place in History!"

"Think of how much money we could make!" I said.

"That, too!"

"How did you . . . ?"

"Please," said Polly. "Allow a girl a few secrets. The point is, I don't feel entirely . . . safe, going after this on my own. I need a partner. And I chose you! Say you're grateful."

"I'm grateful," I said. "Really. But why me? There are any number of other treasure-hunters, far more experienced, who'd be only too happy to help you out."

"I want a partner, sweetie, not someone who'd cut me out first chance he got, or fob me off with a percentage," said Polly. "Besides, I like a man with a lean and hungry look. A man who'll go the distance in pursuit of the big prize. You provide the brawn, and I'll provide the brains. Do we have a deal?"

"You want someone to hide behind when the bullets start flying," I said.

"Exactly!" She clapped her little hands together and gave me a smouldering glance. "We're going to have such fun together . . . So, are you in? Or do I have to go looking for someone with bigger . . . dreams?"

I wasn't entirely stupid, or completely besotted by her charms. Like all good cons, this was just too good to be true. I knew there was a real chance she wanted someone to do all the hard work, then hang around to take all the blame while she disappeared with the prize. But she was pretty, and I was young, and I thought I could hold my own when it came to treachery and back-stabbing. Part of me . . . wanted it to be true. Wanted her to be true.

And I was so very keen to make my name with a really major find.

"To get to the Lady of the Lake," said Polly Perkins, as we left the Bar Humbug and tripped lightly through the dark and sleazy streets, "we need to open a very old, and very specialised, dimensional gate. And for that we need several specific, and very rare, items. Think of them as tumblers in a lock."

"A dimensional gate?" I said, trying not to sound too appalled. "No wonder you didn't want to do this alone. Make even one mistake in opening that kind of gate, and we could end up staring into other dimensions, other realities . . . even

Heaven or Hell. If half the old stories are true, and you'd be surprised how many are."

"I'm not an amateur," said Polly, a bit frostily. "I have done this kind of thing before. Present the gate with the right items, in the right order, and it'll roll over and play nice like a dog having its tummy tickled. So, ready for a little scavenger hunt? Jolly good! First, we need a magic wand. An elven wand, to be exact."

"Oh, this is getting better and better," I said. "An elf weapon? You are seriously loop the loop! The elves never sell, barter, or give up any of their weapons, so they only ever turn up as lost, stolen, or strayed. They are incredibly dangerous, insanely powerful, and nearly always booby-trapped. You can usually tell when someone's found one because bits of him are flying through the air. There are those who say the best way to rid yourself of a troublesome rival is to make him a gift of an elven weapon."

"If you've quite finished hyperventilating, can I point out that you're not telling me anything I don't already know? You wanted into the big league, Larry, and it doesn't get much bigger than this. You have to risk some to get some. Or is my big bold treasure-hunter afraid of a little fairy magic?"

"Too right I am! So is anyone with two working brain-cells to bang together! I do not want to end up transformed into something small and squishy with eye-balls floating in it. But I said I'm in, so I'm in. Where's the wand?"

She grinned, and batted her eye-lashes coyly at me. "How do you feel about a little tomb robbing?"

"Just call me Indy," I said resignedly. Some rides you have to follow all the way to the end.

• • •

She took me to the Street of the Gods, and we strolled down the middle of the Street, giving all the churches and temples, their Beings and their supporters, plenty of room. There was a light rain of fish, a brief outbreak of spontaneous combustion among the gargoyles, and ball-lightning rolled down the street like tumble-weeds. Typical weather for the Street of the Gods. An evicted god sat miserably on the pavement outside what used to be his church, clutching at his few possessions. The laws of the Street are strict; if you can't raise enough worshippers, make way for a Being who can. So the grey little man with the flickering halo would now have to make his own way in the world, as something else. A god no more. A lot of his kind end up doing the rounds on chat shows, selling their sob stories. And even more end up sleeping in cardboard boxes in Rats' Alley, begging for spare change on street-corners. And it's a wise man who'll stop to drop a little something into their outstretched hand, because the wheel of karma turns for us all, and cosmic payback can be a real bitch.

"I don't recognise him," said Polly, as we walked past. "I don't even know his name. Isn't that sad?"

"Half the Beings on this Street are celestial con men, fakes, and posers," I said, with youthful certainty and arrogance. "There's more preying than praying here."

"They can't all be deceivers," said Polly. "Some of them must be the real thing."

"Those are the ones you give plenty of room. Just in case."

She laughed. "Am I to take it that you're not in any way religious?"

"I deal in facts, not faith," I said. "I hunt for treasure, not miracles. There's enough in this world to keep me interested without bothering about the next. Where are we going, exactly?"

"Egyptian royalty had themselves buried in pyramids, to be sure their remains would be protected and revered for all the years to come," Polly said briskly. "We all know how that worked out. But one particular Pharaoh went that little bit further, and used ancient Egyptian magic to send his Tomb through Space and Time, to a place where it would be safe for all eternity. It ended up here, on the Street of the Gods, its original protections boosted sky-high by centuries of accumulated faith from all those who worshipped the God within the Pyramid. This being the Nightside, a lot of people have tried to break in, down the centuries, including a few Beings who fancied its preferred position on the Street. No-one has ever found a way in."

"Hold it," I said. "What has all this to do with an elven wand?"

She looked at me pityingly.

"Where do you think the Pharaoh found a magic powerful enough to do all this? The elves got around, in the old days."

"Cool," I said. "I've always wanted to meet a mummy. And rob it of everything but its underwear."

"The Tomb stands alone these days, unworshipped and uncared for, almost forgotten. Taken for granted, as one of the sights. Tourists take photos, and then move on to more interesting things. And no-one has noticed that the Tomb's magical protections have slowly faded away, along with the worship. We can get in now, provided we're very, very careful."

"How do you know all this?" I said bluntly.

"You're not the only one who likes to do research in libraries. I found this information while looking for something else, which is often the way. And then I found a Looking Glass in Strange Harald's Junkshop." She gestured fluidly, and the Looking Glass was suddenly in her hand. It looked like an ordinary everyday magnifying glass, but I had enough sense not to say that. Polly favoured me with a brilliant smile for my tact, and continued. "He didn't know what this was, or he'd never have let it go so cheaply. This is an ancient Egyptian artefact, and it can lead us right to the centre of the Tomb."

"How are we supposed to get in?" I said. "Just walk up and knock?"

"There's a side-door," said Polly. "And I know where it is."

"Of course you do," I said.

The Tomb of the forgotten Pharaoh turned out to be a surprisingly modest affair, barely twenty feet tall and ten wide. The pyramid's orange-red bricks were dull and shabby, even crumbling away in places, and yet . . . there was something about it. Set between an ornate church in the old Viking Orthodox style, and a Mother Earth Temple covered in twitching ivy, the pyramid still had its own dark and brooding presence. It wasn't there to be liked or appreciated; it was a stark, functional thing of simple style and brutal lines. It had a job to do, and it was still doing it after thousands of years, while any number of neighbouring churches had been ground to dust under the heels of history. The Tomb had been constructed to outlast Eternity; and powered by the magic of an elven weapon, it just might.

I stood before thousands of years of history and felt very small and insignificant in its shadow. But, of course, I couldn't let Polly Perkins see that. So I looked it over and sniffed loudly, as though I'd seen better before and hadn't been impressed then.

"Bit small," I said. "Maybe it's a bonsai pyramid."

"Don't show your ignorance," Polly said kindly. "This is just the tip of the iceberg. The rest of the pyramid descends under the Street, so far down that no-one's ever been able to see the bottom of it."

"Then there'd better be an elevator," I said. "I hate stairs."

Polly ignored me, studying the pyramid carefully through her Looking Glass. She smiled suddenly, and passed the Glass to me. I took it carefully, and held the lens up to my eye. Through it I saw a huge and intricate labyrinth of narrow stone tunnels, criss-crossing the whole structure of the pyramid, going down and down and down. The pattern was so complex it made my head hurt, and I quickly handed the Glass back to Polly. She made it disappear with another sharp gesture, and I looked after her thoughtfully as I followed her round the side of the pyramid. It was finally dawning on me that there was a lot more to Polly Perkins than met the eye.

She led me along the side of the pyramid, down a dingy alleyway half-full of garbage, some of which was still moving. Stepping carefully around and over things, we finally stopped before a section of the pyramid wall that seemed no different from anywhere else. Polly leaned forward and counted off the levels before pushing a series of bricks in swift succession, in a pattern too complicated to be easily grasped. I looked at her sharply, but she only had eyes for the small section of wall swinging slowly back before her. A side-door, indeed. Beyond the opening there was only darkness, and silence.

"Hang about," I said. "I've got a torch here somewhere."

"Boys and their toys," Polly said airily. "Look and learn."

The Looking Glass was back in her hand again. She held it up before her, and a beam of dazzling bright light blasted out, pushing back the darkness like a spotlight. Polly followed the beam of light into the Tomb, and I moved quickly in behind her. We hadn't managed three steps down the narrow stone tunnel before the side-door closed behind us, with only the faintest of grinding noises.

Polly held the Glass up high, but even its light couldn't penetrate far into the heavy dark before us. She still strode confidently forward, taking left and right turns with breathtaking confidence, according to what the Glass showed her. Hopefully it was also warning her about the inevitable booby-traps and deadfalls. The ancient Egyptians were notorious for their appalling sense of humour in that regard.

The tunnels gave me the creeps. I'd been in worse places as a treasure-hunter, nastier and slimier and even more dangerous places, waded thigh-deep in mud and crawled through earth tunnels barely big enough to take me; but this was different. This was a place of the dead. The air was dry and dusty, and I had to breathe in deeply to get enough oxygen out of it. The ceiling was so low I walked slightly stooped, and the walls to either side of me were covered with lines and lines of hieroglyphics, none of which I could read. I had never bothered to learn, never expecting to end up in a genuine Egyptian pyramid. Well, you don't.

The air grew steadily colder as we descended deeper and deeper, leaving the Street of the Gods behind. The silence was oppressive—no sound anywhere except for my harsh breathing and the soft slap of our feet against the bare stone floor. I was actually shivering from the cold, but it didn't seem to affect Polly at all. Being inside the Tomb didn't seem to bother her either; her grip on the Glass was steady as a rock. I really should have asked her more questions.

We went down and down, and around and around, following the light from the Looking Glass as it blazed our way like a searchlight. The hieroglyphics seemed to stir and writhe as the light moved over them, as though desperate to warn us of something, and our footsteps echoed longer than they should have on the still air. Polly was really hurrying by then, striding confidently through one stone passage after another, and I had to struggle to keep up with her. My lungs were straining, and I hugged myself against the bitter cold. But a part of me was starting to get excited. This was how Tombs were supposed to feel.

And finally, finally, we came to the main chamber. No warning, no intimations; we just rounded a corner like any other, and there it was. Polly stopped so suddenly I almost ran over her. She moved the Looking Glass back and forth, the brilliant light flashing up every detail, clear and distinct. The chamber itself wasn't much to look at. Just a square stone box, deep in the heart of the pyramid. The hieroglyphics covered the floor and the ceiling here, as well as all four walls, and surely it was just my imagination that read dire warnings in the deeply etched figures. Polly knelt to examine some of the markings on the floor, frowning with concentration and tracing them with the tip of one long, slender finger. There was no sign in her face of the girlish adventurer who'd picked me up in the Bar Humbug. She looked . . . older, more experienced. And not in a good way.

She straightened up suddenly and shot me a quick smile. "Nothing to worry about. Only the usual generic warnings and curses. Real amateur night. Magic's come a long way since ancient Egypt. Any one of the half a dozen protective amulets I'm wearing could ward off this stuff."

"Let's not get cocky," I said carefully. "Who knows how much power the wand could have soaked up after all these years on the Street of the Gods."

"Oh, hush, you big baby. We're perfectly safe. Look at you, actually shaking at the thought of the mummy's curse."

"It's cold," I said, with some dignity.

"Is it? I hadn't noticed. Hot on the trail, and all that. Still, better safe than sorry, I suppose."

She took a bone amulet out of her jeans, and waved it around vigorously. We both waited, but nothing happened. The silence remained unbroken, and nothing nasty emerged from the shadows lurking outside the Looking Glass's light. Polly gave me a condescending look.

"Did it work?" I said, wanting to be sure about this.

"Well, the amulet didn't explode, and neither did we, and that's usually a good sign, so . . . Of course it worked! Trust me, sweetie. I know what I'm doing."

"Yes," I said. "I trust you to know what you're doing."

"There's a good boy," she said absently, peering through her Looking Glass again. The beam of light moved steadily across the wall before us, then stopped abruptly. "There!" said Polly, her voice breathy with anticipation. "That's it. The entrance to the burial chamber is on the other side of this wall. We are

about to see things no-one has seen for thousands of years . . .
And steal them! Help me with the lock mechanisms."

"You think they'll still be working, after those thousands
of years?"

"Of course, sweetie. They're as much magical as mechanical, and probably still drawing power from the elven wand.
The Pharaoh expected to be revived someday, and walk out of
his Tomb into the afterlife. They all did."

We worked together, examining the wall inch by inch,
and the right places to press and turn and manipulate seemed
to flare up before us in the light from the Glass, as though we
were being guided through the workings of some intricate
combination lock. I found it increasingly hard to concentrate.
It felt like we were being watched by unseen and unfriendly
eyes. As though we weren't alone in the stone chamber, that
some third person was there with us. Only iron discipline
and self-control kept me from constantly breaking off to look
behind me. That, and the knowledge that Polly would be
sure to say something cutting and sarcastic.

The last piece finally fell into place, and the whole wall
sank slowly and steadily into the floor, revealing the burial
chamber beyond. There was a brief stirring of disturbed air
and a sudden scent of preservative spices. The wall continued to fall away, then I almost cried out as a pair of shining eyes suddenly appeared before me. I fell back, reaching
for the gun I kept in a concealed holster. Polly stood her
ground, and the Glass's light settled on a tall statue with
painted features. The eyes were gold leaf. I gathered what
was left of my dignity about me and moved forward to stand
beside Polly again, as the last of the wall disappeared into the
floor.

She didn't say anything. All her attention was fixed on the burial chamber before her.

The sarcophagus lay waiting in the exact centre of the room, surrounded by half a dozen life-size statues, painted as guards with ever-open eyes. More hieroglyphics on the walls, of course, and several large portraits. Presumably the Pharaoh's family. A whole bunch of ceramic pots, to hold his organs, removed from the body during the mummification process. Even more pots, smaller and less ornate, holding grain and seeds and fruit, food for the afterlife. And lying in scattered piles around the chamber, more solid gold items than I'd ever seen in one place.

They say you can't buy your way into the afterlife, but this Pharaoh had made a serious effort.

"Put your eyes back in your head, sweetie," said Polly. "Yes, it's all very pretty, but it's not what we're here for."

"You speak for yourself," I said. "This is the mother lode!"

"And it's not going anywhere. We'd need trucks to transport this much gold, not to mention an armed guard. We can always come back for it later, after we've found the wand. The gold is safe and secure here, but I can't say the same for the Lady of the Lake. That is still our main objective, isn't it?"

"Well, yes," I said reluctantly. "You can always find more gold, but there's only one Lady of the Lake."

"Exactly! Who's a clever boy."

"Any idea of where we should look for the wand?" I said. "I don't see it anywhere."

"Of course not," said Polly. "Far too valuable to be left lying around. The Pharaoh took it with him, inside his sarcophagus."

I considered the casket thoughtfully. Eight feet long,

covered in jewels and gold leaf, the whole of the lid taken up with one big stylised portrait of the inhabitant. Very impressive, and very solid. Polly pretended to read some of the markings.

"Not dead, only sleeping."

"He's not kidding anyone but himself," I said. "Don't suppose you've got a crow-bar about you?"

"Hold back on the brute force, just for a moment," said Polly. She walked slowly around the sarcophagus, studying every inch of it through her Looking Glass while careful to maintain a respectful distance at all times. "There are supposed to be extra-special booby-traps," she said, after a while. "Mechanical and magical protections, all set to activate if anyone even touches the lid. But as far as I can see . . . they're all silent. Deactivated. I can only assume my protections are working overtime."

"Just as well," I said. "We don't want Sleeping Beauty to wake up. I've seen those movies."

"We can handle him," said Polly, dismissively.

"Don't get overconfident," I said. "After all these years on the Street of the Gods, soaking up worshippers' belief, who knows what the mummy might have become?"

"As long as my protections are still working, he's only another stiff in bandages," Polly said firmly. "If he should sit up, just slap him down again. Larry? Are you listening to me?"

I was listening to something else. I could hear the sound of soft, shuffling feet. I could hear great wings beating. I could hear my own heart hammering in my chest. The sense of some third presence in the burial chamber was almost overwhelming, close and threatening. I kept thinking the statues on the edge of my vision were slowly turning their heads to look at me. They were only feelings. I wasn't fooled by them. But I was becoming more and more convinced that someone or something knew we were there, in a place we shouldn't be. That inside the sarcophagus, under the lid, the Pharaoh's eyes were open and looking up at us.

Polly moved in close beside me, squeezing my arm hard.

"Larry, please calm down. We're perfectly safe. If I'd known you got spooked this easily, I'd have chosen someone else."

"I'm fine," I said. "Fine. Let's get the lid off, get what we came for, and then get the hell out of here."

"Suits me, sweetie. The mummy's holding the wand in his left hand. All we have to do is slide the lid far enough to one side for us to reach in."

Even with both of us pushing and shoving, the sarcophagus lid didn't want to move. It ground grudgingly sideways, a few inches at a time. Loud scraping noises echoed on the still air, interspersed with muffled curses from Polly and me. We threw all our strength against the lid, and slowly, slowly, a space opened up, revealing the interior of the sarcophagus and its occupant. The mummified head and shoulders looked shrivelled and distorted, the eyes and mouth just shadows in a face like baked clay. The wrappings were brown and grey, decayed, sunken down into the dead flesh. The body looked brittle, as though rough handling would break it into pieces.

The elven wand was held tightly in one clawlike hand, laid across the sunken chest.

"Well, go on!" said Polly. "Take it!"

"You take it!"

"What?"

"Let's think about this for a moment," I said, leaning on

the lid. "I have seen pretty much every mummy movie ever made, including that Abbott and Costello abomination, and it's always the idiot who takes the sacred object from the mummy's hand who ends up getting it in the neck. In fact, it's usually at this point in the film that the warning music starts getting really loud."

"God, you're a wimp!" said Polly. She grabbed the elven wand, wrestled it out of the mummy's hand, and stepped back, holding the wand up triumphantly.

The whole burial chamber shook violently, as though hit by an earthquake. Thick streams of dust fell from the ceiling. The floor rose and fell, as though a great rippling wave had swept through the solid stone. The walls seemed to writhe and twist, as though all the hieroglyphics were coming to life and screaming silently. And the wall we'd opened into the burial chamber shot up out of the ground, and slammed into place against the ceiling again. I glared at Polly.

"Next time, listen to the music! Is there any other way out of here?"

Polly waved the Looking Glass back and forth, dust dancing in the brilliant beam of light. "I can't see anything!"

"Terrific," I said.

Then the lid of the sarcophagus crashed to the floor. We both looked round, startled, just in time to see the mummy rise out of its resting place. It moved slowly, jerkily, animated and driven by unnatural energies. It was small, barely five feet tall, a shrivelled wretched thing, but it burned with power. You could feel it. The empty eyes in the dead face fastened first on me, then on Polly, and finally on the wand. It reached out a brown bandaged hand, and the arm made dry, cracking sounds as it extended. The mummy kicked the sarcophagus lid aside with one foot, and the lid flew across the chamber to slam into the far wall.

"Maybe we should give him his wand back," I said.

"Unthinkable!" snapped Polly.

"Hell, I'm thinking it, and so is he," I said. "Can you use the wand against him? What does it do?"

"*I don't know!*" said Polly, backing quickly away from the mummy as it advanced upon her with slow, shuffling steps. The whole chamber was still shaking, making loud, groaning sounds as the heavy stone walls flexed, but the mummy's attention was still fixed solely on the wand in Polly's hand. I took out my gun and gave the mummy six rounds rapid. Three to the body, three to the head. Puffs of dust burst out of the bullet-holes, but the mummy didn't even stagger or interrupt its pursuit of Polly as she retreated before it. Her back slammed up against the wall behind her, and she had to stop. I thought about jumping the mummy from behind and wrestling it to the floor, then thought better of it. Some plans you know aren't going to float. I ran past the slow-moving figure, and grabbed the elven wand from Polly. The dead face immediately turned to me, and I smiled. Because the moment I had the wand in my hand, I knew what it could do and how to use it. The knowledge was suddenly there, in my head, as though I'd always known it but only just remembered. I said the activating Words silently, inside my head, and the wand's power leapt forth and took hold of the world.

Time stopped.

The mummy was still, and so was Polly, caught reaching out to snatch the wand back from me. The burial chamber was still, caught between one moment and the next. Falling dust hung suspended in mid air. I moved slowly forward, and

Time did not move around me. I considered the mummy, the shrivelled face wrapped in yards of decaying gauze, like a mask baked from ancient Egyptian mud. Scary, yes, but take away the supernatural energies that drove him, and the mummy was a small, fragile thing. I considered the elven wand in my hand. Two feet long, carved from the spine of a species that no longer existed in the waking world, it shone with a brilliant light while it did its work. There were all kinds of tricks it could play, with Time. I jabbed the wand at the frozen mummy, and Time accelerated around it. The bandaged body decayed and fell apart and became dust, all in a moment.

I hefted the wand in my hand. Why had it spoken to me and not to Polly? Perhaps because it didn't trust her. I knew how it felt.

I started Time going again, and Polly yelped loudly as she saw only a pile of dust on the floor where the mummy had been a moment before. She looked at me, glared at the wand in my hand, and gestured for it imperiously.

"No," I said. "I think I'll hang on to it for a while. It wants me to."

"What happened to the mummy?" she said, studying my face intently.

"Time caught up with it," I said. "Can we get the hell out of here now, before the whole bloody place collapses?"

Polly was a practical soul. She wasted no time with arguments, just hurried over to the entrance wall and studied it through her Looking Glass. Only took her a few moments to work the mechanism again, then we vaulted over the lowering wall and ran back through the shaking stone passages, trying not to listen to the increasingly loud groaning sounds all around us. Dust fell in thick sheets, and we both coughed harshly as we ran, holding our hands over our mouths and noses to keep out the worst of it. I don't know how long we ran, following the light from the Looking Glass, but it seemed like the journey would never end. For years afterwards I had dreams where I was still there, still running through the dark and the dust, forever.

But finally we came to the side-door again and made our way back out onto the Street of the Gods. We kept running, and didn't stop until we were safely on the other side of the Street. We looked back just in time to see the tip of the pyramid crumble and decay, and fall in upon itself, until there was nothing left but a great hole in the ground.

"All that gold," I said.

"All your fault," said Polly.

"How do you work that out?" I said, honestly curious. "Everything was fine until you grabbed the wand from the mummy."

"It's your fault because you hurried me!"

You can't argue with logic like that. "Sorry," I said.

"Now, give me the wand. You don't know what to do with it."

"It wants me to have it," I said firmly.

Polly looked at me.

We took a taxi to our next destination. Most people don't trust taxis, but I find you can always rely on the driver as long as you keep a gun pressed to the back of his neck. Polly had promised the next item on our list would be much easier to acquire, and I relaxed a little as we headed into Uptown,

SIMON R. GREEN

with its many up-market clubs and bars. You meet a much
better class of scum in Uptown. We were looking for a pair
of chaos dice, simple probability changers, and according to
Polly, the very best example of their kind were to be found in
Wu Fang's Garden of Delights.

Everybody knew Wu Fang's scandalously decadent establishment; one of the most exclusive and expensive gambling
dens in the whole of the Nightside. Which took some doing.
The Garden of Delights had been around since the early
1930s, and so had Wu Fang. My father knew them both, back
in the day, and swore the Oriental Gentleman hadn't aged a
day in all those years. There were many rumours about the
man, most of them quite unsavoury, and Wu Fang encour-
aged them all. Especially the nasty ones.

We had no trouble getting in; Polly showed the tuxedoed
bouncers a handful of platinum credit cards, and they all but
fought each other for the privilege of opening the door for us.
The Garden of Delights always stood ready to welcome anyone with more money than sense. Like many establishments
in the Nightside, the interior was far bigger than the exterior.
It's the only way we can fit everything in. Or, as my father
likes to say, space expands to accommodate the sin available.

Inside Wu Fang's, the Garden of Delights stretched away
for as far as I could see; a veritable jungle of Far Eastern
trees and vegetation, where huge pulpy flowers blossomed
in the perfumed air. Tiny birds of startlingly bright colours
fluttered over our heads, or hovered over pouting petals. A
river meandered through the jungle, with delightful roofed
bridges crossing it at regular intervals. The rich scents hanging on the air buzzed inside my head. It was like breathing
in heaven itself.

Polly and I wandered unhurriedly past a tumbling water-fall, enjoying the faint haze of water droplets in the air, and nodded calmly to the celebrities and high-rollers we passed, as though we belonged there just as much as they did. And they nodded politely back, because since we were there, we must belong.

Set out in little clearings were the gambling tables. Every game of chance you could think of, and some Wu Fang had imported specially from other realities. The traditional games predominated, of course, from poker to craps, roulette to vingt-et-un. You could bet money, futures, your life, or your soul on the outcome; and Wu Fang would be right there to cover your bet. You'd find every single way there is of parting a sucker from his money somewhere in Wu Fang's celebrated Garden of Delights.

Amongst the delicate trees and the glorious foreign growths were statues and works of art, modern sculptures that ranged from the seriously abstract to the disturbingly erotic and displays of weapons from all times and places, including some that didn't exist yet. Suits of medieval armour stood at regular intervals, pretending to be decorative. Wu Fang's body-guards and enforcers; ready to step in and get violently physical at a moment's notice. Sore losers were not tolerated in the Garden of Delight. Curious guests in the know occasionally lifted the gleaming helmet visors and looked inside the armour; but it was always empty.

There were any number of trophies on display, prizes acquired by Wu Fang down the years. A severed hand holding aces and eights; Wild Bill Hickok's actual hand, stuffed and mounted, holding the cards he was dealt just before being shot in the back. The cards known forever after as the dead man's hand. Howard Hughes's death masque, smiling a very unsettling smile. The actual roulette wheel ball that broke the bank at Monte Carlo. And a pair of chaos dice. Two small cubes of night-dark ivory, with the points picked out in tiny blood-red rubies.

I couldn't see any protections, but I had no doubt they were there.

I spotted my brother Tommy, sitting at one of the main poker tables.

A lot of things about this surprised and horrified me. First, Tommy had always been famously bad at gambling. Lady Luck wouldn't recognise Tommy if she stumbled over him in the gutter. He could bet on the Nightside staying dark, and the sun would come up just to spite him. Second, Tommy had no card skills whatsoever. Anything more complicated than Snap was beyond him, and he couldn't count to twenty-one without dropping his trousers. And third, to my utter despair, Tommy was sitting in with some really major card-players. Famous faces from the gambling fraternity, men who made the cards dance and change their spots at will.

I was debating whether or not to rush over and shoot Tommy repeatedly in the head, as a kindness, when Wu Fang himself glided over to greet me. A rare honour indeed. Wu Fang bowed courteously, and I bowed back. Polly sank into a deep curtsey. Wu Fang ignored her, his attention fixed on me. A slight and delicate oriental gentleman, in a suit that undoubtedly cost more than I made in a year, Wu Fang was politeness personified. And for a man who had to be at least a century old, he didn't appear much older than me. There were lots of stories about Wu Fang, and most of them had blood in them. His brief smile showed yellow teeth, and his eyes were very dark.

"Larry Oblivion, son of Dash," he said, in a quiet and civilised tone that could somehow still be heard clearly over the general clamour of his Garden. "So kind of you to drop in. Avail yourself of my facilities. Deny yourself nothing. And do give my kindest regards to your father. An honourable foe from times past and a most determined pain in the arse."

Everybody knew my father.

"What's Tommy doing here?" I said bluntly.

"Winning," said Wu Fang. "Much to my and everyone else's surprise. But no matter. The money may move round and round the table, but it always comes back to me, eventually." Another swift smile. "I do so love to see you white boys lose."

He glided away like a Chinese ghost in a Chinese garden, and I hurried over to stand beside Tommy. Polly tried to grab my arm, but I avoided her. Family always comes first. I could feel her angry gaze burning into my back as I tapped Tommy briskly on the shoulder. He looked up and smiled happily at me.

"Oh, hi, Larry. Does Dad know you visit places like this? Ooh, like your new girlfriend. Tasty. Why is she glaring like that?"

He hadn't adopted his effete existentialist act then.

"What are you doing here, Tommy?"

"Winning," he said proudly. "I read this book, you see, and it suggested a whole new approach to cards I hadn't even considered before."

"You should have asked me," I said. "I've always known what you're doing wrong. You're crap at cards."

Tommy laughed and gestured grandly at the piles of poker

chips laid out before him. Some of them were in colours I hadn't ever seen before. Sitting around the table were Maggot McGuire, Big Alois, and Lucky Lucinda. Card sharks, all of them. Professional card-players, red in tooth and claw. They looked as much mystified as upset, though on the whole I think upset was rapidly coming to the fore. Their piles of chips were noticeably smaller. Tommy fanned out his current hand for me to have a look, and I almost fainted. He had a pair of threes.

Big Alois and Lucinda took one look at my face, misinterpreted what they saw, and folded immediately. That left the Maggot, a man not known for losing gracefully. Tommy grinned at him, and shoved all his chips forward, betting everything he had on his pair of threes. Maggot didn't have enough chips to match him, so he pulled a magic charm from his pocket and slapped that down on the pile. Tommy considered, nodded, and produced several handfuls of poker chips from his pockets and added them to the pile on the table. Maggot threw down his cards in disgust, pushed back his chair, and rose to his feet with a gun in his hand. But before he could aim it, two empty suits of armour moved quickly in on either side and grabbed him by the arms. One metal hand squeezed hard, until blood ran down Maggot's fingers, and he had no choice but to drop the gun. Then they dragged him away from the table. Wu Fang's enforcers were always good at anticipating trouble.

Tommy whooped with joy, and scooped up all the chips on the table, gathering them in with both arms.

Polly was suddenly there beside me, elbowing me discreetly in the ribs. I looked round, and she showed me the chaos dice in her hand, before quickly making them disappear about her person. While everyone's attention had been fixed on Tommy's triumph, Polly had got on with the job. Which meant there was now an empty display case on view, and it was well past time Polly and I were leaving. I said as much to Tommy, and he nodded easily.

"Catch you later, brother. I have some serious debauchery to be getting on with."

I had to smile. "What is this wonderful new card skill, that you learned from a book?"

He grinned cheerfully. "Betting entirely at random, with absolutely no rhyme or reason to it. No thought, no studying; half the time I didn't even look at my cards. Baffled the hell out of them."

Polly pulled me away before I could hit him.

I was still trembling and twitching, just a bit, when Polly and I arrived at our next destination: Savage Hettie's Lost and Found. (We Ask No Questions.) Polly's list of ingredients for opening her demon gate called for a Hand of Glory made from a monkey's paw. As if such a thing wasn't dangerous enough as it is, without meddling. Be like walking around with a tactical nuke in your pocket and the pin half-pulled. Savage Hettie specialised in items that were frequently as dangerous to you as they were to your enemies. Mostly because it amused her.

She sat in her chair by the open door, fanning herself with a paper fan covered in filthy pictures. Hugely fat, overflowing her chair on all sides, in a dark sack of a dress that fitted where it touched. Her red sweaty face was topped with a patently obvious wig of blonde curls. Her huge fingers were tattooed with the words *DIE* and *SCUM*. Her front two teeth were missing, and her tongue kept poking through the gap as she sucked the insides out of variously sized eggs that she kept in a sack by her chair. She radiated shifty malevolence but barely looked me over before fixing her piggy eyes on Polly. Savage Hettie sniffed loudly.

"I don't let just anyone in here, you know," she said, in her harsh East End accent. "And you look dead sneaky, girl. Hiding something, aren't you? Ho yes; I know your sort, girl."

"She's with me," I said flatly. "And you know me, Hettie."

She sniffed again. "I knows your father, you mean. Ho yes. I knew him very well, back in the day."

"Who didn't?" I said, resignedly.

She cackled loudly. "But I knew him intimately, as you might say. I didn't always look like this, you know."

I moved quickly past her, pushing Polly ahead of me, and Hettie's cackling laughter followed me into the dark interior of her shop. There are some mental images you really don't want to dwell on.

Hettie's place was always a mess, on a grand scale. All gloom and shadow and heaps of things, set out apparently at random. No order, no rationale, and absolutely no presentation. Handwritten price tags for everything; and no haggling. Pay Hettie's price or go somewhere else; except if you could have found it anywhere else, you wouldn't have ventured into Savage Hettie's appalling lair. There were shelves and boxes and tottering piles, and you had to dig for what you needed. At your own risk, of course. Touch the wrong thing in the wrong way, and it would have your hand off. Or turn you into a frog, or steal your soul. Browser very much beware; and watch your back at all times. Some of the items in Savage

Hettie's Lost and Found had a way of sneaking up on you from behind.

Hettie didn't give a damn. Except to laugh loudly when something really horrible happened.

Polly and I moved gingerly between stacks of magic boxes, enchanted dancing-shoes, and nasty old magazines, careful not to touch anything. There was fabulous and seriously valuable stuff to be found, if a person was not too fussy over little things like provenance, or guarantees. Savage Hettie was a fence as well as a dealer, and didn't care who knew it.

We passed by glass jars labelled *Manticore musk*, *Vampire's teeth* (which clattered and ground against the glass if you got too close), and a wine bottle covered in cobwebs marked simply *Drink Me You Bastard*. I was briefly distracted by a pile of old magazines that I couldn't resist leafing through (once I'd put some gloves on). The private schoolgirls' issue of *Oz*, *International Times* with a naked Paul and Linda on the front cover, and a battered copy of *Playbeing*, with something utterly revolting on the front cover. Polly, though, was not one for distractions. She stalked up and down the narrow aisles, seemingly following her nose, until finally she stopped abruptly before a sealed glass jam-jar. I joined her, and peered over her shoulder. In the jar was a small, withered thing, with half the hair fallen out, the stiff fingers made into candles with delicate little wicks. The stump was blackened, from where it had been sealed shut with a naked flame. I reached for the jar, and the fingers stirred slowly, like spider's legs. I snatched my hand back instinctively. Polly snorted dismissively and picked up the jar without hesitating in the least.

We took it back to Savage Hettie, who shocked me rigid

by refusing to take any payment. She reared back in her chair rather than touch the jam-jar, and leered at Polly, the tip of her tongue poking provocatively through the gap in her teeth.

"I know your kind, missie, ho yes I do. Don't want no dealings with you and yours, and I ain't going to risk being beholden to you. Take the nasty thing. Glad to be rid of it." She sniffed loudly, then looked at me. "Surprised to see an Oblivion boy with one of her lot, but I suppose you knows what you're doing. Blinded by a pretty face and bemused by the smell of pussy. Just like your dad."

Polly and I walked quickly away.

"Do you know what she was talking about?" she said, after a while.

"Haven't a clue," I said determinedly.

"Probably just as well," said Polly.

The last two items were easy. Deconsecrated host soaked in virgin's urine and a fine powder made from the crushed wings of wee flower faeries. Women use the strangest things as cosmetics. We found both items at the Mammon Emporium, the Nightside's premiere mall, and Polly made me shoplift them from their shelves while she kept a lookout. We then stalked imperiously out of the mall, and no-one challenged us. I think I was less scared in the mummy's burial chamber.

"You know," I said afterwards, "we could have paid for these."

"Where's the fun in that?" said Polly, and I was honestly lost for an answer.

• • •

Not entirely to my surprise, we ended up back on the Street of the Gods, standing before a quiet little church in the Street's equivalent of a backwater. A simple stone structure, with no fancy trimmings and no obvious name. People passed it by without looking, but it must have had something, or some other church or Being would have taken over its location long ago. The door was closed, the windows were dark, and there was no sign of life anywhere.

"Not very inviting," I said, after a while, because you have to say something.

"It isn't here for people," said Polly. Her face was full of an emotion I couldn't read, her eyes blazing.

"Does it have a name?" I said.

"It's old," said Polly. "Names come and go, but the church remains. It is a place of power, and it has been here for a very long time. So long that people have forgotten who it was originally created to venerate and preserve."

"The Lady of the Lake?" I said. "She's here?"

"Help me open the dimensional gate, and you'll see," said Polly.

There were no guards, no protections to get past. The door wasn't even locked, opening easily at Polly's touch. There wasn't actually a sign over the door saying *Enter at Your Own Risk*, but there might as well have been. I could feel all the hackles rising on the back of my neck as I followed Polly in.

The interior was no bigger or smaller than it should have been, an open, empty space surrounded by four stone walls, heavy with shadows, only the barest light seeping in through a narrow-slit window at the far end. No pews, no altar, just the open space. The air was still and uncomfortably warm, as though some great furnace were still operating down below. There was no sign anyone had been here in ages, but no dust either, or any sign of neglect.

Whatever might have been worshipped here in the past, it hadn't been a good or a wholesome thing. I could feel it, in my bones and in my water. Bad things had happened here. The horror of them still vibrated on the air, like the echoes of a scream that never ended. I looked at Polly, but she seemed entirely unaffected by the atmosphere. She trotted happily down the length of the empty church, with me stumbling along in the gloom behind her, trying to look in all directions at once. She dropped suddenly to one knee, and her fingers scrabbled against the floor for a moment before finally closing around the metal ring of a large trap-door I would have sworn wasn't there a moment before. The trap-door itself was solid metal and must have weighed half a ton, but she pulled it open easily with one hand before letting it fall back onto the stone floor. It landed hard, but even so, the echoes were strangely muted, as though the grim atmosphere was soaking up the sound. I looked at Polly, only a pale gleam in the gloom. There was no way a woman of her size could have handled that much weight so easily. I'd suspected she was keeping things from me, and now it seemed I was about to find out what.

Beneath the hole in the floor was a set of bare stone steps, leading down and down into darkness. Polly produced her Looking Glass and started down them without even looking to see if I was following. She knew I wouldn't hang back, not now I'd come so far.

I followed Polly and her light down into the dark, and wasn't at all surprised when the trap-door slammed shut again, over our heads.

The steps were rough and unmarked. The bare stone walls to either side were close enough to touch, hot enough to burn the fingers. The air was hot enough to bring a sheen of sweat to my face. I had to wonder exactly how far down we were going. My legs were aching from the strain of continuous descent when the stairway finally came to an end, and Polly stopped abruptly. She held up the Looking Glass, but its light couldn't penetrate more than a few inches into the dark. She laughed lightly, made the Glass disappear, and snapped her fingers imperiously. A harsh light sprang up, illuminating a huge cavern dug out of the bedrock far beneath the Street of the Gods. It wasn't any normal light; long streams of electrical fire crackled up and down the stone walls and crawled across the ceiling like living lightning. The fierce light hurt my eyes, but didn't seem to bother Polly at all. She looked back at me, and smiled.

"What are you waiting for, sweetie? This is it. This is what you came here for. Come on down, Larry Oblivion, and claim your prize."

She bestowed her most winning smile on me and batted her eye-lashes, but it looked grotesque now, clearly artificial, and practised. All of the attraction I once felt for her was gone, perhaps because I was seeing her clearly for the first time. But I went down to join her anyway. Because I'd come this far, and I wanted to know why. I wanted to know what treasure had been buried here if it wasn't the Lady of the Lake. Polly took me by the hand, and my flesh actually crawled at her touch. I went with her, deep into the cavern, until finally she stopped, let go my hand, and indicated with a warm smile what she'd brought me all this way to see.

It hung on the wall before us, opened up and stretched out over twenty feet or more. I couldn't tell whether it had been a man or a woman originally, but the guts and organs had been spread out and pinned to the stone with silver daggers. The skin had been stretched terribly without tearing, to make a background. The face had been expertly peeled from the skull, and extended so far I couldn't recognise any features in it but the eyes, wide and gleaming and very aware. The whole thing was still alive, despite its state. That was the point. The suffering was fuel for the magic, feeding and maintaining the gateway that pulsed like an alien wound deep in the exposed guts of what had once been a man or a woman.

Not a dimensional gate. Not a dimensional gate at all. A hellgate. A doorway into Hell itself.

Awful sounds burst briefly from the gate, screams and howls and endless destruction.

"What is that?" I said. "Is that Hell?"

"No, sweetie," Polly said happily. "That's the future. That's what the future will sound like, in the hell on Earth we're going to make for all Humankind."

We stood facing each other before the hellgate. Her smile was wide with anticipation, her face alive with enjoyment at the secret she'd kept from me, now to be revealed. I should have known it would end up like this. I've always had rotten luck with women.

And when you can't see the patsy in the deal, it's almost certainly you.

"So, Polly," I said, calm as calm could be. "No Lady in the

Lake, and the pretty face was just a come-on. So what's the deal? What do you need a hellgate for?"

"Sometimes, the living can be cast down into Hell," said Polly. "Damned to the Houses of Pain, forever. Unless you can send down a worthy replacement."

"That's why the scavenger hunt," I said. "You didn't need any of those things to open a hellgate. You wanted to test my mettle, see if I was . . . worthy."

"Exactly. I knew your reputation, but I needed to see you in action. After all, reputations are ten a penny in the Night-side. And the items we acquired will make a fine tribute for my long-lost mistress."

"Who?" I said. My mouth was dry, though my face was streaming with sweat, and I had to clench my hands into fists to stop them trembling. "Who are you planning to raise up out of Hell?"

"Can't you guess?" she said, and just like that she didn't look like Polly Perkins any more, or anything human.

She was tall and supernaturally slender, her glowing skin pale as the finest porcelain. Her ears were long and pointed, and her eyes had slitted cat pupils. She wore a simple white shift with the arrogance of nobility and a necklace of human fingers. Delicate elven script had been branded in a straight line across her forehead. Just looking at her now roused a kind of arachnid revulsion in me. There's nothing worse than something that looks like human, but isn't.

"You're an elf," I said, and my voice sounded dull and defeated, even to me. "Never trust an elf."

"Exactly," she said, and her voice was rich and sweet and cloying, like poisoned honey. "You're here to help me bring back our lost mistress, Queen Mab. Oldest and greatest of our kind, thrown down into Hell by the traitors Oberon and Titania. But any living thing damned to Hell can be rescued or redeemed by another living thing. One of the oldest rules there is . . ." She stopped, and looked at me, thoughtfully. "I wonder if the same rule applies to Heaven? What sport, what joy, to drag a noble person back from Paradise! But that's a thought for another day. Bye-bye, sweetie. Give my regards to the Inferno. It's been fun; but now it's over."

She lunged at me while she was still speaking, moving inhumanly quickly, expecting to catch me off-balance. But I was ready for her. I had the wand. She'd been so caught up in her moment of triumph that she'd forgotten to take it from me. I said the Words, and the wand stopped Time. Polly hung in mid air before me, her elongated alien form suspended between one moment and the next. I looked at her for a while. Thinking of what might have been. We'd worked well together, and I had enjoyed her company. But I'm nobody's patsy. So I took careful hold of her, turned her around in mid air so that she was facing the hellgate, and started Time up again.

She screamed, just once, as she saw what lay before her, then the gate sucked her in and sent her down, and she was gone while the echo of her scream still hung on the hot air. I looked at the hellgate, at the suffering human eyes in what had once been a human face, and thought about killing it. I knew how. I'd done it before. But to disrupt the hellgate while the transfer was still in progress could release unimaginable energies. I certainly wouldn't survive it. Wand or no wand. I didn't want to die, not while I still had so much life ahead of me . . . So even though I knew what was coming, I waited and watched, as Queen Mab of the Fae returned to the world of the living. One of the old monsters, Humanity's Ruin.

Something came rising up out of Hell. I could feel it, in the deepest part of what made me human. Something old and powerful, and huge beyond bearing, was rising up out of the dark latitudes, up from the Houses of Pain, forcing her way back into a natural world that wanted no part of her. Rising up, like a shark through bloody waters, like a tidal wave come to sweep away every living thing before it, up she came, Queen Mab, rising faster and faster. Coming at me like a meteor crashing to the Earth, like a bullet with my name on it.

Screaming in an ancient tongue, laughing horribly, swearing damnation and torment on all her many enemies; Queen Mab came back.

She stood before me in all her terrible glory. The hellgate lay in ruins on the wall behind her, incinerated by her passage through it, nothing now but small pieces of cooked meat pinned to the wall. The gate was closed, its victim released. That was something. Queen Mab fixed me with her fierce gaze, and I couldn't have moved to save my life. She was eight feet tall, slender, graceful, overbearingly regal. Horribly abhuman and utterly evil. Her presence filled the cavern, and I knelt to her. I still like to think I had no choice.

"This place was once dedicated to me," she said, and her voice was calm and casual, like a cat playing with a mouse. "Nice to know I haven't been completely forgotten. And I have been brought back by a human through the sacrifice of an elf. Love the irony. You can keep the wand, for now. Never let it be said Queen Mab failed to reward her servant. But now I'm back, and must be about my business."

She laughed, and I wanted to vomit.

"Ah, the things I'll do, now I'm back."

I never told anyone. Who could I tell? Who would believe it wasn't my fault?

FIVE

Everybody's Talking at Me

I listened to Larry's story without interrupting, then offered him my glass of Valhalla Venom again. He all but grabbed it out of my hand and knocked the stuff back in several large gulps. There are times when a stiff drink isn't just traditional; it's a psychological necessity. The vicious liquor didn't seem to affect Larry at all; presumably being dead helped. We both sat silently for a while, each of us considering our own thoughts. A lot of Larry's story had struck home with me. I knew how it felt to be trampled on and used by greater powers.

"I could have stopped her," Larry said finally. "I could have stopped Queen Mab coming through if I'd been willing to die to do it. But I wasn't."

"You can't be sure of that."

"I never will, now. Through my weakness, or at best my

hesitation, I let one of the old monsters back into the world. And now I'm dead, Heaven and Hell seem a lot closer. I can't just lie down and let go; I don't dare. My only hope is atonement; and for now that means finding Tommy. Are you in?"

I thought about it. Several things in his story had struck me forcefully. There were an awful lot of elves in the Nightside recently. Far more than usual. And then there were the Arthurian elements; did Polly Perkins pick them at random to lure Larry in? Or could they be linked to Puck's warning about Excalibur? Something was going on. But then, this is the Nightside. Something's always going on.

To unravel a mess, pull on any strand. So Tommy it was.

"I'll help you find out what happened to Tommy," I said. "But all I can offer is the truth. Don't blame me if you don't like what I find."

"That's what I always say to my clients," said Larry. "Only I usually put it a little more tactfully."

We managed a small smile for each other. We were never going to be close; but we could work together.

Then the whole bar went quiet. Conversations ceased, laughter and tears died away, and the piped music stopped so fast it briefly went into reverse. Heads turned and craned, and not a few lowered themselves and hoped not to be noticed. The whole bar seemed to be holding its breath because Walker had arrived.

He hadn't bothered with his usual slow descent of the metal steps, to let everyone know he was coming and make a grand entrance. He simply appeared suddenly out of nowhere, standing right there in the middle of the bar, leaning casually on his furled umbrella, smiling easily about him. Most of the clientele avoided meeting his eyes, not wanting to draw attention to themselves. Because if Walker was on the scene, it meant someone was in trouble; and given that Walker moves in more mysterious ways than half the Beings on the Street of the Gods, it might just be you. Walker was infamous for knowing things he shouldn't and doing something horribly punitive about it—*pour discourager les autres*.

And whatever he does, no-one ever protests. Because he's Walker.

But there's always one, isn't there? Someone always has to learn the hard way. In this case, it was one of Black Betty's overmuscled goons. She always had half a dozen or so on a leash in case she met a customer. This particular goon decided he was going to impress his mistress, so he stepped forward to face Walker, flexing his steroid-abused muscles in what he clearly thought was a threatening way. Walker considered him thoughtfully. A wise man would have taken the hint and run, but not the goon.

"You're upsetting my mistress, little man," said the goon. "Disappear."

Walker smiled, just a little. *"Shit yourself."*

He used the Voice, which commands everyone who hears it, and the goon made a sudden low sound of distress. Quickly accompanied by other, less pleasant sounds. Black Betty pulled a face and dropped his leash. The goon turned away from Walker, slowly and carefully, and trudged miserably off to the toilets. People he passed by wished he hadn't. The bar as a whole decided the safest thing to do was act as if Walker wasn't there. Heads turned away, conversations resumed, and the piped music returned. I noticed the bar's muscular bouncers, Betty and Lucy Coltrane, lurking in the background, ready to give their all at a moment's notice; but Alex had more sense. He gave Walker his best glare, then busied himself polishing some glasses that didn't need polishing.

Walker looked unhurriedly about him, taking his time. No-one was fooled by his calm exterior. Walker was always dangerous, even when he was being polite. Perhaps especially then. And, of course, in the end he spotted me, walked over to my booth, and smiled charmingly.

"Hello, John. Can I have a word? It is rather urgent."

"You've got a nerve," I said. "Just a few hours ago you were doing your best to have me killed."

"It's what I do," said Walker. "Nothing personal, John. You should know that by now."

"I've already taken a case," I said. "Find someone else to do your dirty work."

"This isn't about work. This is personal."

I sighed. Clearly I wasn't going to get rid of Walker until I'd listened to what he had to say. I looked at Larry, spreading my hands in a *What can you do?* gesture.

"You go on ahead. I'll join up with you outside the Cheyne Walk Underground Station, as soon as I can. That's the last place I saw Tommy alive."

Larry nodded and rose to his feet, then looked at Walker challengingly. "I'm Larry Oblivion. Do you have anything to say to me?"

Walker looked at him thoughtfully. "No, I don't think so. Not for the moment."

"Don't think you can intimidate me, Walker. I'm dead."

Walker smiled. "You, of all people, should know that death isn't the worst thing that can happen. When I want you, I'll come for you."

Larry turned his back on Walker and strode out of the

bar, his back straight and his head held high. And perhaps only Walker and I knew he was running away. Which is often the best way to deal with Walker. Just head for the nearest horizon the moment you spot him. I gestured resignedly to the empty seat, and Walker sat down opposite me, his every movement elegance and grace personified. He stood his umbrella on end beside his chair, took off his bowler hat and placed it carefully on the table before him, and casually adjusted his old-school tie. In anyone else these would have been mere habitual gestures; but Walker was quietly reminding me where his authority came from. Walker wasn't part of the System; he was the System.

"Would you care for a drink?" I said, gesturing at the Valhalla Venom with malice aforethought.

Walker studied the bottle without touching it and raised an eyebrow briefly. "Ah, yes . . . I wondered what had become of that. The steward at my club tried to persuade me to try some, but I had more sense. That stuff could eat holes in your kirlian aura. But you go right ahead, John. Don't let me put you off."

I pushed the bottle and glass to one side. "What do you want, Walker?"

He sighed slightly, as though disappointed by my lack of subtlety. "I understand you've learned my little secret, John. Yes; it's true. I'm dying. And no, there's nothing that can be done. We all die of something. All that's left to me is to make arrangements for what will happen afterwards."

"You want me to arrange your funeral?" I said. "Or just try to keep people from pissing on your grave?"

"I want you to take over my position when I'm gone," said Walker. "I want you to be the new representative of the new

Authorities. Because there's no-one else I can trust to do the job properly."

You think you've heard everything, then the universe rears up and slaps you round the head.

"*What?*"

"I said . . ."

"I know what you said! Are you crazy? I don't want the job!"

"Best kind of person for a job like this," said Walker. "And who more fitting than the son of my oldest friend?"

"Oh please," I said. "Emotional blackmail will get you nowhere."

"Always worth a try," said Walker.

"Look, we just went head to head over the elf, while a whole bunch of your people did their very best to terminate me with extreme prejudice. When you're not trying to have me arrested or stepped on, you're hiring me to investigate cases that will almost certainly get me killed. Now, call me paranoid if you like, but I'm starting to detect a pattern here. So why would you want someone like me, someone you've tried to run out of the Nightside on more than one occasion, to take over your job?"

"I need a man with strong convictions," said Walker. "A man who won't fold when the game gets serious. A man who won't take any shit from the bad guys. You remind me a lot of myself when I was younger."

"Now you're just being nasty," I said.

"I have some time left," said Walker. "Enough to teach you the things you need to know. Including how to avoid my mistakes."

"You mean how to avoid becoming you?" I shook my head

firmly. "I don't want anything to do with this. You know I've always had problems with authority figures. Why would I want to be one? Why pick on me?"

"Doesn't every father want his son to follow in his footsteps; only do it better?"

"I am not your son!"

"Who has shaped your life more than I? Who helped make you what you are? I am responsible for you, John, in every way that matters."

"Only in the sense that I'm determined to be nothing like you," I said. "I know a bad example when I see one."

" 'How sharper than a serpent's tooth,' " murmured Walker. "Come with me, John. Come walk with me through the Nightside and see it as I see it. My portable Timeslip can take us anywhere in a moment. We can take in the whole Nightside in a single night. Watch me work. See what I have to do, to maintain the peace and keep the lid on things. There's a lot to my job that no-one ever knows but I."

"I don't want your job. I have a job, and I'm bloody good at it."

Walker considered me thoughtfully. "You always say you want to help people. How better than by mediating between them and the Authorities? By using their power to protect the little people from those who would prey on them? How many more people could you help, from a position of power?"

"Get thee behind me, Satan," I said, and he actually chuckled.

I thought about it. Despite all my best instincts, a lot of what he said made sense in a seductive kind of way. The things I could do, with the Authorities behind me . . . A lot of the people I couldn't touch, because of their power and connections, would suddenly become . . . touchable. I've always believed that one man, in the right place, can make a difference . . .

"If," I said, "just for the sake of argument . . . If I was to take over your position, I wouldn't be the Authorities' lapdog. I'd go my own way, follow my own conscience . . ."

"That's why I chose you," said Walker.

"Is there really nothing I can do to help you?" I said. "This is the Nightside. There must be something . . ."

"If there was something to be done, I'd be doing it," Walker said calmly. "Would you really try to help me, John? After all the times I've tried to have you arrested or killed?"

"Of course," I said. "You're my father's oldest friend. And . . . for good or bad, you've always been a part of my life. Always there . . . always looking out for me, one way or another. There were so many things I wanted to say to my father, before he died. You always think there'll be time enough . . . until there isn't. Now here I am, wondering what I should say to you. My oldest enemy, my oldest friend. Part of me thinks I should have killed you years ago: for all the people you've trampled underfoot, for all the lives you've destroyed, all in the name of maintaining your precious status quo."

"You're not a killer," said Walker.

"I have killed. When I had to. But I try not to. It would make me too much like you."

"So you're admitting we have some things in common?"

I showed him my teeth in a smile. "Don't say that like it's a good thing."

"I'm not ashamed of anything I've done," said Walker.

"But are you proud of anything?"

"I'm proud of you. One of my better long-term projects."

"Do you have any idea how creepy that sounds?"

"I have kept the peace in the Nightside for thirty years and more," said Walker. "I've stopped the Nightside from tearing itself apart, kept it from spilling over its boundaries into the vulnerable everyday world, and even managed a little justice along the way. That's the best you can hope for, in my position."

"When I look back through my life," I said, "I can see times when you could have killed me, and didn't, when anyone else in your position would have. You didn't because I'm the son of your oldest friend, the man you betrayed and hounded to his death. You can't kill me, Walker. I'm your conscience."

"You keep on thinking that," said Walker. "If it makes you feel more secure."

"What if I told you to take your job and shove it?" I said. "Would you have me killed then?"

"I am many things," said Walker. "But not petty. I'd simply move on to my next choice."

I had to raise an eyebrow at that. "You have someone else in mind?"

"Of course."

I waited, but he had nothing more to say. I nodded, slowly. "I'll have to think about this."

"There isn't much time," said Walker. "I don't have much time. But you think about it, John. I'll see you again."

And he vanished from his chair, gone, just like that. Didn't even use his portable Timeslip. Trust Walker always to have another trick up his sleeve.

I did genuinely consider his offer. Though there had to be a lot more to it than he was saying. Walker wasn't the kind to go gently into that long night. He had to be planning something. But what if he wasn't? What if he was just a man, dying too soon, desperate to put some things in order while there was still time? Experience suggested very strongly that he was setting me up for something, but what if the offer really was genuine? Who else would I want for the job if I was in Walker's position? Someone's got to do it . . . and it was very tempting.

I always thought Walker would kill me someday, or I'd kill him. But things never turn out the way you expect, in the Nightside.

I thought of all the things I could finally put right, with the Authorities' power to back me up. All the bad guys I could take down and put out of business . . . Yes. It was tempting. But could that be the first step down the road of power corrupting? The road that led to the devastated future Nightside I'd seen in the Timeslip? The world where I was responsible for the death of all Humanity . . . I thought I'd avoided that future; but Time does so love to play its little tricks.

The smell hit me first. That familiar, bad smell, of someone who lay down with garbage and dead things and didn't give a damn. I looked up resignedly and sure enough, there was Razor Eddie sitting opposite me. The Punk God of the Straight Razor, his very own smelly and disturbing self. A painfully thin presence wrapped in an oversized grey coat held together with accumulated filth and grease, Eddie looked terrible; but then, he always did. The same gaunt face, close-cropped hair and fever-bright eyes. He was nursing a bottle of designer water, while flies buzzed dolefully around him. The ones that got too close fell out of the air dead. When he spoke, his voice was low and dry and ghostly.

"There's something in the air, John."

"I had noticed," I said. "You should hang some of those little pine trees around your neck. So, how are you doing, Eddie? Still sleeping with the homeless and begging for spare change?"

"I don't have to beg," he said solemnly. "As soon as people see who I am, they throw money at me and run."

Razor Eddie is the only god I know who sleeps in doorways and eats food out of Dumpsters as a form of penance. He has a lot to do penance for.

"What do you want, Eddie?" I said, tiredly. "Seems like everybody wants something from me today."

"You're getting too chummy with Walker," said Razor Eddie. "If you're not one of us, you're one of them."

"I'm not with anybody," I said. "Except Suzie. I go my own way. You know that."

"You've been close to the new Authorities ever since they appeared."

"Is that so bad? They're saying all the right things."

"The only way to stay uncorrupted by power is to turn your back on it. You should know that. Don't let Walker convince you of the rightness of his path. Don't be fooled into thinking you could take his power and not be touched by it. Not be changed by it. The Nightside does so love to break a hero. You can't save the Nightside, John. You can't redeem the Nightside. It doesn't need saving or redeeming. It serves a purpose, just as it is. Or I'd have torn it all down long ago."

"Hasn't stopped you killing a whole bunch of people," I said carefully. "Often in inventively ghastly ways."

"There are always those who go too far. Bad people, who need killing. I'll always be there, for them. But look what that kind of life has done to me. Honour can be a harsh mistress. You have a chance for a real life, with Suzie. How do you think she'll feel when she hears about you sitting down with Walker?"

"Tell me, Eddie," I said. "Why have you never gone after Walker? You've always hated him and everything he stands for. Is it the Voice?"

He smiled slightly, his pale lips hardly moving. "I can move faster than he can speak. No. I never touched him because . . . someone has to be in charge, and better the devil you know. Walker may be a bastard, but he's an even-handed bastard. He doesn't take sides, so we can all hate him evenly."

"But, could you take him?" I said.

Razor Eddie thought about it. "Maybe. Walker has his secrets; but then, don't we all?"

I decided to change the subject. "So what have you been up to lately, Eddie? Killed anyone interesting?"

"No. I've been . . . travelling." Razor Eddie stirred uneasily in his seat. "Ever since Merlin Satanspawn finally passed on, I've felt . . . restless. Disturbed. As though waiting for the storm to break. I've being spending time down in the subterranean ways, listening and learning. There are rumours in dark places, whispers in the shadows . . . People, and others, have talked to me when they wouldn't talk to anyone else. And definitely not to Walker."

"You trust them to tell you the truth?" I said.

"Of course," said Razor Eddie. "I'm a god."

"Of course," I said.

"I first heard the name on the Street of the Gods, passed from hand to hand and mouth to mouth like an isotope too hot to handle. I heard it again in the Moon Pool, and among the Openers of the Way. Something is coming to the Night-side, John, something very old and very powerful, enough to scare even me. It could change everything."

I leaned forward, caught up in his intensity. "How do you mean, 'change'?"

"Something that could save or damn us all." He smiled briefly. "Whether we like it or not. Which rather begs the question: what could be powerful enough to enforce its will upon the whole Nightside and make it stick?"

"My mother is gone," I said steadily. "And she won't be coming back."

"Well, that's good to know. But I wasn't thinking of her. This is a legend that made itself true, an artefact that can rewrite history. A weapon that could sweep the stars out of the sky."

"Does it have a name?" I said.

"Oh yes. And it's a name you'll know. But don't be fooled by the glamour. The stories were rewritten many times, to disguise just how terrible it is."

"Say the name," I said.

"Excalibur," whispered Razor Eddie, Punk God of the Straight Razor.

He got up and left before I could say anything, and I wasn't sure what I would have said anyway. Twice now someone had dropped that name, and not in a good way. I brushed dead flies off the table-top, and thought about it. Could this be the real thing, lost for centuries, come back out of legend and into history again, its time come round at last? How had Puck known about Excalibur? Was there some connection between that ancient sword and the most ancient of races? Supposedly, the great sword could only be wielded by the true King of

England, or by the truly pure in heart; which ruled me out on both counts. In fact, I'd be hard-pressed to name anyone in the Nightside who came even close. So why was it coming here? Had someone summoned it? Or stolen it? Could it be a larger-than-usual piece of celestial flotsam and jetsam, washing up in the Nightside from God knows where . . . Or could its presence here answer some kind of purpose? Or destiny? Destiny can be a real bastard, in the Nightside.

It could save or damn us all . . .

My concentration was interrupted by the tinkling sound of "Tubular Bells," and I got out my mobile phone and answered it, glad to be interrupted. I hadn't liked where my thoughts were taking me . . .

"Hi. It's Suzie. The whole Mother Shipton business was a waste of time. She was warned, and the whole place was empty by the time I got here. Thing is, I'm almost sure the warning came from Walker. Like he wanted me out here, out of the way."

"Could be," I said. "Walker came to see me. He's up to something."

"I'm coming straight back," said Suzie. "Don't agree to anything, and above all don't sign anything until I've looked at it first."

"I did survive for years without you, you know."

"Beats the hell out of me how. See you soon. My love."

And she was gone. Suzie never was one for small talk. I put the phone away. Like a lot of people in the Nightside, I can't help wondering where the satellites are. Or even if there are satellites. I keep hoping someone will hire me to find out.

And then the three witches appeared, advancing on my

booth. Bent-over hags in shapeless shrouds, with warts and hooked noses and evil eyes. They gathered before me, cackling hideously, then bowed deeply.

"Hail!"

"Hail!"

"Hail!"

"All hail John Taylor, who shall be King hereafter!"

I glared at them. "Alex put you up to this, didn't he?"

SIX

Crime Scene Investigators

I travelled to Cheyne Walk on the Underground. After all the more than usually crazy weirdness of my day so far, I felt in need of the ordinary everyday weirdness of the Tube system. From the moment I descended the crowded stairs into the packed station, everything seemed reassuringly normal. The buskers were out in force, singing for their supper with more enthusiasm than talent. A wide-eyed gentleman with multiple personality disorder was doing three-part harmonies with himself, in a rocking rendition of "My Guy." A malfunctioning android in a monk's robe was blasting out Gregorian chants interspersed with quick bursts of hot Gospel soul. And a soft ghost sang a sad song in a language no-one recognised, from a world no-one remembered any more. I dropped a little spare change on all of them. Because you never know. All it ever takes is one really bad day, and we can all fall off the edge.

The tunnels and platforms seemed more than usually crowded, with people—and others—from here, there, and everywhere. All of them full of a restless nervous energy, desperate to get to wherever they were going, as though afraid it might not be there when they arrived. No-one was talking to anyone else, and the crowded conditions led to a certain amount of elbowing and shoving and barging aside, the sort of behaviour that really wasn't safe in the Nightside.

Everyone gave me plenty of room, though. I'm John Taylor.

I leaned against a platform wall and waited for my train, aimlessly studying the posters on the wall opposite. They stirred and changed in subtle ways, advertising movies that could only be seen in certain very private clubs. Weird images that came and went like scenes from disturbed dreams.

A tall diva in all-white leathers led a shaved chupacabra past me on a leash. A clone boy band with seven identical faces slouched arrogantly after her. A dead surfer with rotting jammies came to stand beside me, leaning patiently on the coffin lid he was using as a board. (Though God alone knew where he thought he was going to find a decent wave in the Nightside.) City gents in smart city suits stood close together in their proud little cliques, discussing ritual sacrifice and the *Financial Times* shares index. There were also plenty of the usual creatures trying to pass themselves off as human, with varying degrees of success. No-one ever says anything to them. It's the thought that counts.

A few yards away a group of mimes beat up a pickpocket with their invisible mallets.

Just another day in the Nightside.

By the time the train got me to Cheyne Walk, I was so relaxed I almost dozed off on my seat, and my head came up with a jerk as the train slammed into the station. I made my way up through the tunnels, swept along with the hurrying crowds, and finally emerged onto the street. The air was hot and sweaty, and a gusting wind blew lighter pieces of garbage this way and that. There are no street-cleaners in the Nightside; because there's always something around that'll eat anything. I strolled down the street, taking my time, looking the place over. It hadn't been that long since the Lilith War, but you'd never have known there'd ever been any fighting or destruction here. It had all been repaired, rebuilt, renewed. Old shops and businesses destroyed by fire and explosion and the madness of rioting mobs had been replaced by bright new establishments; like a carnival built on a neglected graveyard.

Heavy-drinking bars stood alongside advanced dance salons, while brightly lit book-shops offered volumes of forgotten lore and forbidden knowledge. In paperback, and usually remaindered. There was even one of those new age soul-massage parlours, guaranteed to put your inner self at rest, and a restaurant from the Strange Offerings chain, specialising in food from other worlds and dimensions. For the more adventurous, there was a branch of Baron Samedi's Bide A Wee; where you can pay to be briefly possessed, just for the kick of it. And for the truly creepy among us, there was the Dreamy Travel Agency, where lucid-dreaming potions allowed the discerning client to go tripping through the Dreamtime, to skinny-dip in other people's dreams.

But still the tourists and the punters streamed this way and that, with eyes bigger than their wallets, on the prod and on the prowl, desperate to give away everything they had for everything on offer that was bad for them. The street was alive with noise and bustle and something very like glamour. Candy-coloured neon signs blazed like beacons, and everywhere you looked there was every kind of come-on. The damned leading the damned; the Nightside doing what it did best.

I stopped half-way along the street, trying to remember exactly where I saw Tommy Oblivion go down; first under a falling wall, then under the clawing hands of a maddened crowd. I always assumed he died here because I saw so many others die that day. Like Sister Morphine, the angel of the homeless. She'd died right in front of me, and there was nothing I could do to help her. There was a war on. I couldn't save everyone. I could still remember the bodies, piled up like refuse, while blood ran so thickly in the gutters it overflowed the storm drains. I could still hear the screams and pleas from the wounded and the dying . . . still see the mobs running wild, driven out of their minds by shock and horror, tearing apart everyone in their path. So many dead, and no memorial for any of them. Not even a plaque on a wall.

Because the Nightside doesn't look back.

I finally caught up with Larry Oblivion at the end of the street. He was standing in front of what had been one of the new business establishments, but was now just a smoking ruin, with broken, blackened walls surrounding a great pit in the earth. A sputtering neon sign had been driven half its length into the ground, like a Technicolor spike. A crowd of interested onlookers was carefully maintaining a discreet distance between them and the blast zone. Or possibly, between them and the heavily scowling Larry Oblivion. They were all cheerfully debating what had happened, how it had happened, why it had happened; and swapping theories on who might be next. Then they saw me approaching and went suddenly quiet. Not so much because they were impressed as because they didn't want to miss out on anything. Everyone knew about Larry and me. The Nightside does so love to gossip. I made a point of giving Larry my most friendly smile as I joined him, to spite everyone.

"Hadleigh's already been here," Larry said bluntly. "I've been talking to people. He scared the crap out of everybody and blew this place up just by looking at it. Typical Hadleigh. At least he only killed a bunch of bad guys this time, and no innocent bystanders. That's something."

"Does he do that, sometimes?" I said. "Kill innocent bystanders?"

"Who knows what he does, these days."

"Why single out this place?" I said, looking interestedly around the still-smoking ruins.

"He disapproved," said Larry.

"And what business was it of his?" said an angry voice from the crowd.

Larry and I took our time turning round to look. We didn't want to be thought of as the kind who could be hurried by an angry voice. I spotted the speaker immediately. I knew Augustus Grimm of old, always ready to appoint himself the spokesman for any aggrieved gathering, whip it into violence, then fade quietly into the background once the whole thing kicked off. A defrocked heretic accountant, Grimm had learned just enough mathemagics to be a nuisance, if not actually dangerous, and had been thrown out of the Accountants' Guild for unethical use of imaginary numbers. (Apparently Grimm could make certain numbers imagine they were in his client's bank accounts rather than where they were supposed to be. The Guild shut him down fast; no-one messes with business in the Nightside.)

"Shut up, Augustus," I said kindly. "Or I will come over there and kick the fractions out of you."

Larry and I waited politely, but Grimm didn't want to meet either of our eyes. We made a point of turning our backs on him.

"Hadleigh objected to the very existence of this place," said Larry. "Turnabout Inc. could swap a mind from one body to another, for the right price. An old man could live on in a young man's body as long as he kept up the payments. Do as much damage to the young body as he liked because he could always move on to another and walk away unconnected from all the evils he'd done. A very popular business; so popular, Turnabout had run out of paid volunteers and taken to snatching kids right off the street."

I nodded slowly. This was the third case of mind-swapping I'd heard about today. Was someone trying to tell me something? Or warn me about something?

"Hadleigh blasted the whole building into kindling with just a glance," said Larry. "Killed the owners and the staff, and all the customers who happened to be there. A handful of the possessed staggered out of the ruins, entirely unarmed, and back in their own bodies again. Not all of them were grateful. A few had gone in with their eyes open because they needed the money. When you've sold off everything you own to pay your debts, all you have left to sell is your body, one way or another. Hadleigh had nothing to say to them. It seems the Detective Inspectre is only interested in crime, not its victims."

The crowd was getting noisy. I looked back, and there was Augustus Grimm, with his pinched, vindictive face, whipping up grievances, pointing the finger at Larry and me. The crowd seemed bigger than before, full of angry faces and raised voices. A slow, cold anger moved through me as I remembered the maddened faces that had killed Sister Morphine, and maybe Tommy as well. No matter where you are in the Nightside, you're never far from an angry mob, eager to get their hands bloody for any good reason or none. Just for the thrill of it. It's in the nature of the Nightside to bring out the worst in us. It's what we come here for.

"You think I don't know you, dead man?" Grimm shouted at Larry. "You're his brother! Which makes you as guilty as him! Who are you, to judge us? To take our fun away? You'll pay for what he did!"

He gestured grandly with one hand, and a long, glowing blade manifested in his grip. I suppose it's only a short step from imaginary numbers to imaginary weapons. There was no substance to the blade he held; it was the concept of a sword. But that only made it stronger and sharper. The crowd growled its approval. Larry stepped forward to address them, and Grimm cut at him with his imaginary sword. The glowing edge sliced clean through Larry's jacket and shirt, and opened up a long thin cut in the grey flesh beneath. There was no blood, of course.

Larry looked down, then back at Grimm. "That was my best suit, you little turd!"

He whipped out his magic wand, and just like that Time slammed to a halt. Every sound was cut off; everyone stood still; everything was struck motionless. The very atmosphere seemed to hang in the balance, caught between one moment and the next. Even the impaled neon sign was caught in mid flicker. Larry put his wand away, then moved swiftly through the crowd, beating the crap out of every last one of them. His unfeeling dead hands rose and fell, dispensing brutal punishments. He punched heads and chests and sides, and the sound of breaking bone was crisp and sharp on the enforced quiet. No blood flowed—not yet. And no matter how hard he hit them, none of the bodies stirred or reacted, or even rocked in place.

I saw it all and heard it all, because even though I was frozen in place like everyone else . . . I could still think and observe. Perhaps my special gift protected me from the wand's magic, or maybe my unnatural bloodline. Like it or not, I am still my mother's son. Either way, I decided to keep this to myself. Larry didn't need to know.

And I might need to use it against him sometime.

Larry finally returned to his original position, not even breathing hard from his exertions. He took out his wand, started Time up again, then put the wand away and enjoyed the general unpleasantness. The whole crowd cried out in shock and surprise and agony. Bones broke, bruises blossomed, and blood spurted from mouths and noses. Some collapsed; some fainted; some lurched back and forth clutching at broken heads and cradling broken ribs. Augustus Grimm lay flat on his back, fortunately unconscious, so he couldn't feel all the terrible things Larry had done to him. Never get the dead mad; they don't have our sense of restraint.

I pretended a certain amount of surprise, then looked sternly at Larry.

"Wasn't that a bit extreme?"

"You're a fine one to talk," said Larry. "At least I don't rip the teeth right out of their heads. Besides, this bunch wouldn't have been quite so mad if they hadn't been customers, or potential customers, of Turnabout Inc. And therefore deserving of what just happened to them, on general principles. Like my elder brother, there is some shit up with which I will not put."

Those of the crowd who could had already departed, leaving the moaning and the unconscious behind. Larry turned his back on them all, studying the rest of the people on the busy street, most of whom were far too taken up with their own wants and needs to notice a minor scuffle. Business went on as usual, and Larry took it all in; and his cold, dead face showed nothing at all.

"I wasn't there that night," he said finally. "I was busy with the war, organising resistance against your damned mother. If I had been here, do you think it would have made any difference? Would my brother still be alive if I hadn't entrusted him to your care?"

"I couldn't save him," I said. "No-one could have. It was a war. People die in wars."

"Is that supposed to make me feel better? Is it?" He didn't look at me. He didn't expect an answer. "You're sure this is the street where he fell? This is where he disappeared?"

"A bit further down from here, but yes. I didn't actually see him die. So there is still some hope."

"Hope is for the living," said Larry. "The dead must make do with vengeance."

He still wasn't looking at me, apparently concentrating entirely on the street.

"I haven't seen Hadleigh in years," Larry said finally. "Don't even know what he looks like, these days."

"Shouldn't think many do," I said. "Only ones who see

him now are his enemies and his victims; and they're not usually in any shape to talk about it afterwards."

"He isn't that bad," said Larry. "Just a really scary agent of the Good."

"You ever met Razor Eddie?" I said.

"Hadleigh isn't a monster," said Larry. "I have to believe that. The last living Oblivion brother can't be a monster."

I looked back at the ruins of Turnabout Inc. and invoked my gift. I concentrated on my inner eye, my third eye, and used it to summon up ghost images from the recent Past. Important events and significant people stamp themselves on Time, for a while. I let go of now, and focused my Sight on what had happened to Turnabout Inc. so very recently. The world went misty and uncertain, then snapped back into focus as the street changed before me. The shop was still a ruin; something kept me from going back any further; but Hadleigh Oblivion was standing right before me.

He didn't look like any of the usual ghost images I See in the Past: shimmering figures, translucent as soap bubbles, sometimes barely there at all. Hadleigh looked firm and solid and almost unnaturally real. A tall, forbidding presence, in a long leather coat so black it seemed almost a part of the night, with a great mane of long, dark hair. He stood tall and proud, arrogant in his certainty that he had a right to be there and to do whatever he felt like doing. There was a power in him. I could See it, feel it, even at such a distance. His head snapped round, and he stared right at me. His face was bone white, dominated by dark, unblinking eyes and a bright, happy smile. He could see me as clearly as I could See him, even though I was in a future that hadn't happened for him yet.

"Hello, John," he said, in a voice so calm and normal it was downright spooky. "Give my regards to Larry. I'll see you soon."

The vision broke, and the Past was gone. He'd dismissed me with casual ease, as though my gift and all its power was a thing of no consequence, next to him. And maybe he was right. My inner eye had slammed shut so tight it was giving me a headache. I looked at Larry, but he clearly hadn't noticed a thing, still lost in his own thoughts. I decided not to say anything about Hadleigh, for the moment.

He might not be a monster, but I wasn't at all sure he was still human.

Then both of us looked round sharply. No-one had said anything; no-one had called our names; but nonetheless, we knew. We looked down the Cheyne Walk approach, and there he was, Walker, large as life and twice as manipulative, strolling along the street as if he owned it. Heading straight for us. People hurried to get out of his way, and he no more noticed it than the air he breathed. Walker was a shark, and he only noticed other fish when he was hungry. He finally came to a halt before us, smiled easily, tipped his bowler hat politely to Larry, then fixed his steady gaze on me.

"I understand you're looking for Tommy Oblivion," he said, not bothering with pleasantries. "I know something of what happened to him, here, on this street on that terrible night; and as it happens, I am in a position to tell you something you need to know. But all knowledge has its price, and I'll only share what I know with you, John . . . if you'll do something for me."

"What do you want, Walker?" I said, resignedly, because I was pretty sure I already knew what he was going to say.

"Come walk with me, John, for a while. Walk with me

now, and when we're finished, I'll tell you what you need to know."

"This is a bit desperate, isn't it?" I said. "You don't normally resort to open blackmail until much later in the game."

"Needs must when the hounds of time gnaw at our heels," said Walker, entirely unmoved.

"We don't have time for this," said Larry. "If you've got anything useful to contribute, Walker, say it. Or butt out. We're busy."

"Do we have a deal, John?" said Walker, conspicuously ignoring Larry.

"I could make you tell me," said Larry; and there was something in his cold, dead voice that made Walker turn to look at him.

"I rather doubt it," said Walker.

"Tell me what you know about my brother. Do it. Do it now."

"Ah, for the good old days," murmured Walker. "When dead men told no tales."

Larry went for his wand and Walker opened his mouth to use the Voice; but I was already there between them.

"Can you both please put your testosterone back where it belongs and save the showdown for another day? This isn't getting us anywhere. I'll go with you, Walker, let you show me all these things you think I need to see; but it had better be worth it."

"Oh, it will be," said Walker, smiling easily at me so he didn't need to look at Larry. "I have such sights to show you."

I had to raise an eyebrow at that. "You're quoting *Hellraiser*? You've watched that movie?"

"Watched it? Dear boy, I was technical advisor."

I never know when he's joking.

I turned to Larry. "Sorry, but I have to do this. He'll never give up what he knows otherwise. I'll be back as soon as I can. In the meantime, talk to people who knew Tommy and are still around. See if they can verify a connection between him and all the people on your list."

"All right," said Larry, not even a little bit graciously. "But don't be long. And don't make me come looking for you."

He turned his back on me and Walker, and strode off. I looked at Walker.

"You just don't give up, do you?"

"Never," Walker said calmly. "It's one of my more endearing qualities."

"You have endearing qualities?" I said. "Since when?"

He took out his gold pocket-watch and opened it, and the portable Timeslip within leapt out and carried us away.

SEVEN

Not Just Another Walk on the Nightside

Come, John. Walk with me.

And so we went walking together, up and down the
Nightside and back and forth, up the Grand Parade and
down the Old Main Drag, in and out of endless rain-slick
streets and shadowed alleyways. Taking in the wildest clubs
and the lowest dives, walking under hot neon and flashing
signs, past the open doors of very inviting private clubs and
terribly discreet dens, where the barkers promised every pleasure you'd ever heard of or dreamed about. Where the patrons
called for madder music and wilder women and danced till
they dropped. One great kaleidoscope of sin, with temptation
on display in every window, at marked-down prices. Love for
sale on every street-corner, only slightly shop-soiled. The twilight daughters out in force, with their painted-on smiles and
switch-blades tucked into their stocking tops. You can find

anything you want in the Nightside if you're prepared to pay the price.

We walked and walked, and all the time Walker never said a word to me. He just stepped it out at a brisk pace, swinging his furled umbrella like a walking-stick, letting the streets speak for themselves. The pavements were packed with people, wide-eyed and eager, in hot pursuit of whatever drove them. But they all made way for Walker and me, so that we seemed to walk in our own little pool of calm, like the eye of the hurricane.

Up and down we went, in and out of every private domain and sphere of influence, and no-one challenged us. Hard men stepped back into doorways, and foot-soldiers for a dozen different crime lords quickly changed direction or disappeared down handy alleyways. Walker led the way and I followed, and no-one wanted anything to do with us. After a while, my legs grew weary, and my feet hurt, but Walker never slowed his pace. I grew so tired I lost all track of time, which might have been the point.

I'd reached the point where I was prepared to swallow my pride and call a halt when Walker beat me to it. He came to an abrupt stop before a shabby storefront in a decidedly grubby area and gestured grandly at the run-down establishment before us. I looked it over and wasn't impressed. The starkly lettered sign on the blank window said *Welcome to the Nightside Tourist Information Centre!* I couldn't help thinking that the exclamation mark at the end was entirely unjustified. A sort of resigned shrug would have been more appropriate.

"All right," I said to Walker. "This is new, I'll grant you. I didn't even know we had such a thing. Does it get much business? I would have thought most people who come here already know what they're looking for."

"That's the point," said Walker. "Shall we go in?"

He pushed open the door, and crumbling bits of paint fell off it. A small bell tinkled sadly as we entered a stuffy little office. A dark figure sat hunched behind a rough desk, half-concealed behind piles of folders, pamphlets, and assorted paper-work. Curling posters had been roughly tacked to the walls, offering picture-postcard views of places I happened to know looked nothing like that, and tall spinners held cheap pamphlets that looked as though no-one had disturbed them in years, There was dust, and cobwebs, and a general smell of futility and despair.

"Carter!" snapped Walker. "Why are you naked again?"

The figure at the desk crouched down even further behind his stacks of paper. "It helps me relax! I've got a lot on my mind!"

I turned away and interested myself very firmly in the contents of one of the spinners. Mostly pamphlets and flyers concerning places of interest for the discerning tourist in the Nightside. All written in that false, cheerful tone so beloved of Chamber of Commerce types, which fools no-one.

Visit the colourful Street of the Gods! (Travel insurance advised, especially against Acts of Gods.) Visit the amazing Mammon Emporium; all the merchandise from all the worlds! Try a bucket of Moose McNuggets, or a Cocaine Cola! Have you seen the Really Old Ones in the World Beneath? (Parental discretion advised. Some parts of the tour may not be suitable for those of a nervous disposition.)

That was about as much as I could stand. I looked back, to see Carter emerge sullenly from behind his desk, now wearing a grubby undershirt and jeans. He looked as run-down and untrustworthy as the place he worked in, which took some doing. Carter was neurotically thin, defiantly unhealthy, and basically disgusting on a genetic level. You got the feeling he'd still be sleazy even if you soaked him in bleach for a week. He did his best to look put-upon and hard done by, but I still felt an instinctive need to slap him, on general principles. He cringed away from Walker and glared at me.

"Don't bother; I already know who you are. I'm Basil Carter, and you're not at all pleased to see me. No-one ever is. See if I care. And yes, this place is a dump. Why not? No-one ever comes here. The last person to stick his head through that door really wanted the karma repair shop next door. What do you want, Taylor? We're closed. Or out for lunch. Or renovating; that's always a good one. There's been a fire, or an outbreak of plague, or the rabid weasels are loose again. Come back later. Or not at all; see if I care. Those are my official responses to any and all inquiries. I'm only talking to you now because Walker will hit me if I don't."

"And quite right, too," said Walker. "I never knew anyone who deserved being beaten repeatedly about the head and shoulders more than you do, Carter. And don't you dare complain. If the people around here knew who you really were, they'd drag you out of this shop and feed you into a wood-chipper, toes first."

Carter sniffed loudly, in a defiantly moist and unpleasant way. "When you offered me this job as an alternative to lifetime incarceration in Shadow Deep, I should have known there'd be a catch. Working in this hell-hole should count as cruel and unusual punishment. At least I don't have to deal with people much. I've never been a people person."

"Then you shouldn't have buried so many of them under your floor-boards," Walker said briskly. "I needed someone for this position whose very existence would discourage people from coming in, and you fit the job perfectly."

"Walker," I said. "Why are we here? You didn't march me all the way across the Nightside just to meet this . . . person, did you?"

"Perish the thought," said Walker. "Walk this way."

"If I could walk that way, I wouldn't need the acupuncture," sniggered Carter.

Walker hit him.

A concealed door at the back of the office opened up onto a much larger room. I followed Walker in, while Carter resumed his post behind his desk again; and just like that, I was in a whole other world. The new room was huge, stretching away in all directions, its walls covered from floor to high ceiling in hundreds and hundreds of viewscreens. Images came and went faster than I could follow them, constantly changing and updating. There were computers everywhere, backed up by unfamiliar machinery working furiously at unknowable tasks. And miles and miles of hanging cables, twisting and turning in great loops, criss-crossing like the web of a spider strung out on acid. Sitting in the middle of all this was a silent figure in a simple white robe, held upright in his chair by a series of tight leather straps. He was utterly still, his face blank, staring at nothing, with dull, unblinking eyes. A dozen thick cables sprouted from his shaven head, where holes had been drilled to allow them to burrow on through into the brain. He didn't react to me, or to Walker. He didn't even know we were there. Walker shut the door firmly and locked it, then strolled over to the silent figure and checked a few of the skull contacts to make sure the cables were secure. He clapped the unmoving figure on the shoulder and smiled happily, like a proud father.

"Welcome to my Secret Headquarters, John. My special place, from where I see and hear everything, hidden behind the perfect off-putting disguise. This is Argus. He makes what I do possible; don't you, dear boy? Argus isn't his real name, of course; it's more of a job description. No-one remembers who he is; in fact, I doubt if even he remembers any more. It doesn't matter. There have been hundreds like him, and no doubt there will be hundreds more. Computers and scrying balls can't do everything; you need human input to pick out the things that matter from all the oceans of information that come pouring in at any moment.

"So, Argus. The god with a thousand eyes. Sees all, knows all, and no personality to get in the way. Though they do tend to burn out fairly quickly . . . Still, not to worry; there's never any shortage of replacements. Don't worry, John; he can't hear us. All his senses are focused exclusively on the Nightside. His higher functions have been surgically removed, so they can't interfere with his observations. His mind has been surgically adjusted, so it can interface perfectly with the computers and watch thousands of situations at once, throughout the Nightside, and never once grow bored or distracted. Nothing happens that Argus doesn't know about, and report on, and draw attention to, if it is red-flagged in his programming. Names and faces like yours, John. He always has an eye out for you.

"What do you think of my Secret Headquarters, John? Admit it; you always thought I had some great underground lair, watching over an army of secret informers and secret police, reporting back on everything they see. Well, in a way you're right, but we'll get to that later. Why are you scowling, John?"

I gestured at Argus. "He's not a volunteer, is he?"

"Well, hardly. That would be cruel. Only the really nasty bastards get to undergo the Argus procedure. People who deserve it. Like Basil Carter out there; why waste time and money locking them up? There's Shadow Deep, of course, but that's for the out-and-out monsters like Shock-Headed Peter, who deserve to suffer. Everyone else gets to do useful things for the Nightside, in recompense for their crimes. This particular Argus ran an utterly foul con scheme, ripping babies from living wombs to sell on. Now he performs a useful function and is well provided for. He gets fed and watered and changed on a regular basis, and he'll spend what's left of his time helping to protect the Nightside from people like him. What could be more fitting?"

"You said something about secret police," I said.

"So I did. Well spotted, John. Glad to see you're paying attention. There are hundreds of other criminals, their heads as empty as Argus, walking up and down the Nightside, their minds linked to him through the computers. They've been programmed to look and talk like everyone else, even though there's no-one at home in their heads. They go everywhere and see everything, and no-one ever notices them."

"And these are more pressed men? More criminals being punished?"

"Of course!" said Walker. "Take your poachers and turn them into gamekeepers. A grand old tradition . . ."

He looked at me for some response, some reaction to what he was saying, but I wasn't ready yet. I gestured at the hundreds of screens covering the walls.

"Ah, yes, those," said Walker. "From here I can talk to everyone in the world." He didn't say it at all grandly, to boast or to preen. It was all just part of the job, to him. "From here I can call on any backup I need, to help me enforce my decisions. I can get armed men from the Church, the Armed Services, the Carnacki Institute, and any number of more specialised organisations. I can talk to the Authorities, the British Government, and places of power all across the world; and there isn't a place on Earth where they won't take my call. Because everyone knows how important the Nightside is, and how dangerous. Of course, only specially trained troops are ever allowed into the Nightside. You couldn't expect ordinary soldiers to cope. I'd say that about the only people I don't talk to are the Droods. They're banned from the Nightside by long agreement. They don't play nice."

He broke off abruptly, as Argus began to rock back and forth in his chair. When he spoke, his voice was rough and harsh, as though he didn't get to use it very often.

"Out of the dark, it's coming. From out of the place that nothing comes from, it's coming. And, oh, it's so bright, so bright!"

Walker moved quickly forward and put his mouth right next to Argus's ear. "What is it? What's coming?"

"So old, so ancient; far older than people think. But it never was what people thought it was. It is mighty and terrible, too . . . and it shines so brightly it hurts to look at it. The only survivor from a Golden Age; because we were not worthy of it. Now it's back. And God help us all."

He stopped speaking, and nothing Walker could do could make him say anything else. Walker didn't know what Argus was talking about, but I thought I did.

"You said he had no personality left," I said. "But he sounded really scared."

"They can always surprise you," Walker said finally. "I wouldn't worry about it. His condition makes him supersensitive to certain disturbances in the aether. He's only repeating what someone else is saying . . . I doubt it's anything important. Bad things are always coming to the Nightside. It's what we're here for." He turned his back on Argus, and spread his arms out wide, taking in the whole set-up. "So, John, what do you think of my Secret Headquarters?"

"Typical of you," I said. "That all your influence and power should be derived from the suffering of others."

"They suffer because they deserve to," said Walker. "And through their penance they serve and protect the people they preyed on." He smiled briefly. "One day, all of this could be yours. Or would you shut the system down and become blind to what threatens us? Let the bad guys go unpunished and let everyone else suffer? What would you replace this with? See? Not as simple as you thought, is it, John? I only do what is necessary for the common good. And so could you, John. All this could be yours to command. All the secret lines of influence, control, and power . . . Tell me you're not tempted."

"Get thee behind me, Walker," I said.

He laughed.

Next he took me to the Londinium Club, that most private and select of clubs, where the elite of the Nightside come together to dine and do business, and discuss the destruction of their enemies. You aren't anyone in the Nightside unless you've been invited to become a member of the oldest club in

SIMON R. GREEN

the world. I am not a member. They wouldn't accept the likes
of me on a bet. Though I have been known to barge, trick,
and intimidate my way in when I need answers I can't find
anywhere else. This has not made me popular with members
of the club, but I've learned to live with that. The current
Doorman saw me approaching and looked like he wanted to
pull up the drawbridge and set fire to the moat; but I was
with Walker, and no-one says no to Walker. The Doorman
bowed stiffly as we passed, his face utterly impassive; but
his body language suggested terrible things were happening
inside him.

"You see what it is to have power?" said Walker, as we
strolled into the elegant embrace of the club lobby. "You can
go anywhere, and they have to smile and bow and let you in.
No door is ever closed, and no-one is ever unreachable."

"And you do so enjoy having the world by the throat, don't
you, Walker?" I said, and he surprised me by considering the
question seriously.

"I try not to," he said finally. "It gets in the way of getting
the job done."

Various liveried servants appeared to take Walker's coat.
They tried to take mine, but I just looked at them, and they
gave up on the idea. The servants concentrated on Walker,
smiling and bowing and asking if there was anything at
all they could do for him; and as I watched them fawn over
him, with their fake smiles and subservient gestures, I had to
wonder if this was anything I wanted. Most people refrained
from upsetting me because they were afraid of my reputation.
They did what I told them because they were afraid of what I
might do if they didn't. Was that really any different?

Walker and I moved on into the dining room, where the

great and the good, the movers and shakers and Major Players of the Nightside all sat down together, like so many predators sharing the same watering hole. A general truce prevailed because the place was so useful. Walker moved easily amongst the various members, greeting them all by name, charming and intimidating and persuading all the right people. All in the same calm, quiet, and utterly assured manner, never once raising his voice. Everywhere he went, good men and bad smiled just a bit nervously and agreed with whatever he said. They took it on the chin as the price of doing business.

Eventually, Walker and I ended up standing before a table set far too near the kitchens, an indication that the people sitting there might be members in good standing but were still very much at the bottom of the Londinium Club's pecking order. Surprisingly, the old man and his wife not only didn't look pleased to see us but made no effort to hide it. Walker tipped his bowler hat to both of them.

"John Taylor, allow me to introduce Dash Oblivion, the Confidential Op, and his wife, Shirley den Adel, once the costumed adventurer known as the Lady Phantasm."

"Oh please," said the grey-haired lady in the pearls and twin set. "Do call me Shirley."

Dash just grunted something, concentrating on his meal. It was a curry, steaming hot, and the smell of it made my stomach rumble. Dash was a whip-thin figure in a smart blue blazer and white slacks. Bald-headed, his face was dominated by an eagle nose and bushy white eyebrows. He had to be in his eighties, but his cold blue eyes were still sharp and piercing. He sat bolt upright in his chair, and his blue-veined, liver-spotted hands didn't tremble once as he shovelled food into his mouth.

Shirley gave her husband a look that was half-exasperated and half-amused. "Don't mind him, Mr. Taylor. He hates being interrupted at his dinner. He's always believed conversation should follow food, not interrupt it. Won't change your ways for anyone, will you, darling?"

Dash grunted again, and she laughed quietly. Shirley den Adel was a well-preserved woman in her seventies, with a faint European accent I couldn't quite place. Her gaze and her voice were both quite firm, and her easy manner did nothing to hide a sense of accustomed power and authority.

"Good to meet you at last, Mr. Taylor," she said, with what sounded very like genuine warmth. "Tommy always spoke very well of you."

"Tommy didn't know his ass from his elbow," said Dash, his voice still dominated by a sharp Chicago twang. He pushed back his empty plate and fixed me with a hard stare. "He should never have been a private eye. It's not for everyone." He glared at Walker. "And stay clear of that one. He's bad news."

"You wound me, Dash," murmured Walker. "After all, it was your son Hadleigh who taught me everything I know. Before he . . . stepped down."

"Before he went crazy and ran off to the Deep School," growled Dash. "The job broke him like it breaks everyone."

"He left to save his soul," Shirley said firmly.

"Or what was left of it," said Dash.

"The job's not for everyone," said Walker. "It's always suited me just fine."

He looked at them both challengingly, and they looked away rather than meet his gaze. Walker glanced at me, to make sure I'd seen them defer to his authority.

"So," Walker said easily. "What are you doing these days, Dash?"

Dash growled at him, apparently deeply immersed in the dessert menu, so Shirley answered for him. I got the feeling that happened a lot.

"Dash is retired now. We both are. He gardens, and I work on our memoirs. Oh, the stories we have to tell! Not to be published until we're both safely dead, of course. It's not everyone who were legendary heroes back in the thirties and forties, then made an even more successful comeback in the seventies and eighties! We could have gone on . . . but we both felt we'd done our best. So now we just consult, on occasion, and let younger bodies do all the hard lifting. Isn't that right, Dash?"

"Even done some work for you, Walker, on the quiet," said Dash, grinning nastily. "I can still show these youngsters how it's done."

"But not too often," said Shirley. "We've earned our retirement."

"Don't you ever miss the old days?" I said.

"Sometimes," said Shirley, a bit wistfully. "We had a good war, really, chasing saboteurs and fifth columnists all over America . . . And the villains were all so colourful in those days. They had style. The Vril Power Gang, the Nazi Skull . . ."

"And Wu Fang," said Dash. "Put him away a dozen times, but he always got out. We should never have let him drink that Dragon's Blood, back in 'forty-one."

"Oh, hush, dear," said Shirley. "He was dying. And he wasn't a bad sort. For a Chinaman."

"Things were different when the Timeslip kicked us out

here, back in the seventies," said Dash. "Appalling place, then and now. So we rolled up our sleeves and got to work. There was a lot to do."

"Never much cared for the seventies," said Shirley. "Terribly cynical times. Though the eighties turned out to be even worse . . . I was glad to retire. We stayed involved, though, helping train our successors. I worked with Ms. Fate, you know, when she started out. She's done very well for herself."

"What do you want with us, Walker?" said Dash. "You never show up unless you want something."

"I'm looking into Tommy's disappearance," I said carefully. "Working with his brother Larry, not Walker. And it would appear that your eldest, Hadleigh, is also involved in some way. I was hoping you could tell me something about him."

Dash and Shirley looked at each other, and they suddenly seemed older and more frail. Dash's hands closed together on the table before him, and Shirley put her hand over them.

"Can't say I approve of what Hadleigh's made of himself," Dash said finally. "Detective Inspectre for God's sake . . . We should never have left him alone, all those years. Not our fault, of course, but . . ."

"He fell in with bad company," said Shirley, glaring at Walker. "We'd hardly been back a year, before he disappeared. And when he came back . . . We don't talk any more. We never see him. He does write us the occasional letter, now and again. But it's not the same."

"He was our first-born," said Dash. "He meant so much to us. We had such hopes for him . . ."

"Larry and Tommy came later," said Shirley. "Good boys, both of them. Nothing like their elder brother. We had hopes for them, too . . . but Larry was murdered by his own partner, and we lost Tommy to the Lilith War."

"Never did like Larry's partner," said Dash. "That Maggie Boniface . . . stuck-up little piece. Just because her family was big in voodoo . . ."

"I never knew what he saw in her," said Shirley.

Dash grinned suddenly. "I could make a good guess. She had a balcony you could do Shakespeare from . . ."

"Oh, hush, you nasty old man," said Shirley. And they smiled at each other.

"Larry hasn't been the same, since he came back from the dead," said Shirley. "We try to look after him, as best we can, but he keeps us at a distance. As though we might be bothered because he's dead. The very idea. He's our son."

"Seen a lot worse than the walking dead," said Dash, nodding. "Lot worse."

"We spent a lot of time and money looking for Tommy," said Shirley. "After the War was over. But it was chaos everywhere, everything in such a mess . . . and there were so many people missing. No-one knew anything. Dash wore himself out, walking up and down the streets, looking for something, some sign . . . until finally I made him stop. We did think about hiring you, Mr. Taylor; but we heard you'd already tried your gift, to no effect, so what was the point? So we got used to the idea that our poor Tommy was gone, another victim of that damned War."

"Larry never gave up on his brother," said Dash. "Always was stubborn as a mule, that boy."

"They were both good boys," said Shirley.

"Good boys," said Dash.

They sat close together, holding hands, their heads bowed.

"We didn't do so well with our children," said Shirley. "Larry's dead, Tommy's gone, and Hadleigh . . . God alone knows what Hadleigh is. Three sons, but no grandchildren, and never likely to have any now. Was all that we did for nothing? We saved the world, on at least three occasions. President gave us medals. In private. And all for what? To grow old and see our children lost to us. Don't we deserve something for all we did?"

"We didn't do it for the rewards," said Dash, squeezing her hand. "We did it because it needed doing."

"Duty and responsibility," said Walker, nodding. "The only things that matter."

"Oh, fuck off, Walker," said Shirley.

I felt like applauding.

After the Londinium Club, Walker and I paid a visit to the Uptown Board of Unnatural Commerce. A big stately building right in the heart of the Nightside business sector. All very solemn, very dignified and businesslike; you could practically smell fresh bank-notes on the rarefied lobby air. Walker took me in and out of various offices, where no expense had been spared, and comfort and ostentatious luxury came as standard. He made a point of introducing me to a whole series of powerful and influential people, who all pretended to be glad to see me. Because if I was with Walker, then I must be a personage worth knowing. They offered me thick, murky sherry, which I declined, and listened to my every casual remark as though each contained the secrets of the world. I smiled and nodded and avoided answering any of their subtly probing questions as to what I was doing with Walker. Let them wonder and worry.

It didn't take me long to work out why Walker wanted me to meet these high city types. These were the people who supplied Walker with private and confidential business information, from the inside. Such as who was on the way up, who was on the way down, and who could be pressured or blackmailed . . . All so Walker could keep on top of things and apply corrections when necessary. More than one top business man with a pale and sweaty face eased me to one side to whisper how Walker had destroyed this person or that, or even made them disappear . . . because they put their personal financial interests ahead of the Nightside's.

No-one was allowed to threaten the status quo, not while Walker was on the job. No matter how rich and powerful they might think they were.

The Street of the Gods came next. Walker's portable Timeslip was working overtime now, slamming us from one place to another. Walker and I strode down the Street, side by side, and a whole bunch of Beings, Powers, and Other-Dimensional Deities decided to retire to their various churches, lock the doors, and hide under their altars until we were gone. Other Beings and their congregations made a point of coming out into the Street, just to be seen conversing amiably with Walker and me and demonstrate to everyone else that they were on good terms with us. And not in any way afraid of either of us. Walker was very polite, as always, and even allowed a few of the gods to bless him.

"Doesn't any of this ever go to your head?" I asked him, as we left our admirers behind.

"It's pleasant enough, in its way," said Walker. "One of the perks of the job. But it's not real. There isn't one of them that really likes or even respects me. It's the position, and the power that comes with it. They'd bow down to you as quickly if you were in my position."

"There was a time when people did that," I said. "Back when some quarters saw me as a potential King in waiting. Can't say I ever liked it much. They weren't talking to me, just who they thought I might be."

"You've made people respect you," said Walker. "You've put a lot of effort into building your reputation. And unlike many in the Nightside, you really have done most of the awful things you're supposed to have done."

"A reputation helps keep the flies off," I said. "But it's there to protect me, not feed my ego."

"And it is a useful tool, to make people do what you want them to do."

"Yes," I said. "But . . ."

And then I stopped, because I didn't know what came next. Walker just smiled. And so we carried on quietly together, for a while.

"Normally, I'd take you to the Exiles Club next," said Walker. "Introduce you to all the otherworldly and other-dimensional royalty in exile; thrown up here on the Nightside's shores through Timeslips or dimensional doors, or some other unfortunate celestial accident. All the lost Kings and Queens, Emperors and Divinities . . . If only to show you that royalty can be a real pain in the arse, just like everyone else. Still, nothing like having a King or Queen bow their head to you to cheer up a dull day. Unfortunately, the Exiles are currently a bit mad at me, ever since I found it necessary to have some of them killed to maintain public order. You remember, John."

I nodded. I remembered their severed heads set on iron spikes outside the Londinium Club. Queen Helena, Monarch of the Evening in a future twilight Earth. Uptown Taffy Lewis, crime boss, and the scumbag's scumbag. And General Condor, a great leader of men from some future Spacefleet; who made some unfortunate alliances in his quest to do the right thing. Walker never hesitated to deal firmly with anyone who might challenge his authority.

Was he trying to tell me something in his own subtle way? Did he have an iron spike ready for my head if I turned him down?

That was Walker's main strength; he always kept you guessing.

Somewhat to my surprise, our next stop turned out to be Rats' Alley; where the homeless scrabble for thrown-out food or a place to lay their heads. Rats' Alley is a wide, cobbled square and a few narrow tributaries, set behind some of the finest and most upscale restaurants in the Nightside. Here, out of sight of the fine clientele who swan in through the front door, exists a small community of those who have fallen off the edge and can't find their way back. The homeless, the beggars, the lost and the ragged, the damaged and the damned, living in cardboard boxes, lean-to shelters, plastic sheeting, or only layers of clothing and the occasional blanket. Refugees from the world the rest of us take for granted.

I spent some time here, once.

Rats' Alley was a rougher, more dangerous place these days, with the loss of their saint and guardian angel, Sister Morphine. Razor Eddie still slept there as often as not, keeping the vultures at bay, and, of course, they still had Jacqueline Hyde. She came lurching out of the shadows to block our way, wrapped in the grimy tatters of what had once been an expensive coat. Walker and I stopped, to show respect for her territory. Everyone knew Jacqueline's story. This grim, bedraggled figure had once been a debutante and a high flyer, until she made the mistake of experimenting with her grandfather's formula. Now she's one of the Nightside's sadder love stories. Jacqueline is in love with Hyde, and he with her, but they can only ever meet briefly, in the moment of the change.

She snarled at Walker and me, and her body exploded suddenly into muscle and bulk. Hyde stood swaying and growling before us, his huge hands clutching at the air, eager to rend and tear, break bones, and feast on their marrow. He towered over us, his brute face flushed with the hatred he felt for all Mankind. Jacqueline Hyde: two souls in one body, together and separated at the same time.

"Easy," said Walker. "Slow and easy, that's the way. You don't want to hurt us, Hyde. It's Walker. You remember Walker."

If anyone else had tried the calm and reasonable routine, Hyde would have turned him into roadkill. But Walker was using the Voice, in a calm and soothing way, rather than his usual abrupt commands. Hyde's great head swayed slowly back and forth, deep-set eyes blinking confusedly under heavy eye-brow ridges, then he turned away suddenly and was gone, back into the shadows.

"I didn't know you could use your Voice like that," I said.

"Lot you don't know about me, John," Walker said cheerfully. "I could write a book. If I only had the time."

He moved easily among the soggy cardboard boxes and the piles of blankets, stepping carefully past and over the filth that covered the cobbled square. He greeted many of the homeless by name, as one by one they emerged from their shelters and hiding-places to crouch uneasily before him, like a pack of suspicious wild dogs. Most didn't want to get too close, but others fawned openly, begging for food or spare change, or a kind word—some sign that they had not been entirely forgotten by the real world. Walker murmured soft words and let them sniff his hands, and they quickly lost interest and retreated back to their own private little worlds. Walker smiled easily about him, in the last place you can fall to before the grave claims you for its own.

"This used to be Peter Pendrake," said Walker, gesturing at a bundled-up figure pressed up against the rear of its mould-covered box. "You used to work for me, didn't you, Peter? Until I caught you with your hand in the till."

"Long time ago, Henry," said a dry, ghostly voice from the shadows at the back of the box. "I'm a different person now. You could take me back. I could still do the job."

"That wasn't all I caught you doing, was it, Peter? You really were a very bad boy. But I'll tell you what; keep your eyes open and keep reporting in, and I'll think about it."

A painfully thin man, stained and filthy, in the ragged remains of a futuristic pressure suit, huddled against the cold under a very basic lean-to. He clutched possessively at his bottle and hugged it to his chest, glaring at Walker with sullen defiance.

"This was the famous Jet Ace Brannigan," said Walker. "Air hero from some alternate time-line. Flew a supersonic jet of his own design, fighting crime in the skies. Then he flew through a Timeslip and ended up here. You used to work for me, too, didn't you, Ace? Hunting dragons in the night sky? Until the drink got to you, and you crashed your jet on a main street, killing one hundred and twenty-seven people. You walked away with hardly a scratch; but I couldn't let you fly again, after that."

"I never used to drink," said Ace. "Until I met you."

The last person Walker wanted me to see was a shivering wreck of a man, trying to keep out the cold and the damp with a single thin blanket. He looked a hundred years old, his face the colour of bleached bone, his features hidden behind heavy wrinkles. He turned his head away, not wanting to be seen. Walker considered him for a long moment.

"This pathetic wreck used to be Somerset Smith, Gentleman Adventurer," he said finally. "Worked for Hadleigh, then for me, taking care of all those important, necessary, but very unpleasant situations that sometimes have to be dealt with quietly, by expendable people like yourself, John. Quite a name in his time, was Somerset; had a hell of a reputation. But then he tried to bring me down, and I broke him. A lot of my enemies end up in places like this. So much more satisfying than simply killing them."

"Are you warning me?" I said. "Or threatening me?"

"What do you think, John?" said Walker.

Everywhere we went, people noticed Walker. They smiled and bowed, glared and turned their faces away . . . but no-one ever ignored him. Walker was the Man. Everyone knew who he was, and what he did. But the one thing they all had in common, when you looked past the smiles and pleasant words, was that no-one was ever genuinely pleased to see Walker. A lot of them faked it remarkably well, so well that perhaps only a trained and experienced eye like mine might have spotted the falseness; but I knew. And I was pretty sure Walker did, too. I had to wonder if Walker had any real friends any more, or if he'd only see that as a weakness others would exploit. He kept his wife and his sons outside the Nightside, in an entirely separate life.

I knew, though, that he used to have friends. Good friends. There were three of them, tight as brothers and thick as thieves, three young men determined to get on in the world and change it for the better. Henry, who became Walker. Mark, who became the Collector. And Charles, my father.

I said as much to Walker, but he just shrugged.

"I don't have time for my family, let alone friends. The job is everything: my life, my wife, my mistress . . . It's very demanding. The thing about duty and responsibility is that they're like the Old Man of the Sea. Once you pick them up, you can't put them down again. Ever. You carry the weight of them until you drop in your tracks, and the best you can hope for is that there'll be someone to take up the burden for you. I thought I knew what I was taking on, when I started; but I didn't. You can't know, you can't understand, how big the job is until you're carrying the whole weight of it on your shoulders. You think this is the life I wanted, John? The life I would have chosen for myself? I don't run the Nightside; it runs me."

"You're not exactly selling me on taking over," I said.

"What about Hadleigh? He was in charge before you. How did he cope?"

"Arguably, he didn't," said Walker. "He gave it all up and ran away to the Deep School, and now he's the Detective Inspectre. Whatever the hell that is. No-one gets to retire from this job, John. We go crazy, or get killed, or drop in our tracks. But . . . it's the only job worth doing. There's nothing else like it."

We were walking through Uptown now, where the very best and the very worst came to wine and dine, to see and be seen. Walker moved easily amongst the celebrities and the Major Players, greeting them all by name and putting them in their places if they got too familiar. All he had to do was murmur his wishes, and people jumped to obey. I never got that, for all my hard-won reputation.

"You see, John?" Walker said finally. "My job isn't to punish the guilty or strike down the wicked. Or even to rescue and preserve the good. It's all about maintaining the status quo. Dealing with all the stresses as they arise, playing one faction against another, encouraging this individual or slapping down that one. I keep the lid on, maintain a steady balance, so that the wheels of business can turn smoothly, and everyone who comes here can get everything they think they want. The Nightside exists to cater to and contain all the darker elements in the world; and it's my responsibility to prevent any of it from spilling over into the unsuspecting everyday world.

"If it were up to me, I'd nuke the whole sick freak show and be done with it. But since the Powers That Be won't let me, I walk the night and do my best to keep the freaks in their cages."

I stopped, and Walker stopped with me. I gave him my best hard look.

"Enough. Enough, Walker. I don't need to hear any more. And I've seen everything I need to see."

He smiled briefly. "You haven't seen anything yet. The Nightside is bigger than you know, bigger than you ever suspected, and so are my duties and responsibilities. I can't hand this over to just anyone."

"How many times do I have to say it, Walker? I don't want your job! I don't want it, don't need it, and I wouldn't be any good at it if I did. Let the new Authorities choose your successor."

"You'd trust them to do that?"

"More than I trust you," I said.

He smiled again. "Very good, John. You're learning."

"I'm not going any further. I have a case, remember? And you know something about Tommy Oblivion. Tell me what it is."

"All right," said Walker. "It was Mark. The Collector has finally lost it. He's moved on from collecting things to collecting people. Famous, important, or interesting people; they're all trophies to him now. Find his current lair, wherever it is, and there you'll find Tommy Oblivion; and all the other missing people. But be careful, John. I can't speak for Mark's state of mind any more. Best of luck. Talk to you again later."

He walked away, not at all tired or troubled, swinging his furled umbrella in a cheerful but dignified way. I watched him go, considering all the things he'd said and all the things he hadn't. First, and most obvious, he didn't know where the Collector was hiding himself these days, or he would have told me. Which was . . . unusual. Where could the Collector have buried himself and his extensive collection that even Walker's people couldn't locate him? And second, why had Walker felt the need to bargain with me, trading his private knowledge for a walk in the Nightside? All right, the man was dying, and time was running out; but I'd never known Walker to deal from anything save a position of strength.

But that would have to wait. I had a case. I'd given my word. I had to find the Collector. I winced as an image of Tommy filled my head, pinned to a giant display card, like a captured butterfly.

Walker and the Collector had worked together, along with my father, during the Lilith War. The Collector had seemed to be improving then; less obviously crazy. What had happened since, to drive him over the edge? And why would Walker want me to lower the boom on the Collector, after tolerating his old friend's nefarious exploits for so many years? Unless . . . Could this be connected to the new time-travel apparatus the Collector had stolen? The one that could transfer his consciousness into another body . . . Such a device would make the perfect escape route, so that the Collector could never be captured or punished, no matter what he did . . . Walker couldn't allow that.

So maybe he wanted me to take down the Collector because, while it had to be done, he couldn't do it himself. Not to the one man who might be his only remaining friend.

That was the trouble with hanging around with Walker. You ended up thinking like him.

EIGHT

I'm Here, Mark

It was raining, a harsh, persistent drizzle, like the tears of some passing god. Just enough to make the night even more miserable. Pools and puddles everywhere, and even more splashed up across the pavements by passing traffic. I hunched my shoulders against the rain and looked around me. It didn't take me long to realise that Walker had walked me round in a circle. I was right back at the Cheyne Walk approach. Larry Oblivion was standing right where I'd left him. Some people just can't be left to get on with things on their own. I strode down the street and hailed him by name, and he looked round, startled.

"Taylor? I thought you were going walkabout with Walker?"

"I did," I said. "We've been all over the Nightside. Why are you still here?"

He looked at me oddly. "You've only been gone a few moments."

Of course. Typical of Walker, to have the last word when he wasn't even there. I hadn't known his personal Timeslip could play tricks with Time as well as Space, but it did explain a lot.

"Walker," I said heavily to Larry, and he nodded. Sometimes that name is all the explanation you need.

"What did he tell you about Tommy?" said Larry, straight to the point as always.

"Apparently the Collector's got him," I said. "The man has gone totally loop the loop, and has taken up collecting people instead of things."

"Why the hell would he want Tommy?" said Larry, honestly baffled. "Nobody wants Tommy. I wouldn't if he wasn't my brother."

"Because of his special gift?" I said. "The Collector has always had a weakness for unique items."

"If the Collector is holding Tommy against his will, then we go where he is and take Tommy away from him," said Larry. "Whatever it takes."

"The Collector is a very powerful personage," I said carefully. "The only reason he's not a Major Player in the Nightside is because he can't be bothered. He's dedicated his life to acquiring rare and valuable objects. To help him in his search, he mastered sciences and magics and a whole bunch of other disciplines most people have never even heard of. Also, he steals time machines. He's a fanatic, and dangerous with it."

"I know," said Larry. "And I don't care."

The rain was getting heavier. I moved us under a candy-striped awning to continue our conversation. Being dead,

Larry probably didn't care about getting soaked, but I've always been susceptible to chills.

"Look," I said, "he isn't in it for the money. His collection is everything to him. So if he has taken to collecting people, you can be sure he won't give Tommy up without a fight."

"I know," said Larry. "And I still don't care. One of the few good things about being dead is that you only have to care about the things you choose to care about. Let him do his worst. He can't hurt me."

"Maybe not," I said. "But he could destroy you. Or make you into one of his exhibits. Or do a hundred other awful things that death could not protect you from."

Larry thought about it. "What are his protections like?"

"Top of the range, magical and scientific, and a few things we don't even have a name for. Weapons and defences he's collected from the past, the future, and any number of alternate realities. Plus his own private army of vicious little rococo robots. And let us not forget his latest acquisition, a time-travel device that apparently allows him to jump inside other people's heads and look out through their eyes."

"Ah," said Larry. "Better kill him on sight, then."

I had to smile at his confidence. "Better men than you and I have tried and failed. I've managed to outwit him on a few occasions, but only because he's not too tightly wrapped. In his own way he's just as dangerous as his old friend Walker."

Larry looked at me sharply. "They know each other? I didn't know that."

"They started out together," I said. "Thick as thieves and twice as tricky. And the fact that Walker is sending us, rather than facing the Collector himself, should tell you something."

"Why is nothing ever simple?" said Larry, wistfully.

I shrugged. "It's the Nightside. Everything's complicated here, including the Collector. He wasn't always crazy. He isn't always the villain. For all his many sins, he did help save us all from Lilith during the War."

"I don't care," Larry said stubbornly.

"What do you care about?" I said. I was honestly interested in the answer.

He didn't hesitate. "I care about family, and friends. No-one else. Nothing else. We're going to get Tommy back even if we have to do it over the Collector's dead and lifeless body."

"I seem to remember you saying something about Heaven and Hell seeming a lot closer, since you died," I said. "Are you really ready to murder a man, before you know the whole story? He could be innocent in this."

"No-one's innocent in the Nightside," said Larry. "Innocent people don't come here. You know the Collector better than me; can you honestly say he hasn't done anything to deserve being killed?"

"No," I said. "I can't say that. But that's not a good enough reason to shoot him on sight. Let me try talking to him first."

"Getting soft, Taylor," said Larry.

I remembered meeting the Collector in a horrible, devastated future Nightside, the one I was supposed to bring about and had worked so hard to prevent. I remembered the horrible things the Collector did there, and the worse things he was prepared to let happen. I remembered how, long ago, he had found my mother for my father and put them together, and all the terrible things that came out of that. Including me. But I still wasn't ready to see him dead. If only because he'd also been Uncle Mark, when I was a kid.

I used my gift to find the Collector's current lair. He was always on the move, hiding his vast collection in more and more obscure locations, away from enemies and rivals and people like me. My inner eye snapped open as my gift manifested, and I shot up out of my head, my Sight soaring higher and higher into the night, sailing weightlessly in the star-filled skies, looking down at the twisting, turning streets of the Nightside.

So much light for so dark a place.

Street-lights and neon signs, and all the blazing multi-coloured come-ons from a town where sin is always in season. Scientific and magical glows, sputtering and flaring and detonating in the night, as a thousand forbidden experiments ran their inevitable courses. The dazzling streaks and smears of light from cars and trucks and other things as they roared endlessly along the Nightside roads, never slowing, never stopping. Neon illuminations, gleaming defiantly from clubs and bars and emporiums, beckoning on men and women with empty hearts and overburdened wallets. Let a thousand poisoned flowers bloom, pushing back the dark with their harsh glamour.

I sent my Sight flying over the Nightside, and it turned slowly beneath me, a city within a city, a world within a world. My Sight showed me the world as it really was and not as we would have it. Huge and transparent, their crowned heads scraping against the sky, the colossal Awful Ones went about their unknowable business, striding through solid buildings as though they weren't even there. Long, sleek, bat-winged shapes soared through the chill upper air, flames leaping up from deep-set eyes and wide, fanged mouths. And wee-winged faeries came streaking through the night in shimmering flocks, speeding and darting back and forth in intricate patterns, leaving behind sparkling trails of sheer exuberance.

But no matter where I went or where I looked, I couldn't See the Collector or his lair. I looked up into the frigid glow of the huge oversized Moon that dominated the Nightside sky. The Collector had a base there once, hidden away deep under the Sea of Tranquility; but he hadn't gone back. It isn't easy, to look at the Moon in the Nightside. There is no man in the Moon in that pallid, cratered sphere. It's so big, so overwhelming, the whole thing seems like one great senile face. And if that face had ever known anything worth knowing, it had forgotten it long ago.

A thought occurred to me. Since the sun never has and never will shine in the Nightside, exactly what light is our oversized and eternally full Moon reflecting? A disturbing thought . . . for another day.

I looked down at the Nightside, spread out before me like the most seductive whore in the world. Promising everything and anything, her wide smile and inviting eyes hiding the cold calculation in her heart. The Collector belonged in a place like this, where we all know the price of everything and the value of nothing. The Collector could be richer than anyone if he'd only sell the smallest part of his magnificent collection. He could give up running and hiding and settle down in comfort. But he'd never give up his collection. It was all he had.

The more I looked down, the more I could feel the Collector's presence even if I couldn't See him. He was there, somewhere. I looked down and down, and my Sight plunged suddenly through the packed streets and further on down, into the places below the Nightside. I ignored the World Beneath, and the subterranean galleries, and the worms of the Earth, following a trail I could sense, if not put a name to. My Sight led me on, like a hound hot on a scent. And all at once I knew where the Collector had gone to ground this time.

The many tunnels and platforms and stations of the Underground rail system spread out spiralling before me, an endless series of branching and interconnecting tunnels, twisting and turning through the bedrock, sometimes diving dangerously deep. I could See travellers on their platforms, and trains roaring through their tunnels, blinking on and off as they dropped in and out of other-dimensional short cuts, to take them to places that weren't really places. And there, hidden quietly away in the heart of the system, deep in the insanely complicated mess of new and old stations, was the Collector's new secret lair.

My first clue was heavy-duty magical shields where there shouldn't have been any. My Sight drifted lightly through the defences, and immediately I Saw signs of life and power and arcane energies emanating from a shut-down station no-one had used in years. There are a great many stations in the Underground that no-one visits any more. Replaced or abandoned, or sealed off and forgotten because they'd become too dangerous, or disturbing. Just like the Collector, to hide his precious collection in a place no-one would want to go. Essentially he now had his own private station, no longer listed on any destinations board, that no-one could get to because they didn't know where to tell the train to stop.

I eased out through his shields, and shot back up into the

light-studded night. I dropped back into my own head and shut down my Sight, carefully re-establishing my mental shields. It's never safe to keep an open mind in the Nightside; you never know what might walk in. I told Larry where we had to go to find the Collector and hopefully Tommy. Larry nodded. We were on our way to rescue his long-lost brother, and go face-to-face with one of the most dangerous men in the Nightside, in his own lair, but there wasn't a trace of emotion in the dead man's face or his cold blue eyes. He'd said often enough that the dead only had room for one emotion at a time. And he was still running on vengeance.

We walked through the rain, not speaking to one another, and entered Cheyne Walk Station. We paid Charon his price, acquired our tickets, and went down into the Underground. There was a time they'd let me ride for free, but nothing lasts forever; least of all gratitude in the Nightside. The crowds seemed thicker than ever, pushing and jostling through the packed tunnels, oblivious to everything but the needs and pressures that drove them. Larry led the way, opening up a path with the impact of his blunt, unfeeling frame, while I wandered along behind, thinking my own thoughts. The air was hot and close, with steam rising from people's damp clothes. There was fresh graffiti on the walls. I don't know where people find the energy. Or the wit. *Walker moves in mysterious ways. Don't let them out of the mirrors! Dagon is back, and this time it's personal.* And, in very neat, educated handwriting: *If this is consensus reality, some of us are cheating.*

There were even new T-shirts on sale, courtesy of Harry Fabulous, the Nightside's premiere con man, fixer, and Go

To man for everything that's bad for you. He'd set up a stall at the bottom of the escalators and was busy being his usual effervescent, bullshitting self, with a big happy smile for everyone, only slightly undermined by dark, desperate eyes. Harry had undergone a close encounter of the spiritual kind, and it showed. I wasn't surprised to find him in the Underground. Harry never stayed anywhere long because someone was always after him. He might or might not have actually reformed, but there were still any number of old creditors and aggrieved past customers very keen to track him down and have a few words with him.

He was currently wearing a T-shirt that said bluntly, *No Questions, No Refunds*, over a pair of cheap knock-off Levis and even-less-convincing trainers. He was doing everything but sing and dance for his supper, thrusting his bagged T-shirts into people's faces as they passed. The display frame at his side boasted shirts with such messages as *Go Down Lilith! Hell Is Other Drivers. The Eyes of Walker Are Upon You.* And the slightly disturbing *Everyone's Damned Except Me and My Dog.* Harry recognised Larry and me as we approached, tensed for a moment as though considering running, then settled for an extra-wide smile and a studied pretence that he was actually glad to see us.

"Hello, Harry," I said. "Keeping busy?"

"Oh, you know how it is, Mr. Taylor," said Harry, shifting nervously from foot to foot. "Make a bit here, make a bit there . . . All strictly legit, of course, these days. The hereafter seems so much closer than it used to be."

"Lot of that about," Larry said solemnly.

"Heard anything about the Collector, Harry?" I said casually.

He tensed again, his eyes blinking rapidly. "The Collector, Mr. Taylor? Not as such . . . But a lot of people have been asking after him just recently. Some of them quite official if you know what I mean."

"But you didn't tell them anything, did you, Harry?" I said.

"I never tell anyone anything, Mr. Taylor. Bad for business. Speaking of which, can I point out that you are quite definitely scaring off my customers, and I do have a living to make . . ."

"Be good, Harry," I said, moving off. "For goodness' sake."

Larry and I made our way down, heading for the more dangerous platforms and the more dangerous destinations. The crowds began to thin out. We passed a whole new bunch of buskers. A burning man stood stiffly among leaping blue-white flames that blackened and split his flesh but failed to consume him, singing a wistful song of unrequited love. A blind busker sang a torch song in Greek, about his mother. And a shadow blasted onto a wall sang a sad song in Japanese. I dropped them all a few coins without getting too close. Larry ignored them.

When we finally got to the deepest platform of all, it was practically empty. Only a couple of knights in dark armour, grim and threatening. They both bore Satanic markings on their breast-plates, daubed in fresh blood. Deep red flames burned behind the eye-slits of their steel helms, following Larry and me as we passed. I couldn't help remembering King Artur, of Sinister Albion. A different history, where Merlin Satanspawn never did reject his father. King Artur was currently missing, presumed killed by Walker. I wondered whether I'd find the dark King in the Collector's lair, part of his new collection . . .

A tall, naked woman, generously daubed with blue woad, ignored Larry and me completely as we passed, immersed in her *Wall Street Journal*. A man with a fossilised penis in a glass tube hanging round his neck sat by himself, looking very glum. And a soft ghost drifted along behind us, barely there at all, tugging wistfully at Larry's sleeve with transparent fingers. Larry just walked faster until he'd left it behind.

We stopped at the end of the platform, and I looked thoughtfully at the destinations board on the wall opposite. All the usual stations on the Infernal Line, from the well-known halts like Shadows Fall, to the disturbing Red Lodge, to the enigmatic Slaughter Towen. But the more I stared at the board, the more my gift insisted there ought to be one more name, at the very end of the line. A very old name, of a place no-one went to any more.

Lud's Gate.

The next train came rushing in, blasting a wave of displaced air ahead of it, heavy with the scent of attar and myrrh. Deep claw-marks gouged into the side of one carriage were already healing. Nightside trains have to travel strange and dangerous ways to get to some of their destinations. Larry and I got into the carriage nearest the driver's cab. The other people on the platform decided to wait for the next train. I get that a lot. Larry didn't even notice. The train waited a moment, just to be sure, then the carriage doors slammed together, and the train set off. The journey was unremarkable, no problems, no attacks, but still no-one got on at any of the other stops. I lounged easily on my seat, while Larry sat stiffly upright, staring straight ahead; and whatever he was thinking didn't touch his dead face at all.

The train finally reached the end of the line, and slowed to a halt at Slaughter Towen. The carriage doors slid open, and Larry and I didn't move from our seats. The train huffed and puffed for a bit, waiting for us to make up our minds, and finally I stood up and addressed the blank steel wall that separated us from the driver's cab. There was no driver, of course. No human driver could stand the strain. In the Nightside, the trains run themselves, and very efficiently, too. The trains are perfectly safe. As long as you're careful to avoid the mating season.

"Hello, train," I said cheerfully. "This is John Taylor. And I want to go to the next station. The station no-one goes to any more. I want to go to Lud's Gate."

The train powered down. The carriage stopped vibrating, the lights dimmed, and the engine was ominously silent. The train was sulking.

"Take us to Lud's Gate," I said, "or I will find out when your holidays are and have them all cancelled."

There was a long pause, then the train powered up again. The lights blazed, the carriage doors slammed shut, and the engine made a series of rude noises before engaging. The train set off, and I smiled a bit as I sat down again. Larry looked at me.

"You fight really dirty, don't you?"

"You just have to know how to talk to them," I said solemnly.

The train ran smoothly through the dark, not turning at all; heading in a remorseless straight line for Lud's Gate. Once, something outside in the dark ran its fingernails along the side of our carriage, a soft scraping sound that made all the hairs on the back of my neck stand up. Larry stared straight ahead, as though he hadn't heard anything; and perhaps he hadn't. There are some things only the living can hear because warnings are wasted on the dead. We travelled on for ages, the air growing steadily colder. Frost appeared on the inside of the carriage, forming harsh abstract faces on the inner walls. I huddled inside my trench coat, my hands thrust deep in my pockets. Larry didn't feel any of it. Not even when frost began to form whorled patterns on his dead face.

The train suddenly screeched to a halt, rocking Larry and me back and forth in our seats. The carriage doors jerked open, a few inches at a time, splinters of ice falling from the frozen metal frame. I got to my feet and moved over to the doors, standing well back as I looked out. Larry got up and stood behind me. Outside, on the platform, the lights were a corrupt yellow glow, more organic than electric, like something from the sick-room. Dust and cobwebs everywhere, and deep dark shadows. Hot sweaty air gusted in through the open carriage doors, heavy with the stench of dying things. The frost on the doors melted and ran away. Larry moved forward to leave the carriage, but I stopped him with a raised hand. There was no-one out there on the platform, no obvious threat, but still I felt uneasy. Someone was watching.

Larry stirred impatiently, and I made myself step out of the carriage and onto the platform. Sweltering hot air hit me like a slap in the face. Larry was at my side, glaring about him. The frost on his dead face quickly melted, running away like unfelt tears. The carriage doors jerked together behind us, and the train roared away, getting the hell out of the station before something bad happened. Ahead of me, the old station sign of Lud's Gate was set out in heavy black Gothic lettering. The bottom of the sign was soaked in old dried blood.

Thick mats of vine and ivy covered the station walls, stirring slowly when I looked at them, agitating in long green tremors beside me as I walked slowly down the platform. Fierce bright eyes peered out of the heavy greenery. Black flowers thrust up through the platform floor, turning slowly to watch as Larry and I passed them by. One of them hissed at Larry, and he deliberately stepped on it, crushing it under his heel.

"Plants should know their place," he said loudly.

His voice didn't echo at all in the quiet. The silence was so deep and long-established it seemed to swallow up all new noises, including our footsteps. It was like walking through a painting of a place rather than the place itself. Larry stopped abruptly and glared about him.

"Is this supposed to scare me?" he said loudly. "I'm dead! My house is spookier than this!"

"Way too much information," I murmured. "And so much for the element of surprise."

"Leave it out," said Larry. "This place is deader than I am. Whatever happened here, it's over. We missed it. This . . . is just the mess it left behind. I want the Collector. Where is he?"

"He must know we're here by now," I said. "But it's a big station. The entrance to his lair could be concealed anywhere. And I really don't feel like wandering around . . . Lud's Gate had a really bad reputation back in the day, before the old Authorities sent a squad in to shut it down."

"Hadleigh led that squad," said Larry. "Back when he was the Man . . . Didn't you know?"

"No," I said. "But the Nightside does so love its little coincidences."

"Couldn't you . . . ?"

"No, I couldn't," I said quickly. "The Collector knows me of old. The number of times I've casually wandered into his secret hideouts and made a complete nuisance of myself, he's bound to have set up booby-traps, keyed to my gift."

"That's right," said Larry. "You and he go way back. What's he like?"

"Crazy, spiteful, and vindictive, and dangerous with it," I said. "He's lots of other things, too, as the mood takes him, but those are the ones to bear in mind."

"I meant," said Larry, "what's he like as a person?"

I thought about it. "I'm not sure how much of a person is left any more. He didn't always use to be like this. He had a name once, a position, friends, and a life. But one by one he gave them all up to pursue his obsessions. And now he's just the Collector."

"So how do we find him?"

"We won't have to," I said. "He'll find us."

We both looked round sharply as a spotlight stabbed down out of nowhere, a brilliant shimmering pillar of light filling one of the exit arches, clear and sharp against the rotten corrupt light of the platform. And in that spotlight, glaring at me: the Collector. A barely medium-height man, badly overweight, wrapped in a simple white Roman tunic. His face was red and sweaty, his piggy eyes were fixed solely on me, and his podgy hands clenched and unclenched at his sides.

"John Taylor," he said heavily. "Once again you come knock knock knocking at my door. How did I end up with you as my personal cross to bear? It's not as if I shot an albatross. And which part of *secret* lair do you find so hard to comprehend? If I wanted visitors, I'd advertise. And who the hell's that?"

"That's Larry Oblivion," I said. "You'll have to excuse his manners. He's dead."

The Collector looked Larry over and shrugged. "I've already got a zombie. And a lich. I used to have a mummy, but the damn thing fell apart when I tried to steam-clean its bandages. What do you want this time, Taylor? Whatever it is, you can't have it. I'm very busy right now."

"What's with the new outfit?" I said cunningly. The Collector never could resist showing off his latest acquisitions.

"Oh, this old thing?" said the Collector. "It is rather fine, isn't it? This is the very tunic Pontius Pilate was wearing when he washed his hands. Would you believe I found it tossed away in a laundry basket? If people can't be trusted to look after things, they shouldn't be allowed to have them." He scowled suddenly as he realised he'd allowed himself to be distracted. "Why can't you just leave me alone, Taylor? What did I ever do to you?"

"You know what you did," I said, and he looked away, not meeting my gaze.

"That was a long time ago," he said. "How many times must a man pay for his sins? There ought to be a statute of limitations on guilt." He glared at me sullenly. "You can't keep on dropping in on me, whenever you feel like it! If I wanted company, I'd put a personal ad in the *Inquirer*! Oh hell, tell me what you want this time, and let's get on with it. I'd keep guard dogs, but they pee on the exhibits."

"You were right," Larry said to me. "Crazy as a bag of arse-holes."

"Shut up, grave dodger," said the Collector.

I cut in quickly. "The last time we met, Collector, you said you were busy with something new. And now you say you're still busy . . . I have to ask: have you taken on a new interest? Something . . . different?"

The Collector stared at me for a moment. He seemed honestly puzzled. "No . . . Not really. I've spent most of my time recently trying to pin down a particularly elusive Arthurian artefact that isn't when it's supposed to be, but that's not enough to bring you here . . . So, what is it, Taylor? Spit it out!"

"Word is, you've started collecting people," I said bluntly. "Unique, important, and significant individuals. Larry thinks you've got his brother Tommy here, because of his gift. Have you?"

The Collector actually gawked at me. "That's it? That's why you're here? *Are you crazy?* What the hell would I want with *people*? Nasty, noisy, demanding things. Which part of *I live alone in secret lairs as far from bloody people as I can get* have you failed to grasp? I collect rare and fascinating objects, from all ages of history. Mainly to protect them from other people, who wouldn't appreciate them. I like things. You know where you are with things. Oh . . . come and take a look, then, if that's what it will take to get rid of you. You can have half an hour to admire my collection and satisfy yourselves that I'm not stockpiling people, then I'm throwing you out of here."

He turned and stalked away into the recesses of the station, and his spotlight went with him. Larry and I hurried after. We'd barely passed through the exit arch when a dozen of the Collector's personal security robots appeared out of nowhere to stride along beside us. I dropped a warning hand on Larry's arm to keep him from reacting, but he shrugged me off. All his attention was fixed on the Collector's back. He hadn't believed a single word the Collector had said. I wasn't sure myself. Walker wasn't usually wrong about things like this, but . . . the Collector was right. He really didn't care about people. Only things.

Like the elegantly long-legged rococo cat-faced robots that were walking with us, which he'd picked up from some future Chinese time-line. Gleaming curves of metal, more works of art than functional servants, topped with stylised cat faces, complete with jutting steel whiskers and slit-pupilled eyes that glowed bright green in the gloom. They moved with an eerie grace, tap-tapping along on their tiny metal paw-like feet. Now and again, one of the robots would flex its steel-clawed hands, as though considering what it would like to do if it wasn't bound by the Collector's commands.

It was dark all around us now, the only illumination spilling out from the Collector's spotlight.

"I have to be careful," the Collector said abruptly. "There are people out there who would stop at nothing to rob me of my lovely treasures. Other collectors, rogue traders—thieves, the lot of them!"

"Indeed," I murmured. "How dare they steal the things you stole first?"

"I appreciate them!" the Collector said haughtily. "And I never give up anything that's mine. My lovely things."

Light flared up around us, and Lud's Gate Station was gone. A new warm, golden glow revealed a huge warehouse, sprawling away in all directions. Massive glass display cases held all the wonders of the world, arranged in rank upon rank for as far as the eye could see, along with shelves and shelves of curios and collectables, the popular trash of decades past and future, everything rare and valuable from every period of Time. It was a maze, a labyrinth, of rarities and marvels, toys and trinkets, objets d'art and objets trouvés . . . If it was bright and shiny, the Collector had an eye for it.

"You can look," the Collector said grudgingly. "But don't touch! Every time I let you in, Taylor, things get broken. But see for yourself: there are no people here! Unless someone's tried to break in again. I haven't checked the traps recently."

I looked at Larry and had to grin. His dead face finally held an emotion, and it was as much shock as awe. Like many people, he'd heard about the Collector's legendary hoard, but the reality was so much bigger. The Collector had promised us half an hour, but you couldn't manage a proper look around in under a month. Not that I felt the need to examine every-thing. If the Collector had started picking up people, they'd have been set out on prominent display, in pride of place, so he could gloat over them. And there weren't any.

I wandered down the aisle before me, Larry stumbling along behind. I pointed out a few things of particular interest. A stuffed waterbaby, covered in thorns; a frozen water ghost in a refrigerated container; and the original sketches for the Turin Shroud. Two of the cat robots followed us at a respect-ful distance, ready to tell on us to the Collector if we got too close to anything. After a while, I stopped before a diorama of stuffed giant albino penguins and looked at Larry.

"Walker lied," I said.

"It would appear so," said Larry. "But why would he lie about my brother?"

"The devil always lies," I said. "Except when a truth can hurt you more. But you're right; why would he lie about this?"

The Collector laughed harshly, and we both looked around. He was watching from a safe distance, surrounded by his cat robots.

"If you've started trusting Walker, you're really letting the side down, Taylor. He always has a plan inside a scheme inside an agenda, and he'll tell you whatever he needs to tell you to get you to do what he wants you to do. Face it, Taylor; he sent you on a wild goose chase to get you out of his way; and you fell for it."

"Looks like it," I said. "Sorry to have troubled you. Show us the way out, and we'll be going."

"No," said the Collector. "I don't think so." He leaned casually against an old-fashioned grandfather clock, with a cobwebbed human skeleton propped up inside it. His gaze was clear and cold, and he didn't seem nearly as out of it as he had before. "I've been thinking, Taylor, and it seems to me . . . that you owe me far more than I owe you. I lost my leg to those giant insects at the end of Time, all because of you."

Larry looked at me. "You do get around, don't you?"

"I've replaced the leg a dozen times," said the Collector, still glaring at me. "I've used machines, cloned tissues, even regrown it using a lizard serum; but it never feels right. I still have nightmares about the insects eating my skin and burrowing into my flesh, while you stood by and did nothing."

"Is that right?" said Larry.

"Sort of," I said. "There was more to it than that. He was planning to do something far worse . . ."

"Shut up!" said the Collector. "This is my moment, not yours! If you'd just left me alone, I might have let bygones be bygones . . . but no, here you are again, intruding and interfering and insulting me in my own home. Relying on my guilt over a few minor past indiscretions to keep me in line . . . Well, I have had enough of you, John Taylor. I don't care if you are Charles's son. I don't care about Charles or Henry or your mother, or any other . . . *people.* I don't care about *people*! They always let you down. I like my things, my wonderful things. You can depend on them to be what they are and nothing else, forever and ever. So I'm going to flush you out of my life, Taylor, because I don't care any more."

"You see," I said to Larry. "Told you that you and he had a lot in common."

"Yes, but I'm dead," said Larry. "What's his excuse?"

The Collector actually stamped his sandalled foot in rage, his face flushed an unhealthy shade of purple. "You never take me seriously, Taylor! You always have to make fun of me, and my marvellous collection! You never appreciated me!"

"You looked after me, sometimes, when I was a kid and my dad couldn't," I said. "I remember that, Uncle Mark. I appreciated that man. Whatever happened to him?"

"No. Don't you dare," said the Collector. "That was a long time ago. We were all different people then."

"And look what's become of us," I said. "All your travels in time, and you couldn't see what was coming? That man with his whole future before him . . . He couldn't avoid ending up a lonely, sad, old man, surrounded by things?"

"Kill them," the Collector said to his robots. "Kill John Taylor, and rip his dead friend to pieces."

The cat robots started forward, inhumanly graceful, taking their time, closing in from all sides to leave us no chance of escape. Their slow, studied approach had something in it of the cruelty of cats. Larry pulled out his magic wand, started to say something, then stopped abruptly.

"That won't work here," I said, looking quickly about for possible escape routes and maybe even a weapon. "The Collector has wards in place for unexpected items like yours."

"Pretty little thing," said the Collector, from behind the safety of his robots. "Elven, isn't it? Thought so. Wasted on a dead thug like you, Oblivion. But it'll make a fine addition to my new elf annex. And you needn't try raising your gift, either, Taylor; I've got shaped charges hanging on the air, bristling with anticipation, ready to do really quite appalling things if you even peek through your inner eye. Should have set them up years ago."

"Come on, Collector," I said, doing my best to sound brave and heroic and not in any way panicking. "You can't kill me. You know lots of people will track you down to avenge me."

"I'll bet a hell of a lot more will celebrate," said the Collector. "Hell. Half of the Nightside will probably throw a party. With streamers and balloons. Besides, no-one will ever know it was me. You and your unpleasant associate will join my collection, as very small portions in a series of very small boxes. Then maybe I'll be able to get some proper sleep at last."

I'd looked everywhere and run out of options. The cat robots had covered every possible escape route, and there were no obvious weapons out on display. None of the usual cursed needles, singing swords, or interstellar blasters. Not even anything heavy enough to pass for a blunt instrument. The robots were all around us now and pressing closer. The Collector didn't allow them weapons, in case they might damage any of his beloved exhibits, but they still had their inhuman strength and wickedly sharp claws.

"Don't suppose you've a gun on you, by any chance?" said Larry.

"I don't like guns," I said. "Besides, most of the time I'm smart enough to avoid getting caught in situations where I might need them. I really thought I had the Collector intimidated . . . or at the very least, sufficiently guilt-tripped . . ."

"On the whole, I'd have to say he doesn't look intimidated," said Larry. "And no; I don't have a gun on me either. I've grown far too dependent on my wand since I died."

"Yes," I said. "Tricky."

"Well, don't just stand there; do something! Those robots are getting bloody close! I do not want to spend the rest of my life as kitty litter! I'm dead, not invulnerable."

"I told you that," I said. "And will you please stop hyperventilating? It's really very unattractive in a dead person. Dead Boy never makes a fuss like this when we work together."

"Dead Boy is crazy!"

"There is that, yes . . . I think we should grab some of the more fragile-looking exhibits, and build a barricade between us and the robots. The Collector won't let them damage anything."

"Are you sure about that?" said Larry.

"I'm betting my life on it."

It didn't take long to drag some of the shelves and display cases into place around us, pushing the more delicate objects to the front. A glass phallus from the Court of Cleopatra, engraved with snake scales; dainty china butterflies from the Court of Versailles, with tiny erotica hand-painted on the wings; and half a dozen paper ghosts from Hiroshima. And sure enough, once the Collector realised what we were doing, he stopped his robots in their tracks rather than have them break anything. Things would always matter more to him than any human emotions, even revenge. He glared at us, and we glared right back at him, and there was no telling where the stalemate might have taken us, if we hadn't been distracted by the sound of deliberate, approaching footsteps. We all looked round sharply, and there was Walker; strolling through the packed shelves and cases, as calm and composed and elegantly dangerous as ever.

The cat robots immediately forgot all about Larry and me and turned as one to focus on Walker. The Collector gestured urgently for them to stand still, and they did. Walker ignored them completely, smiling and nodding to the three of us as though we'd just happened to meet in the street. He walked through the still ranks of robots and finally came to a halt before the Collector. Walker smiled at him warmly.

"Hello, Mark. Been a while, hasn't it?"

The Collector scowled at him. "Don't come the old-chums act with me, Walker. That was a long time ago. We're both different people now. And don't try your Voice, either; it won't work here."

"Never occurred to me that it would," murmured Walker.

"How did you find me?" said the Collector, plaintively. "I put a lot of hard work into choosing this site and hiding it from unfriendly eyes."

"It wasn't difficult," said Walker. "I just followed John."

"I didn't see you!" I said.

"People don't, unless I want them to," said Walker.

"You lied to me," I said. "You used me to find the Collector for you!"

"Needs must, when the Devil's knock knock knocking on your door," said Walker.

The cat robots were still watching Walker with their glowing green eyes, almost visibly straining against the orders that held them motionless. They knew a real threat to their master when they saw one. Walker ignored them all with magnificent disdain. The Collector and Walker stood face-to-face, and when the Collector finally spoke, his voice was quieter, and more human, than I expected.

"It has been a long time, hasn't it, Henry? But with your resources, you could have found me at any time if you'd really wanted to. I've always known that. Why did you stay away so long? We might have been on opposing sides, but that never stopped you with other people. Why did you wait until you were dying to come and see me? Yes, I know; of course I know. All those years we were friends, and I had to hear it from someone else? What were you thinking? Why didn't you come to me the moment you found out? I could have come up with something! I have all of Time to look in!"

"But I am running out of Time," said Walker. "And I couldn't bring myself to trust anything you might find for me. Our relationship has always been . . . complicated."

"And whose fault is that?" said the Collector. "I had such plans, such dreams, before you swept me along with your damned ambitions!"

Walked nodded slightly, accepting the point. "And what have you made of your life, Mark? All the great things you boasted you were going to do . . . and you gave it all up to collect toys?"

"What have you done with *your* life, Henry?" the Collector said angrily. "You wanted to fight the establishment, and instead you became it. You're the Man now; everyone knows that. You've become everything we despised! And for what? To be king of shit heap? Caretaker of a freak show? Errand and bully-boy for the Powers That Be!"

Walker didn't flinch once, even as the Collector spat hot, hateful words at him. He waited politely for the Collector to run down, then spoke calmly and reasonably in return.

"Time changes all things, Mark. You of all people should understand that. And you . . . have become too dangerous and too unpredictable to be left running around loose, making trouble when I am gone. I did help towards making you the man you are; and that makes you my responsibility."

"I made myself what I am," snapped the Collector. "I don't owe you anything!"

"You never did listen, Mark," murmured Walker, almost sadly. "This isn't about what you owe me."

"You always did have too high an opinion of yourself," said the Collector. "I made myself the greatest Collector in the Nightside, through my own hard work and determination. Despite everything you or anyone else could do to stop me!"

"I should have tried harder," said Walker. "But I always had so much else on my plate, and you were my friend, so . . . If I'd known you were going to end up like this, I would have done something. I can't help feeling this is all my fault."

"What are you talking about?" said the Collector.

"Oh, wake up, Mark!" snapped Walker. "Look around you! What kind of a life is this for anyone? No family, no children, no friends; just . . . things?"

"You have family, children, and friends," said the Collector. "Did they make you happy, Henry? Did they make you content? We were never going to be happy, or content, or satisfied. It wasn't in our nature."

"We have come a long way from the idealistic young men we once were," said Walker. "When did we lose our innocence, Mark?"

The Collector laughed harshly. "We didn't lose it, Henry; we threw it away first chance we got. Don't waste my time with nostalgia just because you're dying. Those days, and those people, are long gone."

"No," said Walker. "That was yesterday. And I would give everything I own to have it back."

"What do you want here?" said the Collector. "I'm busy."

"I came to say good-bye," said Walker.

He was standing right in front of his old friend, smiling kindly, holding the Collector's eyes with his, when the knife he'd concealed in his left hand slammed between the Collector's ribs. The cat robots started forward, and Walker's other hand opened to reveal his gold pocket-watch. It snapped open, and the Timeslip inside snatched up every one of the cat robots and whisked them away, all in a moment.

The Collector cried out once as the knife went in, sounding as much surprised as anything. He grabbed Walker with both arms, pulling him close. Walker let go of the knife, and held him, too. The Collector's legs buckled, blood pouring thickly down his side, staining the old Roman tunic. Walker lowered the Collector slowly to the ground. The Collector tried to say something, and blood ran from his mouth. Walker snapped his gold watch shut and tucked it back into his waistcoat pocket. He never once took his gaze off the Collector's dying face. He knelt down and helped the Collector to lie back on the floor, in a spreading pool of blood. The Roman tunic was soaked with gore now. The Collector clutched at Walker with weakening hands, looking confused.

"It's all right, Mark," said Walker, quietly, tenderly. "I'm here, Mark."

"Henry . . . ?"

"It's all right. I'm here. I'll stay with you."

Walker looked at me. "You can go now. I don't need you any more. Leave me here with my friend."

Larry didn't want to go, but I hustled him out. In his current mood, Walker was capable of anything. I only looked back once, to see Walker kneeling beside his dying friend, holding one of the Collector's hands in both of his, saying good-bye. One dying man to another.

NINE

Old Truths Come Home to Roost

In the Nightside, it always pays to expect the worst; but the old girl can still surprise you. Back on Lud's Gate platform, I reached out with my gift to find a train that could take us back to the city, and was pleasantly amazed to find one already waiting for us, right outside the station. It was the same train we'd arrived in, scared to stay but hanging around anyway, in case we might need it. I was genuinely touched and made a point of sending profuse mental apologies for my previous bad manners. The train just shrugged. Apparently trains are used to that sort of thing.

The gleaming steel bullet slammed back into Lud's Gate Station, the carriage doors opened long enough for Larry and I to climb aboard. Then the doors slammed shut, and the train shot out of the station at full speed. Something dark and dripping raised itself from the receding platform, but I didn't look back. Larry and I sprawled tiredly on our seats, staring at nothing in particular.

It's not every day you see a legend murdered in cold blood.

"What about Walker?" Larry said finally.

"He can find his own way home," I said.

"Not what I meant," said Larry. "I meant: what are we going to do about Walker?"

"Nothing," I said. "You can't do anything about him. He's . . . Walker."

"Is he? The Walker I remember from before I died might have been a ruthless bastard, but he made a point of never getting his own hands soiled. Someone else always did his dirty work for him. And usually with at least the appearance of law or justice to back him up. He didn't just stick knives into people he thought he couldn't trust."

"Yes," I said. "He murdered his oldest friend, right in front of us. As though . . . he doesn't give a damn any more."

"Did he ever?" said Larry.

"Oh yes," I said. "Walker was always a stickler for the rules and regulations, even if he did make most of them up himself."

"He can't expect us to keep quiet about this?"

"No. He's counting on us to tell everyone. He wants people to know. When a man knows for sure that his time is running out . . . he can't be bothered with the little things. He wants to tidy up his messes while he still can."

"So I did hear right?" said Larry. "The great and mighty Walker is dying."

"Yes. And that makes him more dangerous than he ever was before. There's nothing left to hold him back."

"I had no warning," said Larry. "Before I was killed. There are a lot of things I would have liked to do . . . Things I could have said, things I could have put right . . . I mean, I'm still here, still around, still taking care of business . . . But there are some things only the living can do and have it mean anything."

I waited, but that was all he had to say. We were, after all, professionals, only partners on a case, not friends. But perhaps there are some things you can only say to a stranger.

"Anyway," Larry said finally, "the important thing is that Walker lied. We have to start hunting for Tommy all over again."

"Looks like it," I said. "And I haven't the faintest idea where we should look next. No clues, no sightings, no suspects to threaten or intimidate . . . We could try some of the augurs or farseers. I know a wishing well that often comes through . . ."

"Hell with them," Larry said firmly. "They'll charge an arm and a leg for a rhyming couplet that will only make sense seven years from now or when it's too late to do any good."

"Sometimes . . . things, and people just vanish," I said. "It's the Nightside."

Larry glared at me. "You're not suggesting we give up, are you?"

"No," I said. "But I'm being realistic. If my gift can't find Tommy, he must really be lost."

"He's not dead!"

"No, I'd know if he was dead." I wasn't actually sure of that until I said it, but it made sense. My gift would have found a body. "We could try the Street of the Gods. A lot of the Beings there claim to be all-knowing."

"Why would they talk to us?" said Larry.

I grinned. "Because Razor Eddie is a friend of mine. And half the Beings on the Street would wet themselves if the Punk God of the Straight Razor even looked harshly in their direction."

"It's nice to have friends," Larry said solemnly.

We sat in silence for a while as the train roared through darkness and dark places.

"What do you suppose will happen to the collection?" Larry said finally. "It did look . . . very impressive. Will Walker put it up for auction, do you suppose?"

"No," I said. "I don't think so. Walker can get sentimental over the strangest things. I think he'll leave it where it is: all the treasures and curios, and the body of the man who collected them. Let it all remain lost, in a far place, and become its own legend. The Collector would have liked that."

"Will you miss him?" said Larry.

"He was my enemy. He tried to have me killed half a dozen times. He was my uncle Mark. Of course I'll miss him."

Larry and I emerged from the Underground again at Cheyne Walk Station, just in case we'd missed anything the last time. And once again, the Nightside managed a pleasant surprise. No fog, no rain, no showers of frogs; rather a pleasant night under a starry sky. The air was heavy with the scents of a dozen different cuisines, drifting out of restaurant doorways, open invitations for meals so ethnic they didn't even have names outside the Nightside. Forgotten food, from countries and cultures that don't exist any more. Kodo and Burundi drums held long, rolling conversations in the distance, and the barkers outside the members-only clubs chanted their harsh come-ons. People came and went and didn't even look around; but that's the Nightside for you. My mobile phone rang, and I answered it cautiously. The ad mail had been getting pretty aggressive recently, even with the best bullshit filters money can buy.

"Hello, John," said a calm, familiar voice. "This is Walker."

I paused. You had to admire the sheer nerve of the man. "What makes you think I want to hear anything you have to say?" I said finally.

"Hadleigh Oblivion has been sighted at the Church of St. Jude."

"And I should believe you because . . . ?"

"Oh, don't take my word for it, dear boy," said Walker. "Ask anyone. If you can get them to stop screaming long enough. The Detective Inspectre has never been one to hide his appalling light under a bushel."

The phone went dead. I thought for a moment, then called my secretary, Cathy. She knew everything. Especially if it involved celebrity gossip.

"Oh hell yes," she said, as soon as I mentioned Hadleigh Oblivion. "Word's coming in from all over the Nightside, according to these gossip sites on the computer that I just happened to be glancing at when you called. The Detective Inspectre is out and about, punishing the wicked with vim and vigour. Hadleigh's blown up a dozen dubious establishments, made twenty-three notorious scumbags vanish simply by looking at them, and no-one can even find Blaiston Street any more. It's gone, as though it was never there in the first place. Not a great loss there, admittedly, but . . . People haven't been this scared since the Walking Man was here last month, mowing down the bad guys and giggling while he did it. Everyone I know is at home, locked in their bathrooms, waiting for the storm to pass. And, I might add, if Hadleigh Oblivion even looks as though he's heading in my direction, I am taking the day off. Possibly the whole year."

"You really must learn to breathe occasionally while you're talking," I said, when she finally paused long enough for me to jam a word in edgeways. "Are there any sightings of Hadleigh near the Church of St. Jude?"

"Let me check." There was a long pause. No doubt she was doing things with the extremely complicated office computers that I paid for but have never been able to understand. "Right, yes, word just in—definite sighting of Hadleigh exploding a fat guy two streets down from the church. Ooh, messy. Ick. That one's going to end up on YouTube."

"Listen to me, Cathy," I said. "This is important. Walker's lost it. He's killed the Collector. Get the word out; warn people. Walker . . . doesn't give a damn any more."

She sniffed loudly. "News to me he ever did. Always said he was mad, bad, and dangerous to be within a hundred miles of, behind all that polite public school façade. You watch yourself, boss. I know you like to think you and Walker have a connection, an understanding; but I've always known he'd cut you down in a minute if he thought it served his purposes."

She shut down the connection before I could argue with her, but I wasn't sure I would have. When a man knows he's going to die, his thoughts can turn in strange directions. Walker had surprised me when he called me son, and again when he asked me to take over his position. And yet again when he murdered the Collector. Who knew how many other surprises he had in store?

I filled Larry in on Hadleigh and St. Jude's, and he scowled. "That's a long way off. Too long by the Underground . . ."

"We could try a taxi," I said. "They can't all be psychopaths, mind robbers, and licensed thieves. You could put it on expenses."

"I think we can do better than that," said Larry, not quite condescending. "I run a large organisation, remember? Just because I'm dead, it doesn't mean I've been lying down on the job."

He got out his mobile phone and called for one of his drivers to come and pick us up. He'd barely put the phone away before a long pearl grey limousine eased out of the traffic and purred to a halt. The driver got out to open the door for Larry and me, a tall, blonde, Valkyrie type in a white leather chauffeur's uniform, complete with peaked cap. She smiled at Larry, winked at me, and was back behind the wheel before I'd even finished doing up my seat belt.

"Image is everything these days," Larry said comfortably. "Act important, and everyone will treat you as though you're important. You might be more comfortable with the traditional ways, walking the mean streets in your iconic white trench coat; but I've always believed in travelling in style. Take us to St. Jude's, Priscilla."

"You see a lot more from the street than you do from a car," I said, but my heart wasn't in it.

The limousine must have been heavily armed, on the quiet, because the rest of the traffic gave us plenty of room. We swept smoothly through the night, leaving the bright lights behind us as we headed into the darker and more obscure areas. Where the shadows have substance, and even the moonlight seems corrupt. Like slipping out of a dream and into a nightmare, leaving everyday temptations behind in favour of darker and more malicious impulses. I watched the streets and squares drift by, swept along in the smooth comfort of the limousine; and all the sharp neon and Technicolor come-ons seemed like a dream within a dream, far, far away.

You find the Church of St. Jude tucked away in a quiet corner, in the back of beyond, far and far from the fields you know. It has no sign outside, no name on any board, no promise of hope or comfort. It's just there for when you need it. The only real church in the Nightside. The limousine eased to a halt a respectable distance away, and Larry and I got out. The night air was cold and sharp, brisk and bracing, alive with possibilities. Larry told his chauffeur to stay put, and he and I headed for the church, neither of us in any hurry. The Church of St. Jude is not a welcoming place.

An old, cold stone structure, older than history, older than Christianity itself, St. Jude's consists of four bare greystone walls with a slate roof, narrow slits for windows, and only one door. Never locked or bolted, always open; and let any man walk into the lion's mouth who would. No priests here, no services or sermons; just a place where a man can talk with God and stand a real chance of getting an answer. Your last chance in the Nightside for sanctuary, salvation, or sudden and terrible justice.

Not many people come to St. Jude's. It is not a place for mercy or compassion. St. Jude's deals strictly in the truth.

It didn't take me long to realise that the church had undergone a change since I was last there. It didn't seem quiet or brooding any more. Brilliant shafts of light blazed out of every window-slit, piercing the dark. A great and mighty power was abroad in the night, emanating from the ancient stone building, pulsing and pounding on the air. There was nothing of Good or Evil in it, only pure naked power. Larry and I looked at each other, hunched our shoulders, and pressed on. The closer we got, the more it was like breasting a tide, or facing into a storm, and we had to fight our way forward through sheer will-power. Whoever or whatever had made itself at home in the church, it clearly wasn't keen on visitors.

"Never been here before," Larry said casually. "Is it always like this?"

"Not usually," I said. "Sometimes it's actually quite dangerous."

"Who do you suppose is in there?"

"Beats me. Maybe someone got a prayer answered."

Larry smiled briefly. "Looks more like a personal appearance."

"Could be."

Larry looked at me. "I was joking!"

"I wasn't. This is St. Jude's."

"Could that be Hadleigh, do you think?"

"What would he be doing in there?"

"I don't know. Talking to his boss?"

"Now, that I have got to see," I said.

The moment we forced our way through the open door and into the church, the pressure on the air disappeared. The sense of power was still there, but it was no longer directed at us. The whole church was full of light, so stark and brilliant it seemed to blaze right through me, throwing all my hopes and needs and secrets into sharp relief, so that anyone could see them. But bright as it was, I could still see clearly without squinting or blinking, for this was no ordinary earthly light. The source was a man, fuelled by heavenly fires but not consumed. The Lord of Thorns had come back into his power again.

He was striding up and down and back and forth, his long white robes flapping about him, raging and raving and brandishing his bony fists. I'd never seen anyone look so purely angry in my whole life. His footsteps were like thunder, slamming on the bare stone floor, and his every movement sent shock waves across the air, as his bearded face contorted with rage. His eyes bulged, and his long grey hair swept about his head as he snarled and roared. His hands worked fiercely, as though eager, desperate, to get a hold on whoever had provoked this fury in him. His presence filled the whole church like an endless ongoing explosion.

Larry and I stopped just inside the door. We both knew a real and present danger when we saw one.

"Who or what is that?" said Larry, leaning close to speak right into my ear.

"That is the Lord of Thorns," I said. "The original Overseer of the Nightside, first and final dispenser of truth and justice for all who live here. Last I saw, he was a broken old man, stripped of his power, nothing but the self-appointed caretaker of St. Jude's. He would appear to have got his mojo working again, and if you and I had any sense, we'd get the hell out of here before he notices us."

"The Lord of Thorns?" said Larry. "*Really?* I thought he was a myth, a legend."

"Anything can turn out to be true, in the Nightside."

"And you've met him before? What am I saying; of course you have. You're John Taylor. All right; fill me in. The short version, preferably."

"The Lord of Thorns was appointed to be judge and protector of the Nightside," I said patiently.

"Appointed by whom?"

"Who do you think?" I said, glancing about me.

"Oh. Sorry. Carry on."

"He was to be Overseer of the Great Experiment; the one place in the world where neither Good nor Evil could intervene directly. The Lord of Thorns was to be our last chance for truth, justice, and revenge; but some centuries back he went down into the World Beneath and slept a long, long sleep. Until I woke him up."

"Of course," said Larry. "It would have to be you."

"He reappeared in the Nightside just in time to go up against my mother in the Lilith War; and she slapped him down as though he was nothing. It broke his heart, and it broke his spirit; because if he wasn't the divinely appointed protector of the Nightside and its people, then what was he? Who was he? He came here, looking for answers; and from the look of him, I'd say he's finally found some."

"Don't think he liked them much," said Larry.

The Lord of Thorns didn't even know we were there. He raged back and forth inside the church, a giant of a man again, with eyes full of fire. So angry he couldn't speak, only utter great cries and roars of rage. His white robes blazed like the sun, and with his long grey hair and beard, he looked very much like an Old Testament prophet, back from the desert to tell us all the bad news. Every now and again, lightning would strike down on the church, discharging harmlessly into the stone floor and sparking the air with the scent of ozone.

The Lord of Thorns stopped abruptly and thrust out his right hand, and a long wooden staff appeared in it out of nowhere. I gaped with equal parts shock and amazement. This was no ordinary staff; supposedly it had been grown from a sliver taken from the original Tree of Life itself. I had seen my mother, Lilith, take that staff from the Lord of Thorns and break it into pieces in her awful hands. Now here it was again, true and whole, powerful and potent; re-formed in the hand of the Lord of Thorns by his will alone.

"I am the stone that breaks all hearts. I am the nails that held the Christ to His cross. I am the necessary suffering that makes us all stronger. I maintain the Great Experiment, watching over it, and sitting in judgement on all who would endanger it, or tamper with its essential nature. I am the scalpel that cuts out infection, and the heart-break that makes men wiser. I am the Lord of Thorns, and I am back; and God help the guilty!"

His voice had the inhuman certainty of a man touched by something far greater.

"Welcome back," I said, stepping forward. "Now would you mind telling me what in God's name is going on here?"

He looked right at me, and his gaze stopped me dead in my tracks, as though he'd slammed a cold hand against my chest. I gave the Lord of Thorns my best friendly smile and hoped that he'd remember me. Preferably kindly.

"Walker!" The Lord of Thorns made a curse of his name. "This is all down to him! He betrayed me . . . I will strike him down for this crime, and the Authorities who ordered it!"

I looked at Larry. "Didn't you somehow know Walker was going to be behind all this?"

"Does seem to be his day," said Larry.

"The Authorities are dead," I said to the Lord of Thorns, with all the politeness I could muster. "Lilith's children killed and ate them all, during the War. There's a new Authorities now. Good people. Mostly."

"They'd better be," said the Lord of Thorns. The more he talked, the more human he seemed, his presence falling away to more bearable levels. Didn't make him any less scary, though. This one man had been set in judgement over the whole Nightside, with power to back it up; and he looked in the mood to pass judgement on every damned one of us.

"Excuse me for asking," I ventured, cautiously. "But what exactly has Walker done? What's made you so angry? And what brought you back from the . . . quiet man I met here last time?"

"That would be me," said Hadleigh Oblivion.

We all looked round sharply, and there he was, standing in the church doorway. In his long black leather coat, so dark it seemed made from a piece of the night itself, with his bone-white face and long mane of jet-black hair, his dark, unblinking eyes and his arrogantly cheerful smile, he looked utterly black and white; because there was no room for shades of grey in his world.

The world of the Detective Inspectre.

He seemed entirely unaffected by the Lord of Thorns' angry presence, or by the power that still blazed so very brightly inside the church. In fact, Hadleigh gave the distinct impression that he'd seen it all before and hadn't been impressed then. And perhaps he had; he was a product of the Deep School, after all. Hadleigh gave the impression that wherever he was, that was where he was supposed to be. He might not have possessed the power of the Lord of Thorns, but there was no doubt he was still a power in himself.

He strode forward into the church, bowed slightly to the Lord of Thorns, nodded to me, and smiled easily at Larry.

"Hello, little brother. Sorry I couldn't make it to your funeral."

"Not many did," said Larry, staring openly at his older brother. "I ended up having to put flowers on my own grave. There wasn't any body in it, of course; I'm still using it. But our parents wanted a grave and a headstone and flowers, so that's what they got. Hell, they miss you more than they do me. Would it kill you to visit them once in a while?"

"I have duties and responsibilities," said Hadleigh. "And my time isn't always my own."

"Do you know where Tommy is?" said Larry, blunt and to the point as ever.

"I'll get to that," said Hadleigh. "But first things first. Starting with you, Mr. Taylor."

Larry looked surprised for the first time. "You know Taylor?"

"I know everyone," said Hadleigh Oblivion. "Whether they know it or not. Hello, John. I've been watching you for some time."

"Okay," I said. "That's actually quite creepy, but moving on . . . What brings you out into plain view?"

"You. And Walker." Hadleigh paused, seeming to consider his words carefully. "Something important is going to be decided, very soon, something that will affect the whole Nightside. I'm here to prevent certain outside forces from interfering. On either side."

"So you didn't come back to help me find Tommy," said Larry. "I should have known."

"I'll help if I can, while I'm here," said Hadleigh. "I would have come back for Tommy eventually, but . . ."

"Yeah, I know," said Larry. "Duties and responsibilities."

"You have no idea what I had to give up, what I had to turn my back on, to become what I am," said Hadleigh.

"Was it worth it?" said Larry.

"Ask me another time," said Hadleigh. "We have business to be about. Let's deal with the Lord of Thorns first, before he explodes from rage and frustration."

"Suits me," I said. Some of those lightning bolts had been getting really close. "What's the connection between Walker and the Lord of Thorns?"

"He sabotaged me!" said the Lord of Thorns, and his voice was flat and harsh and vicious. "To prevent me from ever using my power to overthrow his precious status quo. As long as I still slumbered in the World Beneath, I was no danger to him or the Authorities. But once you awoke me, Taylor, and I ascended into the Nightside again, everything changed."

"Somehow I knew this would all turn out to be my fault," I said.

"I went walking through the streets, and I saw how much had changed," said the Lord of Thorns. "Whole place had gone to hell without me. And then Lilith arose, and all her monstrous offspring, and I went out to face her, to guard and protect you all. It should have been my finest hour. But Walker and his Authorities were fearful."

"Of what?" said Larry.

"That I would take up my function as Overseer again and dispense judgement and punishment, as is my right and duty."

"What put you to sleep in the World Beneath in the first place?" I said.

The Lord of Thorns smiled grimly. "I was persuaded that it was for the best. That the Nightside had changed from what it used to be, and I didn't need to be in touch with everything and everyone, all the time. And I listened, because I had been Overseer for centuries, and I was tired of people and their endless problems. So very tired . . ."

"Who persuaded you?" I said.

"Who do you think?" said the Lord of Thorns. "The Authorities, of course, and their Man. I was so very weary, and I thought a few years of rest would do me good. But they put powerful wards in place, to keep me sleeping, and guards to keep anyone from interrupting my sleep. Even that wasn't enough. The Authorities were taking no chances. In case I should escape from the trap they'd tricked me into, they had a contingency plan. A vile, appallingly simple scheme, passed down through the centuries, from Authorities to Authorities."

"I knew about it," said Hadleigh. "From when I was the Authorities' Man. I never approved, even then. I always meant to do something about it. But there was always so much that needed doing . . ."

"Duties and responsibilities," I said.

"Yes . . . When I was gone, the details of the scheme were passed on to Walker. And the Lilith War presented him with his best opportunity to . . . defuse the Lord of Thorns. Break his spirit, make him harmless."

"But . . . didn't Walker need the Lord of Thorns' power, to help him defeat Lilith?" I said.

"The Authorities feared the Lord of Thorns more," said Hadleigh. "After all, Lilith only wanted to destroy the Nightside; the Lord of Thorns wanted to change it. That's Walker for you; always taking the long view. Just as I taught him . . ."

A quiet chill ran through me, as I remembered that, for all his apparent youth, Hadleigh was at least twenty years older than Walker. He looked strong and sharp, in his prime; but I had to wonder what it was he gave up to become the Detective Inspectre. How much of Larry's older brother was still in there? Was he still human; or was he pretending, for his audience? For his brother? People say many bad things about the Deep School; and a lot of them are true.

"Long and long ago, the Authorities made a deal with the Street of the Gods," said Hadleigh. "Those jumped-up poseurs were always scared of the Lord of Thorns because he was the real deal, and they were only pretenders. So the Beings pooled their power, waited for the right opportunity, and channelled it through Walker's Voice, to shut down the Lord of Thorns' power, when he went head to head with Lilith. She could never have defeated him otherwise. And so he lost his confidence, and he lost his faith; and without those, he was nothing. He crawled away and ended up here: broken, confused, and no threat to anyone."

"What did the Street of the Gods get out of it?" said Larry, practical as ever.

"They got left alone," said Hadleigh. "Free to do as they would, as long as they stayed on their Street and didn't upset the tourists too much."

"That's why you came here," I said to the Lord of Thorns. "To the one place where prayers are answered. But then . . . why did you have to wait for Hadleigh to come and tell you the truth?"

"Because it was my crisis of faith," said the Lord of Thorns. The interior of the church was quiet now, the lightning gone, and his presence returned almost to that of a man. "I lost my faith, so I had to find it again. And I did, here, day by day, serving this place and the stricken people who come to it. You have to fall all the way, before you can rise again. Nothing like being in charge of everything and everyone for centuries to make you an arrogant prick." He laughed quietly at the expression on my face. "I am the Lord of Thorns, but I'm still a man, with a man's failings. Any judge forgets that at his peril. I found my faith again, long before Hadleigh turned up to tell me what I needed to know."

"So why blow your top?" said Larry. "You all but blasted this church off its foundations and slammed it down again facing in a different direction."

"Just blowing off some steam." The Lord of Thorns frowned. "There is justice waiting to be done, and there shall be smiting. I've been gone too long. The people I've seen here, begging for help, telling of terrible things . . . The Nightside was never supposed to be like this! So mean, so cruel, so casually evil . . ."

"I know some people who would agree with you on that," said Hadleigh.

"Hold it, hold it," I said. "As I understand it, and I'm perfectly prepared to be told that I don't . . . there's supposed to be a balance in place these days. You must have heard what happened when the Walking Man tried to lay down the law here. You need to get out and about in the Nightside, Lord, and talk to people, see how things really are, before you start making any decisions. Especially about the smiting."

"Or what?" said the Lord of Thorns. "You'll try and stop me?"

"I wouldn't," I said. "I still remember how you protected me from Herne the Hunter and saved my life, all those centuries ago. But there are others who would stand up to you. Good people, mostly. Like the new Authorities."

The Lord of Thorns looked at me for a long moment, then shook his shaggy head. "Sorry. Can't say I remember. So many years, so many faces; you know how it is. But you did awaken me from my prison of sleep, so you get a free pass. For now."

"How very civilised," I said. "Can I just ask you: do you know anything about the sword Excalibur?"

"I saw it once," said the Lord of Thorns, smiling wistfully. "Golden and glorious, it was. Took my breath away. Why do you ask?"

"I don't care about any of this!" Larry said loudly. "All I care about is finding my brother Tommy! And it's all you ought to be concerned about, Hadleigh!"

"I turn my back on the family for five minutes," said Hadleigh, "and now Tommy's missing, and you're dead. I can't hold your hands forever."

"Where is Tommy!"

"Closer than you think," said Hadleigh.

I really thought Larry was going to explode into a rage that would put the Lord of Thorns to shame.

"What the hell is that supposed to mean? Why can't you speak clearly any more? And what kind of a title is Detective Inspectre anyway?"

"A very descriptive one," said Hadleigh.

"You're not my brother," said Larry. "You don't look like him, talk like him, feel like him. What did those bastards do to you in the Deep School?"

"They opened my eyes."

I butted in, to give Larry time to control his temper. For a dead man who claimed to have hardly any emotions,

I thought Larry was doing pretty well. I was beginning to feel like a referee at a boxing match where everyone else has turned out to be heavily armed. I looked at Hadleigh.

"Why did you come here, now, to tell the Lord of Thorns who did this to him?"

"I know what I need to know, when I need to know it," said Hadleigh. "Comes with the job. And I'm here now because I knew you would be. I need to talk to you, too. Everything you know is a lie."

"What?"

"Only kidding. I've always wanted to say that to someone. No, what you need to know . . . is that a lot of things happening right now, in the Nightside, are the result of long-hidden plots and intrigues finally coming to a head. I'm here because I'm needed here. And . . . by the pricking of my thumbs, something morally ambiguous this way comes."

We all looked round, following Hadleigh's gaze, and there, standing in the doorway of the church, was Walker. Calm and composed, smiling easily, as though he hadn't just murdered his oldest friend. There wasn't a spot of blood anywhere on his smart city suit, and his old-school tie wasn't an inch out of place. He might have come from his club, or a board meeting. He let us admire him for a moment, then strolled unhurriedly forward to join us, the steel ferule of his umbrella tapping loudly on the bare stone floor.

"My ears are burning," he murmured. "The only thing worse than being talked about is being sniped at by enemies. Don't you want to hear my side of the story?"

The Lord of Thorns stabbed a bony finger at him. "Betrayer!"

Walker ignored him, his calm gaze fixed on Hadleigh,

who stared thoughtfully back. Two of the most powerful men in the Nightside stood looking at each other, and I felt like diving for cover. If they decided to go at it, even the Church of St. Jude might not be strong enough to contain the explosion. For all I knew, Walker had a whole army waiting outside to back him up; and I didn't even want to think what kind of forces Hadleigh Oblivion might be able to call on. And if the Lord of Thorns decided to get involved . . . I drifted surreptitiously to one side, so there was nothing between me and the exit.

"I knew my talking to the Lord of Thorns would bring you here, Walker," Hadleigh said finally.

"No-one brings me anywhere," said Walker. "I just go where I'm needed."

"We have so much in common," said Hadleigh.

"I wouldn't put money on it," said Walker.

"Your time is up, Henry," said Hadleigh. "Time for you to step down and let others take over."

"Not just yet," Walker murmured. "There are still loose ends to be taken care of first. Like the Lord of Thorns. Yesterday's man, who can't seem to understand that he isn't needed or wanted any more."

The Lord of Thorns thrust his wooden staff at Walker, and the temperature inside the church plummeted.

"You betrayed me! I am the Overseer of the Nightside!"

"That was then; this is now," Walker said calmly. "Yours was a simpler office, for a simpler time. We've all moved on since then. Things are different now. More complex."

"More corrupt!"

"You see? You don't understand the Nightside at all. These days, it exists to provide a safe haven for all those people and forces too dangerous to be allowed to run free in the outside world. The old days, the days of the Great Experiment, are gone. It's all about business now, satisfying needs and appetites, making money by entertaining the tourists. Just one big, very profitable, freak show. And your old-fashioned ideas of what is and is not permissible . . . are bad for business."

He used his Voice then. The Voice that compels all who hear it and cannot be denied or disobeyed. The blunt force of its power swept through the church, pushing everything else aside, settling over us like a spiritual strait jacket.

"Be still," said Walker. "Be calm. Listen to me. You know I have only your best interests at heart."

It worked on Larry. It even worked on Hadleigh. They stood still, smiling at Walker with open, empty faces. Ready to do whatever he told them because, for all their unnatural status, they were still men, and Walker's Voice had power over the living and the dead. It only partly worked on me, because I am my mother's son; but while I was still struggling to throw it off, the Lord of Thorns laughed mockingly and threw Walker's Voice back in his face with one sweep of his staff. The power trembling on the air shattered like glass, and Walker actually fell back a step, staring blankly at the Lord of Thorns.

"Do not seek to command me with our Creator's Voice, little man! I am closer to Him than you will ever be! Defend yourself, functionary! Or will you claim you tried to rob us of our free will for the greater good?"

"I told you," said Walker, pulling the remains of his dignity about him again. "I don't do Good, or Evil. I support the status quo. I keep the wheels turning, and I keep the natives from getting out of hand. Tell him, John. You've seen what I

do and why it must be done. Surely you of all people understand that what I do is necessary!"

The Lord of Thorns looked at me. "Time to choose a side,
John Taylor."

"Yes," said Walker. "Whose side are you on?"

I looked at him. "Anyone's but yours."

"You always have to do things the hard way, don't you,
John?" said Walker.

He flipped open his gold pocket-watch, and the Timeslip
within leapt out, enveloped Walker and me, and swept
us away.

TEN

And He Took Him Up to a High Place

When I could see again, I could see *everything*, laid out before me like a corrupt banquet.

The whole of the Nightside lay sprawled out below me, its fierce lights blazing against the dark. But this was no vision born of my Sight, no mental soaring in search of answers. This was real; this was here and now. I was standing on top of a mountain, looking down on my world, a cold wind hitting me hard. I knew where I was immediately; I'd been here before. I was on top of Griffin Hill, or at least, what was left of the top of Griffin Hill.

Once upon a time, and not so very long ago at that, this whole mountain and everything on it had been owned by one man: Jeremiah Griffin. He owned a lot of the Nightside, too, and far too many of the people who lived there. Back then, Griffin Hall had stood at the very top of Griffin Hill, a huge and magnificent mansion, home to the immortal Griffin family. But everything that man had he owed to a deal he made long ago with the Ancient Enemy; and I was there when the Devil rose up out of Hell to claim the Griffin's soul, and his family, and even his magnificent mansion. The Devil dragged them all down to Hell, and now nothing was left at the top of Griffin Hill but a great hole in the ground, a huge pit full of darkness, falling away further than the human eye could follow.

I turned my back on the Nightside view and stared thoughtfully down into the pit. The cold wind blew handfuls of dust into my face, from the narrow circle of dead earth that surrounded the huge crater. Nothing else remained. It seemed to me that the whole place was spiritually cold, as though the very essence of life itself had been taken away, torn away, leaving nothing behind.

The pit itself seemed as though it might fall away forever, nothing but darkness all the way down. Light from the full Moon directly overhead bathed the top of Griffin Hill in a stark blue-white light, but it only penetrated a few feet into the pit, as though the moonlight itself was repulsed by what it found there. The pit's ragged edge and interior were scorched and blackened, as though exposed to incredible, impossible heat. Someone wanted everyone to remember exactly what had happened to the Griffin.

I shuddered, and it had nothing to do with the cold wind.

I looked away, and there was Walker, maintaining a polite distance, smiling easily. The gusting wind barely touched him at all, and I knew that although what was left of Griffin Hill was creeping me out big-time, none of it bothered him in the least. He'd seen far worse in his time, and right now he only had eyes for me. His chosen son, his successor.

So I deliberately looked away, staring down the long slopes of Griffin Hill, where once a huge and magnificent garden had sprawled, full of amazing and incredible plants and blossoms and trees, some so rare they were the last of their kind, others brought in specially from other worlds and dimensions. The flowers had sung and the bushes walked, and the trees swayed even when no wind blew.

Now . . . it was a dark and corrupt place, touched and changed by the awful thing that had happened so close to it. Tall, distorted growths lashed at the air with curling branches, while things like bunches of twigs lurched up and down narrow trails. There were blossoms the size of houses, thick and pulpy, their diseased colours fluorescent in the night. Great slow waves moved through long green seas, as underneath the surface hidden species went to war. It wasn't a garden any more.

"It's a jungle," said Walker, following my thoughts. "No-one dares go in any more. The Authorities are talking about sending in armoured squads with flame-throwers, and burning it all down. Before something comes crawling down the mountain . . . I've always had a fondness for the scorched-earth policy. A shame, though, I suppose . . . There are species in there unknown to history or botanical gardens. The Collector would have loved them."

"Mark," I said. "His name was Mark."

"Oh no," said Walker. "He hadn't been Mark for a long time. Have you been up here since . . . ?"

"No," I said. "When a case is over, it's over. I've never felt the need to revisit old battle-fields. Besides, I've heard stories of strange manifestations. Visions stark and frightful enough to scare off even the Nightside tourists. They might come here to indulge in a little hell, but they don't want to get too close to the real thing. Still, there are always some who think they've seen everything . . . and they tell stories, in whispers, of ghost images of Griffin Hall, all its many windows blazing with hell-fire light, while terrible shadows of agonised men and women beat against the inside of the glass, desperate to get out . . ."

"Really?" said Walker. "A whole mansion, floating in mid air, over a hole? I don't think so. There are always stories, John; you should know that. I came up here, just the once, to see for myself. And to make sure nothing was coming back up out of the hole . . . It's a bad place now and probably always will be, but that's all. No ghosts, no apparitions, no distant screams from the Griffins burning in Hell. A really quite spectacular view, though, I think you'll agree."

"You don't . . . feel anything here?" I said.

He pursed his lips briefly. "A sense of horror, and lingering evil. About what you'd expect."

"You must feel right at home, then."

He gave me a stern look. "Now, that was just rude. Behave yourself. The Authorities sent the Salvation Army Sisterhood up here, a while back, to run some really heavy-duty exorcisms; but I can't honestly say I feel any difference."

"There are those," I said carefully, "who say that if you stay here long enough, the Devil will rise up out of Hell and offer you the same deal he made with the Griffin. All your heart's desires, in return for your soul. Is that why you've brought me up here, Walker? To offer me a deal?"

He laughed and indicated the whole of the Nightside spread out below us with one sweep of his arm. "All this could be yours, John, if you'll agree to be me. Take up my role. Keep the peace, whatever it takes."

"But what price would I have to pay?" I said, still looking at him rather than the Nightside. "I'd have to do what you do, think like you think, become the kind of man you are. And I think—I'd rather die."

"I've done this for so long, John," said Walker. He sounded suddenly tired, and old. "I've carried this weight for longer than you've been alive. All the things I've done, and none of it for me. Never any of it for me! Dying doesn't bother me; it'll be good to get a little rest at last. But how could I ever rest, knowing I'd left the Nightside without a steady hand on the tiller? Without a proper successor? And who else is there but you, John, who could take over from me? Who else would you name?"

"Julien Advent," I said.

"Yes," said Walker. "A good choice. A good man. The Great Victorian Adventurer, come through Time to be a hero here, too. Yes; I did consider him. But as a part of the new Authorities, he's too busy making policy to enforce it. And besides, the knight in cold armour has always been a strictly honourable man. He can't know—the Authorities can't ever know—what must sometimes be done in their name."

"All right," I said. "Let's go in the opposite direction. How about Razor Eddie, Punk God of the Straight Razor? The most distressing agent for Good the Good ever had? He's spent most of his life pursuing and punishing the wicked."

Walker smiled sadly. "The population of the Nightside would plummet."

"True," I said.

"I'm dying, John," said Walker. "I hate to keep reminding you, but time is not on my side. I need your answer. Now."

"You already know it," I said. "I don't want your job. I protect people from people like you. I know what your job leads to. I watched you murder your oldest friend in cold blood!"

"I have always been able to do the hard, unpleasant, necessary things."

"That's it? That's your justification? That it's not what you do, but why you do it?"

"Exactly! The end justifies the means."

"Only sometimes," I said. "And only some ends, and some means. I have always drawn a line I will not cross, no matter what, because to cross that line would mean betraying who I am."

"And what is that?" said Walker. "An honourable man?"

"Sometimes," I said. "The difference between you and me . . . is that you believe in protecting the System, and I believe in protecting people from the System."

"People!" said Walker. "Never put your trust in people, John; they'll always let you down. You have to put your faith in something bigger. Something that will last."

"The System?" I said. "There is no System, no State; just us. Men and women, struggling to get by, pursuing their own little desires and accomplishments. It's people who keep the wheels turning, Walker. We don't all want to rule the world, only the chance to live in peace in our own little part of it."

"We may all be cogs in the machine," Walker said calmly. "But some cogs are more important than others. They achieve more, and so they matter more, and they must be protected. Sometimes at the expense of certain minor cogs."

"Is their pain any less? Their deaths any less final? Do their children suffer and miss them any less?"

"It always comes back to you and your father, doesn't it, John?"

"You and Mark sacrificed my father, for the sake of your careers!" I said. And my voice sounded cold and vicious, even to me. "You broke him, ruined him, destroyed him. But who was it saved us all, in the Lilith War? You? Mark? No; my father sacrificed himself to save everyone."

"We all sacrifice for what we believe in," said Walker. "Will you sacrifice the bitterness of your past? Your blinkered, limiting sentimentality . . . for real responsibility? You say you want to protect the people of the Nightside; well, this is your chance. Your chance to stand between the people and the Authorities; to punish the wicked, stamp out corruption, make the world run as it should. Think of all the good you could do, with real power to back you up."

"Power," I said. "It always comes down to power. To be able to say, *Do what I tell you.* Whether I'm right or not. Power tends to corrupt, said a wise man, and absolute power tends to corrupt absolutely. The Nightside is living proof of that. I couldn't do your job without becoming you, Walker. And for me that would be a fate worse than death."

"Ah, well," said Walker. "I had to try. I knew you'd never see sense, but I had to try. You always were far too much like your father. I didn't want to do this, John, really I didn't . . . But unfortunately for you, I have a backup plan. I always have a backup plan. Do you know what this is?"

He held up a gleaming high-tech circlet for me to see. In the cold moonlight it looked like a crown of thorns, made out of steel and glass and diamonds. The more I looked at it, the more fiercely it blazed, until I had to look away.

"This," Walker said proudly, "is the time-travel device the Collector acquired recently. Not sure where he found it, some obscure alternate world or future time-line . . . but this really is something rather special. It was designed to let you travel in Time without interfering by putting your thoughts inside the head of any individual, at any Time. The perfect observer, of Time Past, Present, and Future. Very noble, I'm sure. But I have a more practical use for it. This is why I had to kill the Collector; so I could get my hands on this device. I knew he'd never give it up voluntarily. This is power, you see. Real power. To step inside anyone's head and take over. To drive them like cars and make them do or say anything."

"You didn't kill Mark because you were afraid to leave him running around loose," I said. "You killed him because he was in the way."

"Quite," said Walker. "I needed you to get me in there, because the Collector didn't trust me any more. So I told you what you wanted to hear, a simple, plausible story, and off you went like a good little hound on the scent. And all I had to do was follow you."

"You haven't a clue where Tommy Oblivion is, have you?" I said.

"Of course not. Why should I care about some minor private eye who never did anything that mattered? Glad he's gone. I have more important things on my mind. Do pay attention, John! This is the last conversation we're ever going to have. Because, you see, with this marvellous little device, I don't need you any more. Or at least, not as such. This device will put me inside your head. Since you wouldn't agree to take my place, I'll take yours. I will become you and dispose of you in my old body in this handy bottomless pit. As you, I will then take over my old position and continue my work. I'll have to kill off all the people who know you well, of course, even the ones I approve of; but it shouldn't be too difficult. They'll trust your face and your voice, right up to the point where they realise they shouldn't have. It won't be the first innocent blood on my hands, after all. Comes with the job."

"Yet another reason why I don't want it," I said.

Walker advanced slowly on me, holding the device out before him. "You failed the test, John. I gave you every chance. But unfortunately, you're just not worthy. Far too limited in your thinking and far too sentimental. You're not what the Nightside needs. I am. I can't die, John. I've far too much left to do."

He lifted the circlet with both hands, as though to crown himself with it, only to discover at the last moment that he'd forgotten he was still wearing his bowler hat. It was so much a part of his outfit, so much a part of his persona, that he'd honestly forgotten he still had it on. And as he hesitated, I stepped slightly to one side to get the full force of the wind blowing behind me, and threw the handful of pepper I'd sneaked out of my coat pocket into Walker's face. The wind blasted the vicious stuff into his eyes and up his nose, and he cried out in shock and pain before sneezing convulsively. He staggered backwards, sneezing so hard it shook his whole body, while tears streamed down his face. It was the easiest thing in the world for me to step forward and snatch the circlet out of his hand, then step quickly back out of reach.

Being the tough old bird he was, Walker quickly had

control of himself again. He glared at me through puffed-up eyes.

"You bastard, John! You bastard . . . You and your damned tricks!"

"Keep it simple," I said. "You taught me that, remember?"

"You don't know how to work the device!"

"I don't want it," I said, slipping it inside my coat. "Now, after everything I've heard, what am I to do with you? You were going to walk around in my body, killing Suzie and Cathy and Alex and Eddie, and everyone else who knew me; to keep yourself safe. You were going to walk up and down the Nightside, with my face and my reputation, dispensing your own idea of justice. Undoing everything I ever achieved and believed in. Could there be any greater betrayal?"

"Oh, grow up, John," said Walker. He had his old calm back again, but his voice was flat and cold. "I do what needs doing. Always have done. What are you going to do?"

"Well, first, I'm going to try and get this time-travel device back to where it belongs. It's far too dangerous, and too tempting a thing, to have here."

"And then? What will you do, John, to the man who always tried to be a father to you?"

"I've never had much luck with fathers," I said. "Probably why I've always done my best to go my own way."

Walker sighed, looked out over the Nightside, then back at me. He smiled briefly. "We always knew it would come to this; didn't we, John? That eventually one of us would have to kill the other."

"You always were a closet drama queen, Walker. It doesn't have to end like this."

"Yes, it does."

I thought about it for a while and nodded slowly. "Yes; it does. You crossed the line."

"Two good men and true, who never could agree to disagree. And here we are, at the end of a very long road, standing on the edge of the pit. How very Nightside. So, what's it to be? My secret weapons against yours?"

"No," I said. "For all you've done, and for all that you meant to do, I'm going to beat you to death with my bare hands."

"Excellent," said Walker. "Wouldn't have it any other way."

I moved forward, and Walker came to meet me, drawing his long, narrow sword from where it lay hidden inside his umbrella. He threw the shell away, and I stopped abruptly. Walker smiled widely as he swept the long blade back and forth.

"Did I mention I was captain of the school fencing team? I had this lined with silver, John, just for you. No werewolf blood regenerations for you this time. My enemies stay dead."

"Good-bye, Walker," I said.

We went for each other like fighting dogs, as angry and vicious as only two old friends can be. I was young and fast and strong, but he had his blade, and his expertise, and a lifetime's hard-earned tricks and tactics. He stabbed and cut at me with his sword, and I evaded it, forcing my way closer. Again and again I went for him, and every time he drove me back, with blood streaming from cuts that wouldn't close. He cut chunks out of my reaching hands, and hacked at my arms when I lifted them to defend my throat or breast. Soon enough my white trench coat was soaked with blood. I was almost too angry to feel the pain, and what I did feel drove me on. I wasn't fighting for myself, but for Suzie, and for all my friends who would inevitably die at Walker's hands. At my hands, driven by his will. I thought of Suzie; and the blood and the pain didn't matter a damn.

We stamped back and forth on the edge of the pit, with me fighting to get to Walker, and him fighting to hold me off. But in the end, I was willing to die to bring him down, and he . . . was dying. He stumbled, just briefly, as he mistimed a lunge, and I hit him in the head. His foot turned under him, and he fell suddenly sideways into the pit. He reached out instinctively to me for help, and just as instinctively I lunged forward to grab his hand. But it was too late.

Walker fell into the pit. I knelt at the side, reaching helplessly after him. He didn't scream, didn't cry out, and in a moment he was gone. Nothing left but the darkness. I called after him, but there was no reply. He was gone. Swallowed up at last, by the dark.

ELEVEN

Bringing Them All Back Home

I sat on the edge of the pit, my legs dangling over the impenetrable darkness. The cold wind was still blowing, ruffling my hair and striking tears from my eyes. I watched blood drops slowly form on the bottom edge of my trench coat, then fall into the pit. I felt tired, and hurt, and strangely numb. As though a major part of my life was finally over. For good or for bad, Walker had always been there in the background, defining my life by my resistance to everything he stood for. He protected me and threatened me, but he never once ignored me, like my father did. I could always depend on Walker . . . to be Walker. I'd gone out walking earlier in the night because I was unsure about my life, and now I had just destroyed the one sure thing in it. I'd wanted change, and now I had it. You should always be careful of wishing for things in the Nightside because you never know who might be listening. There was the slightest of sounds to my left, and when I looked around, there was Hadleigh, standing next to me.

"Hello, John. You look like shit."

"How the hell did you get here?"

He shrugged. "There are short cuts in reality if you know where to look."

"How did you know I was here?"

"I know what I need to know when I need to know it."

"That answer is getting really irritating."

"I know." He looked thoughtfully down into the pit, leaning dangerously far over. "So Walker's really gone, then?"

"Yes." I studied him thoughtfully. "Did you know this was going to happen?"

"Not as such. The future's not set in stone; there are many possible futures. Which one we end up in depends on the decisions we make. And you and Walker have always been very difficult to predict. You're hurt, John. Allow me."

He took a firm hold on my shoulder, and a sudden shock ran through me, like a bucket of cold water thrown right in my soul. I gasped, and the pain was gone; and I knew without having to check that all my wounds had been healed, all damage repaired. I scrambled up onto my feet, suddenly full of energy. Hadleigh chuckled briefly.

"You see, I'm not only here for the bad things in life."

I arched my back and stretched my arms, relishing the freedom from pain and tiredness. I didn't feel numb any more. I felt like kicking the whole damned world in the arse and making it take notice. I gave Hadleigh one of my best hard looks.

"What did you do to me? I'm not used to feeling this good. It feels . . . strange."

"Let's just say I jump-started you. The technicalities would only upset you."

"What is your job, exactly, Detective Inspectre?"

"I could tell you," said Hadleigh. "But then I'd have to haunt you. Some secrets cannot be revealed because the burden is not mine to share. To put it simply, I walk between life and death, the better to deal with crimes against reality itself. Because somebody has to."

I looked down at my once-white trench coat, now tattered and torn and soaked with drying blood. I looked at Hadleigh. "Could you . . . ?"

"No, I couldn't," Hadleigh said firmly. "I'm a healer, not a tailor."

We stood together for a moment, side by side, looking down into the pit. Walker was gone. Let the neon lights be dimmed and the traffic brought to a halt. Walker was gone, and we shall not see his like again. If we're lucky. After a while, I deliberately turned away from the pit and frowned at Hadleigh.

"You know where Tommy is, don't you? When Larry asked, you said, *Closer than you think.*"

"Yes," Hadleigh said equably. "I know. I've known all along. But I had to wait until you and Walker had put an end to your business. That was more important. What just happened here will affect the Nightside for generations to come."

"How . . . ?"

"Tommy is in no danger where he is. He's just . . . lost, and needs our help to find his way home. Come on; Larry's waiting. Impatiently, I have no doubt."

I looked down the mountain side, at the dark and angry jungle that covered its slopes. "You going to call one of Larry's limousines?"

"Oh," said Hadleigh, "I think we can do better than that."

He seemed to turn sideways, then keep on turning, and the sheer force of his unnatural motion dragged me along with him. In a moment we were both back at the Cheyne Walk approach, and Larry actually jumped as we appeared out of nowhere right in front of him. The few remaining onlookers took our reappearance as their cue to be getting along. I grinned at Hadleigh.

"Nice trick. Could you teach me to do that?"

"Depends. How attached are you to your sanity?"

"We're still on speaking terms, which given my life is actually quite an achievement."

"Where the hell have you been?" demanded Larry, glaring at both of us. "I thought you were here to help find Tommy, Hadleigh, but all you've done so far is stand around looking enigmatic, then disappear after Taylor."

"Tommy's right here with you, in a sense," said Hadleigh. "It's time to bring him back. I had to wait for John to acquire the last necessary piece of the puzzle. You do have the Collector's device, don't you, John?"

I took it out of my coat. Larry regarded it dubiously, while Hadleigh nodded a bit smugly.

"Put it on, John, and raise your gift. Then focus your gift through the device, and it will lead you right to Tommy."

I raised the device with both hands, then hesitated as I remembered Walker doing the same thing. I cautiously lowered the future-science thing onto my head, while some small part of me gleefully thought, *I crown thee King John the First of the Nightside.* The device settled itself onto my head, feeling a lot heavier than it had in my hands. A series of small pin-pricks ran around my scalp as the device established contact, and sharp stabs of lightning detonated inside my head, as long-quiet parts of my mind woke up and made themselves known.

I raised my gift and a huge charge ran through my mind, blasting my inner eye wide open. And suddenly I could See a whole lot more of the world than I ever had before. All the secrets that had been hidden from me, all the wonders and terrors that my Sight either couldn't or wouldn't See; because the world is so much more full than we ever realise. I made myself concentrate on Tommy, and immediately I was sur-rounded by ghosts. Soft ghosts, people worn thin and ragged at the edges—vague, undefined, faceless. Walking through the hard places of the world as though they weren't there. Haunted by their own past, forever always just out of their reach. Dazed, confused, helpless . . . lost.

One of them was Tommy Oblivion. I was looking through his eyes now, Seeing the world he saw. He had become a soft ghost. I could sense his presence, his drifting, unfocused thoughts. More than dreaming, but far from awake. The Col-lector's device brought our two minds together, and I could actually feel his thoughts concentrating, his identity coming into focus for the first time in a long time, strengthened and stabilised by my presence.

"John?" said Tommy Oblivion. "John Taylor? Is that you?"

"Yes, Tommy. I'm here with you. I've been looking for you. I've come to take you home."

"Home . . . I've been trying to find my way home for such a long time . . . What happened?"

"I was hoping you could tell me, Tommy. Do you remember the Lilith War?"

"Hell, yes! There was a mob . . . out of their minds, swarming all over me, trying to kill me. There was no way to escape, so . . . I used my special gift and made myself existential. Neither one thing nor another, neither here nor there, living or dead. It saved me from the mob, but in that existential state I drifted out of reality, or turned sideways from it . . . and became enduringly uncertain. In reality, but not of it."

"A soft ghost," I said.

"Yes . . . I drifted through connecting dimensions, lost as any other soft ghost, set adrift from my moorings in the Nightside by what I'd done to myself. I saw seas on fire, under howling moons. I saw a dark labyrinth where the dead made candles out of the living. I saw men and women screaming in agony as they were burned alive in gigantic wicker men, under a bloody sun, at the orders of a great castle full of knights in terrible armour. Someone in that awful world opened a door into our reality, and I followed them through it, unobserved. But even though I was back in the Nightside at last, I still couldn't change the state I was in.

"Ever since, I've been collecting people I knew and making them like me. Sometimes just to keep me company, sometimes to save their lives when they were in danger. I made them existential, too, made them soft ghosts like me. I was too far gone to realise what a terrible thing I was doing. It's been a long time since I could think this clearly. I've been drifting back and forth for what seems like forever, reaching out to people I thought I recognised, trying to get their attention . . ."

It was only then I remembered the soft ghost who'd been following Larry and me around all night, plucking at our sleeves, calling out to us. All the time we'd been looking for Tommy Oblivion, he'd been right there with us, closer than we thought.

Hadleigh was suddenly there, a solid presence standing firmly in the midst of the soft ghosts. They all turned to focus on him, attracted by his certainty like moths to a flame.

"Well done, John," he said. His voice was everywhere, permeating the uncertain scene. "Now that you've made contact with Tommy, I can help you bring him back to reality. Make him real and solid and certain again."

"And all the others, too," said Tommy, his voice clear. "Not only the ones I'm responsible for; all of them. I can't leave anyone here, like this."

"Of course, Tommy," said Hadleigh. "Everyone gets to go home. That's what I do; that's what I'm here for. I had to wait until John and Larry were working together because I needed both of them to do this. You've located Tommy, John; but you don't have the power to bring him back. I can open a door between this place and the Nightside; but I can't directly affect Tommy, or any of the others. Only Larry can do that, because he's neither one thing nor another. Neither living nor dead, strictly speaking, a man suspended between two states of existence. But now, John, hang on to Tommy. I've opened the door. Larry, bring us home!"

I could sense Larry's presence, cold and sharp like an

unsheathed blade. I could feel him reaching out to us; and Tommy and Hadleigh and I reached back. And just like that we were all back in the Cheyne Walk approach, real and solid. Tommy looked about him, wide-eyed, grinning uncontrollably. Larry punched the air with one grey fist. Hadleigh folded his arms across his chest and nodded slowly to himself. I snatched the device off my head, and immediately my thoughts were my own again and the world was happily limited. I shuddered briefly and tucked the device away inside my coat.

A whole crowd of new people stood around us, solid and real and aware again for the first time in God alone knew how long. Some were laughing; some were crying; others sat down hard and hugged themselves tightly, as though afraid they might drift away again. Larry suddenly hugged Tommy, actually lifting him off his feet.

"All right, yes, I'm glad to see you again, too!" said Tommy, breathlessly. "Now, put me down before you break something! You never did know your own strength, even before you died. And bloody hell, you're cold."

"Circulation problems," Larry said solemnly. "Good to have you back, Tommy."

"Good to be back. Damn, look at them. I didn't know there were so many of them . . ."

There had to be at least a hundred men and women, lost souls with their lives and identities finally restored. I recognised some of the faces. Larry and I had been talking about them earlier; familiar faces from the Nightside scene who hadn't been seen in quite a while. Strange Harald the Junkman, in his assorted rags and tatters, asking plaintively if anyone had seen his horse. Bishop Beastly, splendid in his great scarlet cape, calling on all the spirits of the earth and air to avenge this slight to his dignity. Lady Damnation, with her corpse-pale face and fierce green eyes, licking her dark lips, eager to be about her nasty business again. Sister Igor, delicious as ever. Salvation Kane, gaunt and saturnine in his drab Puritan garb, glaring at everyone. Mistress Murmur, in a long pink ball gown, carrying a blood-soaked hatchet, as though she'd been interrupted in the middle of something. And many more besides, good and bad and somewhere in between, long gone and long thought lost. Not all of them Tommy's fault, by any means.

We'd brought them all home, every lost soul of them.

"All right," said Tommy. "Enough of the hugging, Larry! We were never that close. Thank you. I want to know what's happened while I was away. Where's Lilith, for starters? Did we win?"

"We won," I said. "She's gone; and she won't be coming back."

Tommy blinked at me, heard something in my voice, and decided not to pursue it. "How long have I been gone? Feels like years . . . Like being caught forever in one of those horrible dreams where you try and talk to people, but they can't see or hear you . . ."

"That's all over," Larry said firmly. "I'm taking you back home, to Mum and Dad. They've been worried. They'll look after you, put you back on your feet again."

Tommy pulled a face. "You know very well I hate being fussed over. Mum'll try and feed me up, and Dad'll nag me about getting a proper job."

"All the comforts of home," said Larry. "You're back, so be grateful. Or I will slap you one, and it will hurt. Hadleigh? What about you? Think you could find time in your busy schedule for a home visit?"

"Why not?" said Hadleigh. "Just for a while. I could use a little downtime."

"Well, well," I said. "The Oblivion Brothers, together again for the first time. Let the Nightside tremble, and evildoers cower in their lairs."

"I've got this slap in my pocket I still haven't used yet," said Larry.

"Hold everything," I said. "What about all these other returnees? We can't walk away and leave them here. They're going to need a lot of help and support, fitting into their old lives again or making new ones."

"Not my business," said Larry.

"Or mine," said Hadleigh. "My work here is done. Thanks to you, John."

And he looked meaningfully at me. I knew what he meant, and swore under my breath. In the past I would have contacted Walker, and he would have arranged care and comfort for these people. He might also have killed a few if he thought they needed killing . . . But there wasn't any Walker any more, thanks to me. Which meant . . . it was up to me to do something. Because there wasn't anyone else. The world has a way of arranging what it wants, and to hell with what we want. I'd have to take up Walker's old position, for a while, because I didn't have it in me to turn my back on people who needed help. That was why I'd become a private investigator in the first place, after all. Because there'd been no-one there to help me, when I needed it.

I'd take the position. Only until the Authorities could find someone better suited.

"I'll phone Julien Advent," I said. "Have the new Authorities send some people down here."

"Where's Walker?" said Larry. "Why isn't he here?"

"Walker has gone to the Devil," I said.

EPILOGUE

When I finally got home, Suzie was in the kitchen, scrubbing blood and gristle off one of her gutting knives. She was supposed to be bringing them in alive these days, but old habits die hard. I came up behind her and gave her a hug, and she leaned comfortably back against me.

"I may have a new job," I said. "Though with any luck, I'll fail the interview. How was your day?"

"The usual," said Suzie. "I'm out of shotgun shells again. Oh, and there's some post for you. I put it in the living room."

I went through into the next room—and there on the table was a long, sword-shaped parcel.

Also from *New York Times* bestselling author
SIMON R. GREEN

A HARD DAY'S KNIGHT

A Novel of the Nightside

John Taylor is a PI with a special talent for finding lost things in the dark and secret centre of London known as the Nightside. He's also the reluctant owner of a very special—and dangerous—weapon: Excalibur, the legendary sword. To find out why he was chosen to wield it, John must consult the last defenders of Camelot, a group of knights who dwell in a place that some find more frightening than the Nightside.

penguin.com

Look for the brand-new series
from *New York Times* bestselling author

SIMON R. GREEN

GHOST OF A CHANCE

A Ghost Finders Novel

The Carnacki Institute exists to *Do Something About
Ghosts*—and agents JC Chance, Melody Chambers,
and Happy Jack Palmer will either lay them to rest,
send them packing, or kick their nasty ectoplasmic
arses with extreme prejudice.

M755T0810

New from *New York Times* bestselling author

SIMON R. GREEN

From Hell With Love

It's no walk in the park for a Drood, a member of the family that has protected humanity from the things that go bump in the night for centuries. They aren't much liked by the creatures they kill, by ungrateful humans, or even by one another.

Now their Matriarch is dead, and it's up to Eddie Drood, acting head of the family, to figure out whodunit. Unpopular opinion is divided: It was either Eddie's best girl, Molly. Or Eddie himself. And Eddie knows he didn't do it.

M687T0410